PEACE ON DRACO

KARINA SHEERIN

Edited by Lynn Colletti-Stamos

ISBN: **978-0-692630-37-2**

Foreword

Girls' Power of Transformation for a Safer World

A girl needs space to dream. A teenager will commit her life to her inner beam if only she sees a little light in the shadow, and this light is she. To keep that space open, as Einstein puts it: "The important thing is not to stop questioning." Like millions of scarred girls before her, she must question herself, others, and the world, and keep pushing. What was done in the past may not work. Nonetheless, she, because it is she, can seek original responses in herself and boldly attempt them, because life must prevail over death, even in the worst ordeals. Beyond the initial paralysis, the inquisitorial mind can navigate gently in the most alienating places and eventually transform.

She can *transform herself first*. Every teenage girl has the capacity to grasp the strange environment where she was transported. Why is she here? She draws on her incredible force deep within, like the young Eleanor Roosevelt or Rosa Parks, who refused to be thrown into this world only to do nothing about it, who knew that like all the women of any world, they had to fight hard against injustice and chaos, and to contribute to stronger relationships for a brighter future. But, first of all, they had to create their own safe space. They questioned their inner self-inflicting doubts, learned to tame them each time they threatened to harm their self-worth, which allowed them to carry on. Similarly, our teenager had to overcome her doubts and grow, establish her confidence and moral compass,

1

because that world out there needs her steady and ready, with her personal sense of purpose and responsibility.

Transforming others is hard and requires patience, as futile reluctance of adverse forces borrows from routines, prejudices, bigotry, and sometimes the arsenal of meaningless wars and endless suffering. However, beyond apparent certainties, fighting souls, who seem so alien to kindness and social grace, can feel equally desperate and in query. That is why our young hero will patiently and persistently engage them, relate to them, work hard, and touch them under the armor, maybe not with her usual humor, but with her murmur, voice, and indirect questioning. She can ask them to hang on, pause, stand back, and discover other ways forward. She can evoke the timeless principles of nonviolence and make them allies in the responsibility to protect.

Yes, she can even *transform the world* around her to make it a safer place. See Petronille Vaweka, a Congolese leader who scolded the warlords in Ituri, as a mother grounds her children, telling them to stop harming the population and to better behave in the future. Bravery might cost such nonviolent heroes their own lives, as it happened to Salwa Bughaighis, our Libyan sister and human rights activist, who stood, and died, for the rights of women to cast their vote. Whatever the setbacks, the fight will prevail, like with Leymah Gbowee, the Liberian peace activist who woke up one day from a dream and then led a mass peace movement with women. She organized peaceful protests to push the arms bearers to stay at the negotiation table and sign an agreement. She won, and kept questioning and learning. Women and girls serve as beacons of hope in nonviolence, the same way Antigone or Lysistrata are symbols against hormonal dominance in Greek literature.

These female movers and shakers resemble our teenage heroine in *Draco*: they first wondered what to do with the mess around them, and then they scrutinized old routines and renewed the answers to everyone's benefit. They found the meaning of life in these responsible negotiations with themselves and others. Our life on Earth feels sometimes so small and the world's challenges remain so vast. *Star Trek*, where the people of Earth live in perpetual peace with each other, pushed the next generation "to explore new worlds, new civilizations where no one has gone before." *Draco* brings us to a world where peace seems unlikely. It just sounds like home.

A girl needs space, to expand and express. The teenager builds her place in Draco, as you will find out soon; she leverages all her strengths to make a difference. As a father myself, this is what I hope for my daughter, that she finds her dream like so many of her sisters did before her and pursues it relentlessly. Parents and kids can dream together for a safer world for themselves and others. Where they find meaning is where everyone feels alive and provides positive energy to fill the world around them.

Alain Lempereur is the Alan Slifka Professor of Conflict Resolution and Coexistence at Brandeis University and Affiliated Faculty of the Program on Negotiation at Harvard Law School. He has a lot of experience as a mediator or facilitator of dialogues in conflict situations. He is passionate about science fiction, and in particular he is a big fan of Star Trek, *where the successive captains and crews have to learn how to handle the dialogue and negotiations with new species and civilizations.*

Alain Lempereur

Alan B. Slifka Professor & Director, Graduate Program in Conflict Resolution and Coexistence

Executive Committee Member & Affiliated Faculty, Program on Negotiation at Harvard Law School

Chair, Scientific Committee, Humanitarian Negotiation Exchange at ICRC & Harvard Kennedy School of Government

Grand Canyon

Dear Diary,

You are all I have. I might never see or talk to another human being before I die. You might never be found, read or even understood but I know if I do not share my experience with someone I will probably get consumed by the weirdness of my new reality.

It was an ordinary day. I was sitting on an edge of the Grand Canyon reading a book and enjoying the magnificent view when my three sisters arrived to pick me up for dinner. It was summer and we were free of family obligations but not the summer camp routines, which our emotionally distant militaristic colonel of a father insisted on sending us to every year since the death of our mother at our birth.

Needless to say the man was out of his element and his comfort zone with four helpless infants. No amount of military training could have prepared him for the endless diapers, crying or girlie requirements. Our dad shouldered his responsibilities the best way he knew how: delegate to insubordinate underlings. For the most part, Dad's unit became the most disciplined. My sisters and I could salute before our first word; we lined up for our three daily rations; and our floor faced more toothbrush time than all of our teeth together.

The only time we got to see him was if we majorly screwed up. I viewed the effort as exhausting and was happy just being the shy family bookworm everyone thought I was. This made it very easy for me to sneak out and do whatever I wanted, whenever I wanted. Naturally, I did not involve my sisters; my adventures were mine alone. Now I find myself needing to share this unbelievable situation with anyone, even my diary, or I shall truly go mad.

The first time I picked up a pilot outside of the officers bar, I was at the tender age of 15. How surprised he was when he discovered not only my age, but how quickly his promising career would deteriorate with only one word to my father if he did not acquiesce to my demands. What fun I had watching the big strong men bend to the will of a young girl. It could be said that I was the base bad girl, but I would disagree. I was just having fun. Sure my activities threatened them; but my sweet and presumed innocent disposition kept them trusting. No one was ever hurt. None of my 'boy toys' talked about me for fear of ruining their careers. My secret was safe from my father. This little mean streak of mine allowed me to keep all of my boys on a retainer, call it black mail, when I needed a favor. I am proud to say my little black list was getting longer by the minute, and I was looking forward to an influx of new boy toys when we returned to the base in the fall.

I digress; let's get back to the canyon. I was contemplating how to describe the breathtaking vistas stretched out before me but was having trouble formulating a passage that did not mimic the entries from prior years, when my sisters called out to me. I got to my feet and turned, too quickly for the steep hillside, and I stumbled and fell backwards. I desperately tried to grab on to something, anything, to stop my momentum downhill but ended up with dirt, sand and stones in my hands instead. As I was falling and screaming, all my life choices seemed so empty and useless. I heard my sisters yelling my name as my body was pulled in all directions simultaneously. It hurt so much, the pain knocked me right out.

New place

I woke up and found myself in a terrible lightning storm, gasping for air. I was surrounded with wispy tendrils of mist that burned my lungs. With every breath I felt like I was drowning in acid. Instinctively I wanted to breathe deeper to get more air; but, instead, I inhaled more burning mist flooding me with pain and adrenalin. I tried to get up but my body was too heavy and I felt pain throughout my bones. I could feel slippery mossy grass underneath my fingers, making it difficult to catch hold. Conclusively, I thought that I had fallen and punctured my lungs and broke all my bones. It was so dark I could not see anything and could no longer hear my sisters. I was thankful that the intermittent lightning allowed me to see my surroundings sporadically now and then. I wanted to cry out for help, but for that, I couldn't take in enough air.

I thought if I could move to higher ground, just a few feet away, I could signal for help or at least I would be better visible to the search party. I moved a few centimeters at a time. Every move crawling on this slippery soft ground was as exhausting as climbing up a cliff. Moving at a snail's pace, I headed toward a little hill a few feet away, although it seemed to be miles away. The slimy ground got slipperier and softer with every move. I was so exhausted I just wanted to lie down and die. I put my face to the ground and with a jolt I noticed that the ground was undulating slowly beneath me.

I looked closer and realized to my disgust that I was crawling on top of giant worms. I immediately tried to scream, and with all my remaining energy, attempted to crawl towards the hill. I was never so freaked out in my life. With every move I seemed to sink deeper and deeper between the worms. Now they were crawling all over my body under my neck and fingers.

"This is what Hell really must look like." I was convinced that I must have died from the fall off the cliff and now I was in hell! My heart was pounding in my throat. At this point I was treading worms, and completely lost the ability to move forward. Then I felt something grabbing my leg. I wanted to turn around to see what it was but drained of all energy, I resigned. I just wanted it to be over quickly, whatever "it" was. With peace I welcomed the black out that followed.

I woke up still gasping for air, lying on the ground in some kind of dark cave. A soldier with a helmet and a black uniform that looked like a space suit was leaning over me. Another soldier was firing at something with very bright lasers making sounds like lightning. Was I in the middle of a war zone? Who was shooting at us? And who were they shooting at? The soldier leaning over me looked a little like a videogame soldier from the future. He got up and was about to leave. Desperately I wanted to scream, "Don't leave me here! Please help!" but I could not get a word out. Instead I collected all my strength and reached out to him. He was beyond my grasp. He looked over his shoulder while he was walking away and froze. Warily he turned around still looking at me. Slowly he bent over me, extended his hand and pulled me up. Limply I leaned into him noting that he appeared to be larger than any man I had ever encountered. He held my hand like he was waiting for something. I kept trying to say, "Air, I need air," but he didn't respond. Instead he tapped at his helmet, which retracted backwards. I still could not breathe, and did not know where I was or what was going on, but the way he held my hand made me trust him, that all would be OK.

When he finally looked at me, I noticed his strange dead

looking eyes. I thought he had very weird contacts. His eyes were vibrant green outlined with a sharp black line. I could swear the inside of them was moving like it was alive. I found myself staring, unable to look away or focus properly from lack of oxygen. Yet I could not help thinking that his eyes looked sad. His face was covered with scars and he was very pale with short black hair. His hand never let go of mine, and I was grateful he did not leave me there. He picked up a vial and pressed it against the base of his skull. It made a sucking noise and appeared to cause him lots of discomfort, but he did not make a sound. Then he took the same vial and placed it at the base of my skull. Why did I trust him? The injection stung like hell. A pulling pain spread from the point of the injection over my entire body. Terrified I looked at the strange soldier, who still held my hand, wondering what he did to me. He did not appear like he wanted to hurt me, yet he had calmly caused me a lot of pain.

With an unprecedented force the pain spread over my body, causing seizures and convulsions. The word hell had a completely new meaning now. The soldier looked into my eyes and placed his other hand on my chest. With another hissing sound came more pain, but only for a brief moment, then all pain completely disappeared. My body was still seizing and convulsing but at least there was no more pain. I felt secure feeling his hand still tightly holding mine. Then I passed out again.

Where am I?

I woke up again in a semi-dark, sterile and quiet room. Thankfully, there was no pain or seizures and I could breathe normally. I was on top of a slab that was covered in sandy gel, and I was dressed in fibrous grey bandages. I looked up and saw a three dimensional hologram of my body above me. I was sore but didn't feel any muscle weakness. I got up, turned around and jumped in place. I felt light like a feather. When I looked back at the image of my body, I could see my skeleton, muscles, organs and veins with my blood circulating in them. I've never seen such advanced technology before. My lungs looked funny, not like what I remembered from biology class. Strange fibers were winding over and around my muscles.

The hologram had a magnified portion of my blood vessels, where I could see bugs moving inside of my veins. I looked closer and they looked more like microscopically small robots or nanites, but biological. At least I was hoping that's what they were. It was a little too advanced for my taste. But I was glad I was out of the worm jungle.

There was nobody in the room except the soldier who saved me. He was so tall, at least seven feet or so. I felt naked and exposed in my bandages. I took a look around and found my clothes. I put them on making sure the soldier was not looking. I walked up to him and tapped his back. He looked at me, but no matter what I asked him, he wasn't answering. I was getting angry that he was ignoring me. So I decided to look for someone else, anyone, who would give me some answers. I went through a door into a hallway. I looked left then right, but saw nothing that would give me any clues about where I was, only a long endless hall. I looked back at my soldier, but he gave me no direction.

Determined to find answers, I went right. The next room down the hall was similar to the one I just left; this room was filled with scientific-looking equipment and more green eyed, seven-foot tall people who looked like scientists. They all looked at me curiously when I entered the lab. I started firing questions.

"Where am I? What happened to me? Where are my sisters and my father? Can I talk to them?" But they just looked at me, like my soldier, in silence. I kept repeating my questions, getting louder and more agitated. I even pulled on some of their arms, angling for some kind of a response, but nothing. Spinning on my heels I left abruptly intending to visit each room until I got answers. My soldier followed me although he kept his distance.

After a handful of rooms, I became frustrated. Finally, I slid down onto the floor in the corridor and started crying. What kind of a strange hell is this? What is going to happen to me? Is this a nightmare? Or am I in a coma? I wanted answers badly and I was scared. I had not been this scared since I was 5 years old when I was convinced there were monsters in my closet holding my childhood stuffy hostage.

Ironically, my dad was the last person to come to mind to ask for help. He would tell me to calm down, assess the situation by observing everything, and then regroup. In short, "take a knee." When I was five, "taking a knee" did not make much sense to me. But for some inexplicable reason I took comfort in his advice and knew what to do now. So what were all the details and facts in this situation? We had worms, seven foot tall, green-eyed soldiers who were most likely enhanced, difficulty breathing, first an inability to get up and now the ability to walk, a strange base, mysterious fabric, futuristic equipment, and it looked like they injected me with nanites. Was I an experiment? It was very weird that people did not talk.

The list was very long, and when I added it all together, I knew that my imagination was not good enough to come up with all of this. Therefore, I could not be in a coma. So if it was not in my head, then what was it? I was determined to collect more information. I got up and started walking again. The long, empty corridor had many more rooms of different sizes. Some were small, like the one I awoke in, and others were huge, like a concert hall and even bigger. All of them had equipment and scientists, dressed in military-like uniforms. At least that is what they looked like to me. I felt nauseous and shaky and that's when it hit me that I was starving. I checked my pockets for anything edible I could have stashed away, but found nothing. To my delight, I found my phone in my pocket. How stupid of me not to think about it sooner. The battery was almost dead and, as expected there were no bars. A top-secret facility like this would have jamming devices to prevent unauthorized calls. However, I was glad I had my music. It had taken me a long time to create my perfect playlist. I checked the time and realized that 32 hours had passed since my accident.

Wow. It was time for me to eat something. I looked at my soldier and tried to tell him with my hands that I was hungry. I touched my stomach. I even pointed at my mouth, but he was just so incredibly non-committal. He was like a porcelain doll, expressionless and never changing. I wished I could shake him out of his stoic state. He probably had orders not to talk to me, but the least he could do was to bring me to someone who could. Frustrated, I screamed, "HUNGRY." He stood there like a statue. I slid down the wall and started thinking about all the food I could eat. I could almost taste it. After everything, I was not getting any closer to figuring out where I was or what was happening to me. So I took a deep breath and got up. It was time to keep going and maybe, by chance, find a kitchen or mess hall.

Further down the hall a giant laboratory that looked like an airplane hangar caught my attention. I walked in and saw hundreds, maybe thousands, of glass containers with humans suspended in fluid. Horrified, I turned around and started running. I screamed for help with little hope I would get any but I had to try. My soldier ran after me. I was convinced he would catch me and I would end up in one of those tubes. I ran blindly screaming with him right at my heels chasing me. My knees weakened and I stumbled, but he was so quick he caught me midair. He carried me back to the lab I came out of. This time there were three soldier-like scientists in the room. As soon as I was laid on the slab with the sandy gel, my body anatomy was displayed overhead. My soldier backed away and placed himself next to the door like a guard. I wondered at this point if I was a prisoner and what they would do to me next.

One of the scientists, a tall, brown haired man with a short forehead, approached me with something similar to a syringe. I was about to jump off the slab when I felt my soldier's soothing, but strong, hand in mine. What was it about him and his touch that calmed me down and made me blindly trust him? With my guard there I let them inject me with the syringe. I immediately felt better and energized but I still felt hungry. The tall scientist with the short forehead gave me a large petri dish with dry chunks in it. The chunks reminded me of dog food. The tall scientists placed a chunk in my mouth. It tasted strange, like fish, meatballs, potatoes and various vegetables, all mixed together, dried and processed into this chunk. I was so hungry I ate without hesitation.

I emptied the dish and jumped off the slab. Replenished, I wanted to see if I was a prisoner or free to continue exploring. My soldier, or guard, let me pass and, as expected, continued to follow me like before. Not wanting to push my luck I went back to the room where I saw people suspended in fluid. Maybe I could help them. For some reason I was not put in one of those containers and that did not appear to be the soldiers' intent. I kept walking down the hall, suspiciously checking back at my companion, wondering whether his behavior towards me would change. I arrived at the lab hangar and walked in thinking that it did not make any sense for them to let me walk around unless it was a mistake shortly to be corrected. The room was filled with military like scientists, similar to those taking care of me before. They were walking everywhere and obviously monitoring the humans in those fluid tubes.

I started checking each tube to see if I recognized anybody. I was terrified at the thought that I could potentially find one of my sisters or all of them in there or even my father. Even though I hated him, he did not deserve that. On closer inspection, I saw fetuses, infants, children and young adults. The oldest appeared to be in their 20's. I did not see any older people in those containers. Were they killing everybody 30 and over? What about my father? Is that why I was still alive?

"Oh!" I exclaimed with a sharp intake of air, when I finally recognized someone.

Unwilling to believe my eyes I looked back at my companion. It was him! The man in the tube had no scars and looked significantly younger. They were definitely related. A younger brother maybe? Emotionless he kept staring at me. The logo on the canister was the same logo on his left shoulder. The same logo was on the next five containers, but the bodies varied in age by about 5 years. Was this his family? Looking closer I noticed that all of the glass containers were about 8 feet tall. They were the perfect size to fit a grown man like this soldier. The fact that none of the people I met in this facility were older than 20 was also very bizarre. My mind was whirling. Cloning?

With all I had seen that day, I deduced that this must be a cloning facility. I turned to the soldier and asked hesitantly if this was how they came to be. He just kept looking at me. I thought about the natural reproduction and birth cycle and how much better it was than this artificial cold and distant process. I understood his emotionless demeanor better. Anything was better than this! I looked at those containers and for the first time in my life I was grateful for my upbringing. I took a last look around the giant warehouse and realized this could never have been kept secret on Earth. Not for the 30 years or so it would have taken to experiment and create the first clone. I went cold and my vision narrowed as I realized, I wasn't on Earth any more. Unable to move, my face must have resembled the soldier in color and expression.

The soldier instantly picked me up and carried me out of there. Back in the hallway, he placed me slowly on the floor and kneeled right in front of me looking directly into my eyes. I think this is the first time I saw him show any sign of emotion. A glimpse of questionable compassion was revealing itself, melting the porcelain expression.

I was clearly in shock. My breathing was shallow and rapid and I was deathly cold. I had read about it but never experienced it myself. He held my hand and looked right at me, as if to say snap out of it. Maybe this was just what I knew needed to happen. I kept my focus on him, as I realized he was my only constant in this never-ending nightmare. He saved my life more than once and he always reset my mind. He made me feel safe and hopeful, like a friend I never knew I had. The feeling in my legs started to come back, my heart slowed and breathing got easier. He kept holding my hand, and I felt his warm skin and raw strength. I felt strangely safe.

It looked like we were going to be together for a while. I needed to give him a name other than 'my soldier,' 'shadow' or 'companion.' He was not offering any suggestions. I studied him, trying to come up with the right name, when I noticed his logo resembled cards stacked on top of a dragon. I was playing around with the names Dragon, Dragan and Drache. I rolled the name around in my mind and smiled. Yes, he looked like a Drak. Drak from the planet Draco. I liked that. I felt better. Now I knew who he was and where I was, even if I had to name everything myself. Assuming this would be my future home, I was determined to find out all I could about it. In the spirit of exploration, I got up and started walking down the same corridor. The base was huge, hundreds of pathways and rooms and corridors filled with marching soldiers in uniforms. There were soldiers everywhere; the base was teeming with life.

I passed the small labs and the cloning lab and paused at the huge armory, where hundreds of Draco soldiers suited up into their combat suits and got their weapons. The combat suits were actually just top-heavy backpacks on top of a black rubbery one-piece suit. I saw a soldier activate one, without any physical activation of any kind, right before me. It rippled outwards, converting the rubber into a full body hard-shell armor over their entire body. It was so cool.

In addition to weapons, the room was filled with all kinds of strange robots, vehicles, and male and female human-looking soldiers like Drak. They noticed my presence but ignored me. Not threatened by me at all, they resumed their activities. I could not help but notice that they all were well toned and moved with alacrity, purpose and unison even when dismounting the layers of light but robust armor. It was quite beautiful. I could have watched them all day. I was feeling better noticing that, despite the fact they were relatively giant compared to me, some soldiers were cuter than others, but so far I preferred Drak. I looked back at Drak and blushed.

In my new and bizarre world, the most shocking thing wasn't the clone lab or that I was on another planet. This place had another giant surprise for me. I slowly walked towards the next room. My jaw dropped when I arrived at a plane hangar or, should I say, a shuttle hangar!

Being convinced I was on another planet was one thing, but seeing it with my own eyes gave me the chills. Additionally, as insanely incredible as it would be to be on a base on another planet, this was a space station. In space! I could see the stars from there as clearly as I could see Drak. Who gets to see that? No longer a nightmare, it was something from a dream. I was on an alien space station; and ironically, I was the alien! I looked back at Drak to confirm that I was not dreaming. He looked surprised at my reaction. I guess it was nothing special for him but I never imagined going into space. What would my father think if he could see me now? In space among aliens! More disturbingly, what would he do if the situation was reversed and Drak, the alien was on Earth? I was convinced that after painful interrogation and tests, Drak would find his end on a research table being cut open. It was a morbid and gruesome image, and at that moment, I swore to myself that I would protect and save Drak with my life just like he protected and saved me back on the planet, if that would ever happen.

Looking at the vastness of the stars, I needed to share this overwhelming view with someone. I moved closer to Drak and reached out backwards to grab his hand. He tilted his head questioning, when I settled my head against his chest while admiring the view for a little while longer. My mind grew sluggish. I needed sleep. I was physically and mentally exhausted. I had spent 32 hours in my new reality and was feeling overwhelmed.

Sleep

I wondered if my soldier would wait by my side if I fell asleep in one of the hallways or somewhere in a corner. I did not think I could find my way back to the gel slab lab. Honestly, the thought that I would wake up alone in this place, among all the other aliens, terrified me. Something about my soldier made me feel like he was close to me, and I would rather forfeit my sleep than risk losing him in this ginormous place.

I think another hour or two passed before a female soldier came. She was tall like the rest of them and had weird eyes like the others, although hers were slightly different, resembling snake eyes. Her facial features and many scars made her look intimidating and yet exotically pretty. It looked like she came to relieve Drak from his post because she began watching and following me, and he walked away from me. I wanted to know where he was going so I followed Drak and she followed me. I kept talking and asking questions, I guessed by now it was fruitless to expect a reply, but I wanted to break the awful silence.

Drak went to a part of the station I hadn't gone to before. It was filled with hundreds of pods. The Dracos went in and out of them and Drak seemed to wish to do the same. He waved his hand over the sensor panel and it opened. He placed himself in it and was about to close it when I stopped the lid by pushing against it. He pointed at the pod next to his, but I did not want to go in there. What if he left and I did not notice? I would be alone in there, scared and nervous the entire time. Why did they go in there anyway? Were those revolving oval, slick-looking pods going somewhere? What did those pods do? I freaked out when I realized I was holding up the line of Dracos behind us patiently waiting to go to the pods.

I think out of desperation, Drak waved me into his pod. I wasn't convinced I would fit, and it felt very awkward, but it beat the alternative. I wanted to go wherever he was going. I hesitated but he grabbed my hand impatiently. Next thing I knew, the lid had closed over us. Swallowing my panic, I inspected the inside of the pod. It was laid out with a very dry sandy gel, the same consistency as the lab slab. It was dark; but I felt a sudden itch in my eyes, and then I could see everything. My eyes must have been altered just like my lungs, bones and muscles. I had developed night vision.

Drak was lying on his back with his eyes closed like a new G. I. Joe doll in its package. I tried to make myself as small as I could, so that I touched him as little as possible. I was worried that he would regret allowing me in to the pod. I thought about the situation and concluded that I was all right, really all right given all that happen to me, which was strange. It took about a minute before I fell asleep to the soothing thrum of his heart. The next thing I knew the lid was open, revealing in all awkwardness that I had cozied up to Drak and drooled all over his shoulder. His eyes were still closed and I hoped he was sleeping and did not notice. I jumped out of the pod quickly and Drak gracefully followed me. The woman solider was still standing outside waiting for me. She looked at me with suspicion and disapproval then she looked at Drak and walked away. I did not like her at all.

I deduced from her absence that her watch was over and Drak was back on duty to watch me. Meanwhile I was rested and strangely I felt clean, like a newborn baby. I wondered if there were also little bugs or nanites in the sandy gel taking care of our hygiene while we rested. This of course would make sense given their advanced technology. I made sure I did not lose my phone. The music on it was, at this point, invaluable to me, and as I glanced at it, my heart skipped a few beats when I noticed that the battery was fully loaded. I guess the pods purpose in this case was self-explanatory. No need for me to look for a wall outlet anymore. Wonderful as that might have been, I was distracted by hunger again. I figured if I walked to the lab where they fed me last time, they could manufacture that disgusting but nourishing dog food for me again. It made me feel like a dog trying to explain to his master he is hungry.

Is that what I was to them? A pet? I looked at Drak, hoping at least he would not see me that way. In an afterthought, demeaning as it was, at least I was not their lab rat. Following my plan I arrived at the lab, picked up one of the glass dishes and showed it to one of the scientists. He actually filled it up for me. It was a small victory that gave me hope that I could possibly find a way to communicate with them one of these days until I found a way home. After I satisfied my hunger, I was ready to explore all possibilities to find my place and purpose in this new society I belonged to.

If I was ever going to find a place for myself in Drak's world, I needed to learn my options. So far, I observed that there were 4 casts: soldiers, scientists, probably pilots for the shuttles and someone who gave orders. You always have those. I did not have enough confidence to become a pilot, general or scientist, so the only thing left for me to try out was to become a soldier. I was 5 foot 7 and, compared to these 7 feet units, I was a dwarf. I was not even half as strong or fast and I lacked endurance. And there was the little detail of lack of communication. As far as I could tell they all moved as if controlled by one mind. I could not relate because, sometimes, I had more than one mind in my own head. But giving up was not an option and at least I could have fun trying. The first step: How would I explain to "Mr. observe me, shadow me but don't talk to me" that I wanted to enlist?

I could not imagine how a boot camp would look in this sort of place. I started saluting and pointing at myself, but he did not get it. I pointed at his uniform and at my outfit, but nothing. I even did some push-ups in hopes he would understand, but no such luck. I must have looked pretty funny to him. And then I did something awkward. I reached for his gun strapped to his right thigh. That move of course was very stupid even for me. I have never in my life seen anybody or anything move as fast as he did in that very moment, grabbing the gun before me and dangling it over my head. If I had been on Earth my guard would have shot me on the spot for this move or tossed me, at least, into the brig, but not him. It was almost like he was toying with me, dangling the gun, just out of reach, not threatened by me at all. Resigned to this failed attempt, I moved on as I explored the station, when something changed. He put his gun away and indicated with his eyes for me to follow him. Then he turned around and started walking.

Ok that was new. I was incredibly curious. Where were we going? Had he understood my request? We arrived in a darkened room and again my eyes switched into night mode. I could actually see something. Drak handed me a relative to his own, a much smaller version of his gun, and pointed at tiny red flashes dancing all around us. I picked up the gun, which appeared heavy, but was light, and looked for the trigger. Growing up on a military base, needless to say, I know my way around guns, but I had never seen anything like this. There was no trigger! How was I supposed to fire this thing? I looked it over from right to left, bottom to top and found nothing. Was he making fun of me? He noticed my conundrum and gently took the gun out of my hand. He pointed with the gun, closed his eyes and gently touched my head. The gun fired.

He handed the gun back to me and stepped out of the room leaving me alone. I guess the instruction part was done. I pointed the gun just like he did, closed my eyes, and hoped that it would shoot. When this didn't work, I thought, "Shoot." Again, nothing happened. I felt silly and was too embarrassed to walk out of that room unsuccessful. He finally trusted me with something he thought I actually could do. I tried again, and again, and again but no shots were fired. I spent half a day trying. It felt like forever. I was just too proud to come out without at least one shot. I sat down on the floor and started crying. Useless! That was what I was! I couldn't even shoot in this stupid place! With the gun in my hand, over my lap and tears pouring over my face, I imagined how simple it looked, he just pointed and shot. Flash! – I screamed in pain as the laser penetrated my calf. The gun had gone off and shot me in my leg. I was in pain, but I was ecstatic with happiness. I DID IT!!!! Ow. Ow. Ow.

Funny, I thought a gun wound should hurt more than a paper cut, but seconds later, that's what it felt like. Dark as it was, I could not examine the extent of my injury, so I decided to repeat the shot before I forgot how I did it, and then call Drak for help. So again I thought, "Shoot." Again, nothing happened. I was growing more frustrated, then I thought about how Drak did it, imagined him shooting and it fired. I was not sure if I could repeat it. Then I was down on the floor. It was covered in wet, slippery fluid. My face bathing in it, I tasted iron. Could it be blood? My blood? Soon I felt Drak pick me up and carry me away. I wanted to share my revolutionary success but the effort was too great and everything was so blurry. I woke up in the lab, again. At this point I was hoping I had insurance in this place given how often I needed medical services. After quick review the diagnosis was clear even to me. Apparently I had a hole like a fist through my leg. I had lost lots of blood which caused me to fall to the floor. The little gun I was handed had quite the punch.

23

They put something on top of the hole and I could instantly see the wound closing. It was like a miracle to me, but I imagined something perfectly natural to them. And why didn't it hurt more, I wondered. In fact the last time I remembered excruciating pain was when Drak injected me with something out of his spine the first time we met. Whatever painkillers he gave me, I was glad they were still working. It took only a couple of hours before this huge wound was fully closed, leaving me with a scar I was very proud of. I looked at Drak and the many scars on his face and hands. There was not much exposed skin and the little I could see was covered in them. Either way all his scars made him even more exciting and handsome in my eyes. Now I looked a little more like a soldier, but still had to learn how to fire this damn gun. I worried a little that after I almost killed myself and showed my enormous incompetency, they might not let me touch one again. Like handing a loaded gun to a kid, the next person I could hurt could be one of them! That would explain also why Drak showed me how to shoot but then left the room. To my surprise, as soon as I was able to get up from the slab, Drak was walking me right back into the shooting range.

Adapting

The next few days I spent eating my food chunks which I called chow chow, sleeping a little and going to the shooting range. There was no sun to rise and set but the rhythm the Dracos had was 20 hours working and 10 hours recharging in the pods. Almost like battery-operated bio-robots, they didn't sleep. It was rough in the beginning for me. I was used to sleeping in, but my body adapted relatively quickly. I now slept in the same pod with Drak, no questions asked. I knew it was weird but this place was too cold and strange for me, and I was afraid to be alone. With Drak it was practice, practice followed by a small or big injury and trip to the infirmary, and then some more practice. There was no fun, entertainment or just hanging out. The Dracos were like machines, purely mission and purpose oriented and all of them had a very outlined and defined duty to fulfill like casts.

Every so often Drak and his unit were called to go on a mission. I would observe them suiting up, choosing their guns and equipment, always wishing I could go with them, or even better, for them not to have to go at all. Especially Drak. Losing Drak was for me like losing my anchor, like losing Earth all over again. One mistake and he could be gone. They could activate his clone, but the last download would only include his memories last recorded in the pod and only data, no emotions and not what he thought and felt living his final moments or, most importantly, anything he felt for me. To me, that felt like the clone would be his double and knew what he knew, but it would not be my Drak.

Every time I would watch him gear up, I felt anxious because it could be the last time I would see him. He was the only one I had a connection to. I could not bear to lose him. On his way to the ship I always squeezed my hand into his, as this might be the last squeeze I would feel in this place. I liked to believe he felt the same way. Each time he would slow down slightly and look into my eyes, as if committing my image to memory. Maybe he was just calming me down.

The waiting was torture, but as soon as I saw them return, it was like getting the best birthday present ever. My life resumed and all was good again. Those were the times I was the most lonely and lost. On his way back from the ship, as soon as he would walk by me, I made sure my hand was in his and our eyes locked into each other's for a brief moment. This brief act was like a warm blanket covering my torn sole. I was a Draco now, and I liked it as long as he was there. Resuming with my training was just a way for us to move on from whatever he came back from.

After a while, getting a laser injury or a broken limb here and there was just part of my practice; and I became quite good at shooting. It was hard to believe that this was my life now. I was by far not as fast as Drak, or any other Draco, but for a human I was incredible. My aim was 7 out of 10 and fast like lightning. With the training I wasn't so bored anymore and I was proud of myself. I felt as though I was taking control of my situation, but I felt hollow and longed for human contact. I missed my family, especially my sisters. I never really let them in, because I always thought I was better on my own. Now when I was on my own, I would give my life to be with them again. I even missed my father. I had thought I was so independent, yet here I was missing their playful banter and companionship. With everyone here so self-contained and icy, it was unlikely that I would find a replacement... No, I cannot go there, I will get back, I will...

Drak must have sensed my distress because lately he sat next to me when I ate and he walked with me instead of following me. I also noticed his subtle hugs in the pod making me feel wanted and safe. I wondered whether he was capable of deeper feelings or if he was doing it for my benefit. I was thankful and impressed that my Draco instinctively knew what I needed.

Exploring

With my body adapted to the long days, I wasn't tired right away. After I entered the pod, many things went through my head keeping me awake. I was freezing; the temperature in this place sometimes dropped real low so I moved closer to Drak and wrapped my body around his. Drak had the uncanny ability to withdraw as soon as the pod covering was in place. He did not move. I tried to adapt and follow his example, but my mind was in overdrive. After reviewing the events of the day and congratulating myself on my small accomplishments, like avoiding the physical recalibration injury room, I investigated the pod. Since there was not much to examine I turned to Drak. Tentatively I touched his uniform and immediately noted the texture. How many times had Drak picked me up and I never noticed the texture of his uniform? I mused.

I slid my fingers gently along the seam and I felt a prickle on my fingertip. I had assumed that Drak's uniform was similar to the material they had given me to wear but after close inspection I would not describe Drak's uniform as material. Although it had the feel of cloth, the outer layer felt like gel or the plastic wrap used to cover leftovers. Beneath the plastic lining were millions of iron dust particles in varying degrees of thickness, thicker over the muscle groups. They reacted to the slightest pressure from me.

As I moved my fingers over his uniform, the iron dust under the plastic flowed and moved. It reminded me of a toy I had as a child. We would move a magnet around to coax metal filings over a face to decorate it with hair, mustaches and beards. But this was different in that the filings moved intuitively as one. It reminded me of a diving expedition to a shipwreck I did with a Navy SEAL.

We swam into a school of sardines so thick that I could not see the sand below. As I watched the diver move through the school of fish, the sardines disbursed and then came together to their original shape once the diver was through, like he had never existed or even disturbed their formation. I would have played with the material more but I did not want to wake Drak with my uninvited explorations.

If it undulates and sways under non-aggressive actions would it shield and protect from aggressive actions? Does this layer have a purpose beyond basic clothing decency or is it armor-like in its functionality? I did not dare try anything rash with Drak or any other Draco, but I watched and drew my own conclusions. When you really think about it, our skin is not much different. It is made out of millions of cells forming a layer over our body. The only difference is that it does not readily move. Now that I was thinking about it, I wondered if his uniform was his skin. Was there another layer beneath? I had never seen Drak undress or change. Is Drak a male in the sense of a human male? I suddenly felt hot and knew that if I could see myself in the mirror my face would be bright red. At this point I didn't think I would care, but thinking about it felt intrusive, and given that I saw him as my guardian, it felt somehow wrong.

Thinking about the uniform, or skin, I wondered if the cells were different on different parts of his body. Did his hands have a different skin color than his torso, and were they the same substance? Ignoring my initial reservations, within the confined area of the pod, I searched for something like a zipper or buttons or any other mechanism to open the uniform so I could see if he had skin underneath it. After a cursory search, I did not find any way to open it. Curiosity got the best of me; I wanted desperately to see beneath. I wanted to know that the dark fabric I was touching and drooling over during my sleep was not his skin. I was not going to be able to rest until I found a reasonable answer.

I gently touched his cheek, but he did not move. Drak's skin felt so warm and supple, like the soft skin of a baby, not at all what I would have expected of a roughed up soldier. Then again, he was probably only a couple years old. Fresh from the cloning pods, I thought, as my mind envisioned Drak in the cloning pods at various ages. I could see the lifespan of a Draco soldier body was not very long because of the fighting with little regard for their own body and injuries. As far as I knew, when they die their mind was simply transferred to the next clone, ready and waiting in the cloning lab. All the experiences and memories of a seasoned hundred-year-old fighting machine, stored and recorded in the pods each and every time they go to recharge, would download to the next clone. Brilliant when you think about it. They could skip the whole training and learning and just go.

I kept sliding my fingers from his chin to his ear, and caught myself enjoying it more than I would have anticipated; but it did in fact feel different from his uniform. So the uniform wasn't his skin. Thank god! I felt relieved. It was awkward enough that I was with him in the pod, but imagining being with him and lying on top of nothing but his skin was a tad too much. At least not unless I wanted it, and I knew about it, I guess. I moved my fingers along the surface of the uniform again but this time I imagined his naked pectorals and chest and how nice they must look from his well-trained physic. Rather than seeing him as a person, I felt like I was lying next to a huge Ken doll I could play with. To my surprise, this time, the black sandy particles, of which his uniform was made, parted like the red sea as if wind had blown them away dragging the translucent gel right with them and exposing his skin.

I brought my hand back with a startle. That was unexpected.

I looked up at Drak to see if he was disturbed by my explorations. He still had not moved a muscle. That was good. I wasn't sure how I was going to explain why part of his uniform was no longer covering his body. It was so much fun moving the dust, but any attempt to put it back, backfired on me and exposed more of his chest. At some point the initial square inch was so big that his entire chest was exposed. While I took the time to admire his bare chest and confirm his incredible build, I also began to wonder about my ability to control the nanites with my mind. First the gun, now Drak's uniform. Is that why no one here speaks? They transfer their will through their minds. I mean I had suspected something like that but I was thinking about transferring thoughts in a sense of saying something without using your vocal cords. Yet this was different. You don't just think a command and the nanites do it, following orders. You have to actually picture the end result of what needs to happen. And boy, I can picture so many things… My hand swiveled around his abdominal muscles. Quickly I caught myself drifting into the forbidden zone. If that was the case, then I was going to have to control my imagination or there was going to be a lot of explaining to do. And given my situation, I was not sure that I was up for that right now.

Okay, mind out of the gutter, back to basics. The weapons only fired if I imagined them firing and his suit opened and reacted to me when I imagined it actually open. Was this the key to their communication? How could I use it? Were they more than telepaths? For some reason this made perfect sense, and something inside said, 'Finally!'

I never saw them move their lips or use hand signals. They did not appear to have a language, but individuals understood each other. It would make sense that they didn't need language or words, if they were able to transfer images and feelings to each other. But, why did they appear not to have any feelings? Or at least not act upon them?

Perhaps it was not efficient and would only get in the way of progress? I could see where anger and other emotions would transfer from one person to another like a virus, spreading throughout society and causing harm and confusion. Communicating with images, I can work with that, I thought, smiling to myself. I was not a telepath but I was good at Pictionary!

I got distracted thinking about the cute guy next to me, asking me to explore his incredibly sculptured body, using nothing but my fingertips. All the while, thinking about communicating? What is wrong with me? I had to get my priorities straight. I thought about how awkward it would be if he caught me undressing him. Thinking about consequences never stopped me before, but knowing about those consequences required me to have a plan B, just in case. I decided to continue my research. I removed the pesky dust from his top and let me tell you, he was firm and his chest was warm like an oven. I got goose bumps as I felt his skin, and my fingers traveled again slowly downwards toward his six-pack. It was exhilarating. I told myself I would stop a little below his navel, or rather where I thought his navel should be if he had one, and then leave him his privacy. After all, he was not a Ken doll. But then, sliding over his well-formed body my fingers developed a mind of their own.

With my newfound understanding I found myself unable to stop and my mind went far beyond just looking. I suddenly found myself seeing him with me. I felt a chill, then heat, a strong heartbeat, flushed cheeks, and soft, slow breathing. Warmth flooded my body and butterflies fluttered within. This new energy forced its way out, finding an outlet on any surface where Drak and I connected. Butterflies became prickles of static electricity, which went right through my fingers increasing in intensity and discharging onto his skin. With the intensity of my fantasies, the intensity of the static energy increased substantially, to the point where a mini lightning zapped Drak with a micro charge, waking him up. I heard about sparks flying when you meet the right guy, but this was something completely different. Drak's eyes flew open in surprise but nothing else moved. Both of us were deadlocked, eyes held, mine in guilty pleasure, his in confusion. Like a small child, caught in the act of stealing a cookie before supper, I withdrew my hand as if I could erase what I had been doing.

To my surprise Drak took my hand and placed it slowly and gently back on his warm chest. His heartbeat was stronger than I remembered and he kept hold of my hand while it rested upon his chest. I did not mean to, but I sighed again. For the first time, I wasn't in control and I kind of liked it. Drak holding my hand on his firm partially exposed body and looking deep into my eyes, made me realize that I could maybe go further or even all the way. Was I ready for that?

I decided to take it slow. This time. I rolled onto my side and settled against Drak. I almost sighed again but caught myself. Maybe it was my imagination, but Drak gave my hand a slight squeeze, so I cuddled closer to him turning the exploration to an intimate hug. Over the next few days all I could think about was him. A stranger became my savior, then my guard, then something like a friend; one could even say my best friend, and now I was afraid I had ruined it. I avoided direct eye contact and his touch, yet I could not stop myself from staring at him and was terrified of him catching me doing so. What made it worse is that we could not talk about it. And even if we could talk, I am not sure what I would have said. It did not help that he possibly could read my thoughts. And if he really could read my thoughts and I had not ruined whatever it was we had, why wasn't he responding or doing something? My head was buzzing like a subway with all the discoveries I had made in the pod and the conclusions I had drawn, right or wrong; but they were overshadowed by the mischievous side of my brain and my fantasies about him. I saw Drak in a different light now. Did he view me differently too? While I was torturing myself with my own thoughts, Drak continued my soldier education, as if nothing had changed between us, and graduated me from gun skills to physical training. From previous experience, I expected injuries, and naturally I was very, very apprehensive, but welcomed the diversion.

The physical skills area was dark and consisted of obstacles and traps. Over the hills, under the hills, through rabbit holes and swinging from ropes and branches were just some of the intense training activities. I had not spent much time on the planet surface, but imagined that the hills and the rest of it were a much smaller version of what could be found out there. If that were not enough, they added some shooting androids looking and bleeding like their enemy, which I later learned were the sixth species to be recognized as alien to the planet. I just called them Hexadoids. They were very intelligent, armed, animal like creatures, similar to armadillos on Earth, with antlers growing over their armor. The lasers fired at irregular intervals and various intensities. There was no discernable pattern, which made it harder to navigate the course.

With my new and revamped muscle and bone structure I could do so much more than a regular human and even any soldier my dad had trained. I was now faster, stronger, and able to leap tall buildings in a single bound. I was a real superwoman, but I knew that even at my best condition, I could not match the genetically enhanced and designed soldiers. This course was designed to challenge them, but given I was now a hybrid, I had to try my best. I wasn't going to try to outdo the Dracos, but I was eager to discover my new personal limits. For weeks I practiced tirelessly and tried to complete the obstacle course but always ended up injured or out of time. It appeared I was battling the course and it was winning. Despite it all I was slowly gaining better reflexes and spending more time battling the course than recovering in the medical room.

One day Drak brought me to one of his unit practice runs on the obstacle course. I wonder if he did that to show me how they do it to impress me or maybe to teach me how it should be done. I was not actually allowed on the course with his unit, but left alone in a room with a vividly accurate 3D model of the course. In the safety of the lab, plugged into my phone, listening to my music, I observed their well-rehearsed, synchronized pairs drop from the shuttle onto the target site. This was followed by skilled advance and secure of a 360-degree perimeter around the site with a symphony of 100% accurate laser fire. This uncanny beauty of military performance could only be achieved by a millennium of targeted practice, refined and adapted life style and undisturbed focus. While practicing there, Drak and his Unit could go through a hundred corpses a day without flinching. This was not at all the image of him I had in my head previously but was an accurate picture of who he was. I had forgotten it and needed to be reminded of it.

All my life I took military life as a daily fact, yet in this moment seeing Drak and his unit performing this stunning display of unity, made me love it. I decided to find my own way to do my best. Most girls see the ballet and dream of performing on stage as the prima ballerina. After witnessing the Draco's performance, I wanted nothing more than to fight with the Draco's on the battlefield against the evil enemy. I was not playing anymore. Like the Draco's I needed my focus to be at peak performance and I had decided, since that awkward night, to sleep in my own pod. I had crossed a line and I wanted to avoid too much contact and temptation at least until I decided whether I wanted to move forward with him or not. He was still my bodyguard and protector and therefore still in charge of my daily life.

To my surprise Drak had different plans. During one of my quick meals he set himself next to me and unexpectedly touched my hand. Normal as that might sound for us humans, it wasn't for Drak or his people. All the personal contact we had before had a purpose or I initiated it. He only held my hand when I needed comfort, to calm me down, make me feel safe or when it was required that I be compliant, or on those rarer occasions when he felt it necessary to pick me up and carry me to a destination point, like when I needed medical attention.

Even the subtle-hugs in the pod were for my benefit and not at all for his. But, this was different; he touched my hand because he wanted to. He appeared to be curious. His normally stoic face had changed slightly; he was wrinkling his forehead and twisting his head inquisitively. I was thrilled that I cracked it with just a touch. I guessed my little exploration of his skin in the pod and the electric charges had something to do with this. Thoughts of relocating to a different pod were quickly replaced with thoughts of unexplored nights. It would be selfish of me to move, after introducing Drak to the pleasures of touch and waking his curiosity. He must have surprised himself with this spontaneous act because he suddenly paused and gave me a stare as if asking for permission to continue. My cheeks were warm with pleasure and I stared back at Drak giving him permission and not denying the contact. I was very interested where this was going, particularly because, for the first time in a long time, I knew more about something than Drak did.

Encouraging him to continue, I took off my jacket and

offered my entire arm for his study. His fingers moved slowly and gently from my hand upwards to my shoulder creating small static electric sparks in the process. It was like observing a little boy playing with his new electric train for the first time. I loved watching his facial expressions as they struggled to take shape on his previously android like face. For a few brief moments he resembled a real human, catapulting me back home to Earth. How this perfect being could be so intimidating one minute and so adorable in the next was completely beyond me.

There was so much work to be done for me now. I was determined to conquer the obstacle course, which I decided to call OC as well as help Drak nurture his feelings. I may not be a Draco, but in this hybrid form I was going to show them a thing or two about how an Earth soldier does it. Unfortunately as resolute as I was to prove myself to the Dracos, it now took a backseat to my decision to teach Drak about human feelings. I called it, Human Feelings 101. I am sure that Drak's new fascination was directly related to the electric charge he received from me. After all except for the nanite/clone thing we were almost genetically alike in makeup. So why was I able to do that? He had touched many other Dracos as required by duty, but obviously this spark was new to him. He appeared to approach the sensation systematically, mentally checking off pros and cons, searching for a conclusion or some explanation of the event. I noticed before that the intensity of the charge was directly linked to feelings associated with our touch. For me it made sense that it did not happen between any other Dracos. They avoid feelings like a disease. I had to admit to myself that I was deeply attracted to Drak, more so than any other person before now, and had to wonder whether there was ever any time Dracos felt attraction and if Drak could feel it for me.

Drak was curious about his physical reaction to me, but was

that curiosity technical or was he beginning to realize that there were other purposes beyond soldiering? What I knew, and he still had to learn, was that those feelings had something to do with attraction, at this moment my attraction to him, but hopefully also his to me. I was afraid that Drak was light years away from developing any real feelings for me; therefore I resolved not to fall in love with him. Outside of the sleeping pod, he innocently wanted to explore the electric charge on other parts of my body. I was torn between stealing moments alone with Drak and guarding my emotions. I successfully diverted his attention and my resolve back to my original goal, the OC. Without hesitation or disappointment, Drak led me back to the course. I admit that I was a little disappointed that he did not insist on perusing it further, but only momentarily.

We relocated to the OC. But instead of starting my training, I walked in and sat down. I saw his puzzled face but I had to take a moment. Faced with the immensity of the OC and the realization that I did not have the luxury of millennia induced experiences, I would have to find my own way around the OC. I needed time to evaluate the situation. I was surprised that I keep referring to my father's words of wisdom as I assessed the situation, observed all the details and categorized all of the known facts. It seemed impossible for a petite little human to finish the course in the required time, without the skill and speed of a Draco. Not unless you had millennia to practice. I am a patient person but if this could not be done reasonably in the next few weeks I would be stuck here forever. I needed a loophole or shortcuts and that was going to require outside-the-box strategies.

I sat, lied down, even did a few handstands with and without music. Drak watched my efforts with calm stoicism as I attempted to see the OC for what it was, waiting for my mind to discover kinks in its perfection. Deep in thought, I caught myself staring at Drak. My thoughts drifting, I began to wonder how a human/Draco relationship would even work. It was then I had an epiphany. I got it! It was so simple. What I had originally seen as a weakness was in actuality an asset. The key was petite. I was everything that the Dracos were not. The last thing the enemy or this course was prepared to fight was me.

I saw the OC in a new light; where the Dracos had to go over the obstacles, I could slip under some of them tirelessly. My light weight and stature would allow me to swing over obstacles using branches and vines like Tarzan. I may not have the synchronous assault, but I do have the panther-like ability to blend and hide. I can get to the target much faster and easier using my vast expertise as a teenage movie watcher. I was ready to beat this course. In lieu of the full body armor and supplies preferred by the Dracos, I suited up with the casual black under-suit they wear around the base. Of course their suit was all nanites. Mine could not be since I do not have Draco skin and the nanites cannot feed off of my energy through it, but with a little help from the scientists, I had my generic, fabric suit modified with targeted padding and protection. I did not need the hard shell armor. In addition I armed myself with the small handgun Drak had given me, the one with the punch to it. I was intimately familiar with it and it suited my plan.

With purpose, I followed my loosely formulated plan knowing that I would have to adapt to individual situations as they arose. I was so busy enjoying the challenge it took me a while to notice that I had completed the course for the first time. When realization struck, I was high fiving the air and bouncing around in my victory dance. When Drak came in to collect me I bounced over to him elated and ready to hug him, but was stopped short by his body language. He was not happy at all. Something was wrong and I was beginning to believe that the something had everything to do with me. Had I violated some rule or protocol or was this how the Draco showed surprise? Sure, my victory did not have the finesse of the Draco troops but I did complete the course. That was the objective wasn't it? I guess the objective was the practice and not the goal. But I did not have hundreds of years. By the time I would have finished the Practice I would be dead! Wouldn't I? How long will I actually live with this new body? Will I be cloned too? All good questions, I just did not have answers for them.

Attraction

Of course the day was over and it was time to go to the pods. As we walked down the corridor I was energized after my win, confused by Drak's response and looking forward to some down time with Drak in the pod. As he opened the lid and settled himself in as always, I very carefully placed myself in my spot, right beside him sure not to touch. I was bashful, which was a first for me. While he was off line, I had to constantly control my thoughts. This was agony and totally unfair. He got to shut off while my mind tried to run a mile a minute with unchecked thoughts, which I could not share or act upon. And the power surges. The stupid power surges. Every touch in combination with my unchecked thoughts would cause them. It was exhausting wrestling with this one sided attraction. Should I stay or should I go? Should I rave or just say no? Should I walk away or feed this crazy dream. Great, now I was rapping. This had to stop. I kept looking for some sign that Drak was feeling something towards me. I mean we clearly had chemistry so why wasn't it happening?

Once I planted the seed it should have grown. Maybe I needed to water it a bit. Since I had mastered the course, maybe my next training session should be some good old-fashioned yoga. Maybe I can teach Drak the art of relaxation and in the meantime show off some of the more sensual moves associated with yoga. I pictured myself in my tight yoga pants bending ever so skillfully. Drak is going to watch me anyway; maybe it was time to give him something to watch. Please don't forget that in the art of teasing, I was a genius yet to be discovered.

With my new and elastic body it was easy to perform yoga and endurance wasn't a problem either. Although I can imagine that for someone who had never seen yoga before it must have looked a little silly. So in the spirit of exploration and trying new things, I dared Drak to do it with me. Boy was that funny. I've never seen any of the Dracos being so clumsy before. It was laugh out loud amusing. I tried desperately to stifle my amusement when Drak tried to follow my stretching examples and almost bellowed when Drak got caught in a full split that threatened to rip him in two but only sent him spilling onto the floor sideways instead. All the while he stared intently at my movements with, what I assumed was, wonder and some determination as I showed off my abilities. Honestly he was no different than any other human boy asked to participate in an activity with a girl of interest. His reaction was similar. I felt vindicated. He was reacting to me. I was having fun.

As his skill improved, I introduced him to more elaborate positions, which sometimes required me to assist his positioning. As funny as it was watching him, it was more amusing watching him become unbalanced. At one point he took me down with him and I could not stop laughing as he lay flat on his back with me sprawled across his chest. I was holding his hands when we fell over and I found that he was still holding my hands, staring into my face, not showing any emotion, but waiting. I stopped laughing and stared back. It seemed like an eternity that we lay there, connected. And then it happened. His eyes were gorgeous and so clear that I could see myself reflected in them. He was not helpless but vulnerable, allowing me to unbalance him. I could not help it. I kissed him. His lips were firm but resilient, sweet and sensual. I could have stayed there all day tasting and exploring just those lips. But the kiss and my thoughts were violently interrupted by a massive prickle and discharge through my lips. It made me push off his chest.

This was not a static charge you get from scuffing your socks over a plush rug. This was high voltage and it was strong enough to scare me. We both felt the jolt, but where I was visibly shaken, Drak looked as he always did with one exception, his eyes were dilated. I could tell that this was something new but welcome for him. Drak reached out a hand to help me up but I quickly sprang to my feet hoping to delay contact. My heart was racing, whether from the shock or the intense connection, I was unsure. What I did not want was a repeat of that electrical charge.

Over the next few days Drak and I returned to the OC and I was trained in traditional Draco maneuvers. Apparently I missed the point of the practice, and was no longer allowed to train on my own. At night I retired to my own pod, hoping to avoid contact with Drak. Avoiding his touch and his eyes was the only way I knew how to deal with my confusion. I wanted him to like me but at this rate I liked him more than I wanted to, and I really wanted to avoid those electrical charges. I was falling in love with him. God I hated my human weakness. Leave it to me to fall in love with a guy incapable of feeling. Why couldn't I just have fun, and like him, explore the technical application of our electric chemistry? I wanted so badly to be the old me. The one who used boys for fun and did not have a care in the world. If I wanted to be honest, I was no different than the Draco when I was on Earth. Unattached exploration in the name of science and curiosity was my motto. What changed? Was there a way to teach him to have feelings for me without developing stronger ones for him? Maybe there was a way. Yes there was a way. Instead of seeing and hating my weaknesses I needed to explore his. If I was right and Drak was reading my mind, I could show him very vividly and in full strength intensity, a human relationship. Show him what it was really about. Make him want it. His weakness was his curiosity and innocence. I wanted to introduce him to love, intimacy and desire and I wanted him to explore those emotions with me on my terms. Was it evil and manipulative to exploit his weaknesses? Yes and I was willing to do my part to find out.

Logically, the perfect vehicle to transport my thoughts was meditation. From now on I would include meditation training at the end of every yoga class. Experimentation through meditation and the unsuspecting participant was Drak. In each of the session's Drak would receive a small dose of Introduction to Relationships 101. Not too little or too much, just enough to digest in the pod during his recharge. Alone! If I was correct he would think about what I showed him in my mind during my meditation and relive it multiple times before he woke up.

A little brain washing would do him some good. Following my evil plan, over the course of the next couple of weeks I tortured Drak with my idea of the perfect relationship. Meditation started with flirtation, dating and flowers and continued all the way through the first kiss, letting nature take its course right to the mutually awesome love. This time I was not just going to place the seed and wait for it to grow. I was determined to make sure the seedling became a tree and produced juicy, sweet fruits! My plan was set, the execution flawless and complete. Now I was waiting, again. But nothing seemed to change.

Waiting for him to show any sign of affection towards me was unbearable. I thought I was more than patient and it was time now for me to confront him and see how he felt about me, and more specifically, whether he was even capable of feeling anything for me in the future. When I made up my mind, it was now or never, so when we were in the lab picking up my chow chow, I turned towards him and placed my hand on his chest the same way my hand was on his chest in the pod during my guilty exploration, in hopes that he would remember. Then I looked into his eyes imagining the two of us in a human like relationship.

I hoped that he saw it as a question and to support this notion I removed my hand slowly from his chest, wishing and hoping that he would grab it and place it back the same way he did in the pod that night long ago. But as I removed my hand, still looking deep into his eyes, he did not budge. My eyes welled with tears. His inaction spoke volumes; he was rejecting me, the answer was no. I thought my heart would stop. I was having trouble breathing, my knees were giving in, and I knew that I could no longer be around him day after day and act as if nothing happened. With tears blurring my vision I gathered all of my courage, looked directly into his face and asked him, using images, for another guard. I wheeled about and started walking away; I did not want to weep in front of him. Then he jerked my hand pulling me towards him and placed a deep warm kiss on my lips. He kissed me like a real human boyfriend would, ignoring the power discharges completely and sliding his open hand upward on my back, pressing me close against him. Surprisingly the electrical hum did not bother me at all. It just made me feel warm and fuzzy this time.

My heart beat faster and stronger than ever before. I wasn't sure whether this was just wishful thinking or reality but I was never happier. He slowed down his kisses, stepped back and handed me an obviously artificial rose. I loved the effort he displayed mimicking a human ritual including the kiss and the rose. I took the rose which instantly fell apart in my hands leaving behind the core, which to my big surprise was a red stone necklace. That was totally unexpected and so sweet! I jumped at his neck giving him a kiss. No response but this time I was okay because I know spontaneity is not natural for Dracos. One step at a time. Returning to the floor, I wiped the tears off my face and took a closer look at this marvelous present.

It was not a gemstone or anything shiny, but it meant more to me than a castle. My whole world was based on this one pivotal moment and it was a dream come true. I would remember this moment forever, I realized, as I focused on the necklace, heavy in my hand. I could feel Drak next to me radiating heat, and nothing else mattered. My own personal fairy tale, tailor made for me, my prince charming liked me!

I let him put the necklace on me and he placed it properly in the middle making sure it wasn't just hanging outside on top of my clothing, but touched my skin directly. It appeared the trinket had a purpose. What I took for a token of courtship was in actuality a cleverly designed translator for Drak's thoughts. In my meditation exercises, I had inadvertently given Drak the idea to give me the device. In his own way he was strengthening our relationship by giving me the ability to communicate with him. I loved it. The necklace appeared to be charging from my body heat. It lit up and I could suddenly see three dimensional images, like holograms, displayed in front of me in my mind that were not my own. I saw myself kissing Drak. Were these memories or was he trying to tell me to do something? Everything was silent. I was receiving images of an alien world. As I stared deep into his eyes I began to understand that the images were Drak's memories being replayed, like a movie. I saw the moment of awareness when he first heard my call for help.

That day Drak and his unit were returning to the pick-up point after their mission, when Drak heard me the first time, in his head. I was unable to talk, even less so cry out for help, but he heard me telepathically. Luckily for me, or I would be dead now. I must have been about 10 miles away and right in the middle of Hexadoids enemy lines, yet he somehow heard me. Against orders, he and his unit went to investigate and found me dying and drowning in worms. By disregarding protocol he lost most of his unit that day to the Hexadoids, except "Snake Eyes," the woman soldier who guarded me in the beginning. Even in the replay, I could sense that Drak himself could not explain his decision to rescue me, but he pulled me out of the worm pool anyway. I was unrecognizable; banged up, slimy, weakly gasping for breath and obviously close to expiring. Against their version of *Star Trek*'s Prime Directive, which limits them for the most part to study and not interfere, except to protect their research, he injected me with his nanites to save me, making me a human-Draco hybrid in the process. As consequence, I was now his responsibility. He not only had to reconstitute his unit but he had to find a way to integrate me into his society or give me up for recycling.

I was touched that he felt compelled to rescue me against his direct orders. It was then that I realized how much he had given up for me, before he even knew me. A strange connection between us led him to me. This same connection made me blindly trust him. I wondered if we were each other's destiny or a fluke. Whatever it was, I knew then that there was never a question that he would have feelings for me; it was just a matter of time. I was unchartered territory for all Dracos, and more personally to Drak, but I was now one of them. The present he gave me was so much more than just a decoration; it was a tool for furthering my integration. Drak had cleverly incorporated the device into what he perceived as my relationship fantasy.

Like a blind person seeing shadows for the first time, I was overwhelmed. I wasn't able to be a telepath and receive the full spectrum of thoughts, feelings, and sensations. But the images were good enough for me. I had a new ability to communicate which worked in both directions. Before only Drak could hear me; now with this device, other Dracos could see what I want to share with them. I tested my newfound abilities with Drak and was soon exhausted. Who could have imagined that analyzing someone else's thoughts would be so tiring? But it was so enlightening. Drak's motives had seemed so cut and dry, but now I saw they were complex as well as completely orderly and reasonable—

except where I was concerned. I was amazed that he had not tossed me aside earlier for all the trouble I had caused. But he had never given up on me.

We kissed some more before I fell asleep in Drak's arms, in perfect happiness, on the lab table. When I woke up he was gone and a soldier, unfamiliar to me, was my new guardian. Using my new necklace I asked where Drak was. It worked like a charm; unfortunately I got the wrong answer. Drak is gone, was the reply. Gone? Not getting any more specifics and feeling uneasy, I went looking for Drak. He never just left me before; something was not right. I ran into the OC, then to the armory. I took a deep breath when I finally found him. He was standing with his back to me, taking a weapon from the shelf. I walked up to him and gave him a huge hug relieved to see him. When he turned, his scars were gone and something in his face made me very uneasy. "You are not Drak," I said with crushing certainty. Like a cold shower, I was shocked with the reality of facing Drak's clone. There was only one reason they would activate a clone. Drak, my Drak, was gone. I felt hollow and drained. No! It was so strange to look into his face knowing it was not him. He clearly had Drak's memories since he recognized me, but I could see in his eyes all feelings toward me were gone. He looked to me like an empty shell with downloaded memories but no soul.

I confronted the Drak-clone, and demanded to know what had happened to my Drak. He offered to take me to their commander; my hysteria was obviously not something he was prepared to handle. The commander would be able to explain it better. He took me to a part of the station I never even thought of entering. My Drak had avoided this area as if it was under quarantine. Command Central was filled with dozens of commanders overseeing and directing multiple active missions in various stages of preparation. Drak's clone presented me to the commander who oversaw Drak's unit. In Draco society each commander has an infantry which specializes in a particular field of interest. Each infantry is made up of researchers, analysts, pilots and a complement of fighters who do their bidding. Dedicated to their directive, Commanders coordinate independently but get overall approval from the high council, a group of the oldest Dracos. The function of the council is to ensure that the main objective of the Dracos is not violated or compromised. Thou shall not interfere with the natural development of an indigenous species; intruders, threats to the object of interest, and potential catastrophes have to be dealt with on occasions.

The explanation was brief but went on forever. Lots of *blah, blah,* relatively important information, but completely not what I wanted to hear at this point. I waited wearily through the rest of it. Finally he came to the part about Drak. The commander was all business as he laid out the details surrounding Drak's mission and failed return. I never meant for him to get hurt but inevitably shared with him my unspoken desire to get back to Earth. In his futile attempt to do something for me, Drak went on a mission to explore the portals looking for a way to send me back home, and he got reckless. During the mission, lightning from the clouds above hit the ship, disabling all functionality and sinking it in an ocean of worms. Apparently this was not typical lightning or a small pool, but one of the largest accumulations of the worms yet encountered on this planet.

The Dracos currently occupied this planet for the sole purpose of studying the worms. There is a connection between the worms, energy clouds and the portals. The Dracos felt compelled to understand the connections, the science, the limitations and possibilities associated with this phenomenon. After prolonged study of the planet's relationship to the worms, the understanding of how and why the worms themselves used the cloud energy to stay alive and create portals eluded them.

Recently the Hexadoids activity had ramped up around the pools. With the enemy getting more aggressive and creative, the Dracos had to step up their actions to contain the events without violating their prime directive and still be productive. The planet was teaming with large numbers of newly arrived Hexadoids from the portal. Although the Dracos had not definitively determined whether the portals connect planets or dimensions, they suspected the Hexadoids plan was to use the portals to invade other dimensions or planets. So much talk but no answer to my most urgent question: Where is my Drak?

However interesting the explanation would have been for me under different circumstances, I was desperate to know what happened to Drak. I could feel that he was not gone. I knew it was the truth but do not ask me how. I assumed it was the telepathic connection we had. So I interrupted the commander very rudely asking about it. He graciously showed me, using my necklace, the events of the mission in question, ending with an image of Drak's ship being engulfed in the middle of the worm ocean.

The commander ignored my agitation and continued to lecture me on the Draco's directive and physiology in relation to the worms and planet. Apparently the worms deplete Dracos of their life energy by direct contact. The Draco ships offered some protection, except against the lightning. The energy traveling from the clouds to the worms is the same the Dracos are using in the ships. Upon contact, the ships' skin transfers the massive amount of energy to the generator, and that one blows. Acceptable loss, and usually they know not to travel under the clouds when they are about to discharge. In short, the unit was finished and the next generation called into service. All neatly explained. The currently captured Dracos, including Drak were inside the ship without options, and just waiting for their death. I wanted to shout that Drak is not expendable. Taking my father's advice again, I stood still realizing that the only way to help Drak was to take a breather and gather my thoughts.

Logically, the commander had moved on. Their situation was declared unsalvageable so their Draco clones were activated. Had I heard right or was I just in denial? Did he say they were unsalvageable? So they were still alive. Drak was just dead to the commander. Is this yoyo telling me to forget him? I was so glad that, unlike Drak, he could not read my mind. He only could read the clunky translator, otherwise he would have felt my rage and disregard for his prime blah, blah.

If the existence of the Drak clone wasn't enough, the commander was telling me to move on. That wasn't an option in my book. Feelings aside, I had to think quickly since it looked like the commander was finished with his explanation and about to go back to his research. I was dismissed. I became rigid, clenched my hands and my jaw tight and shouted, "NO! STOP!" Too late, my emotions were thundering in the quiet control room, attracting the attention of everyone within earshot and then some as I dumped all my frustration on the unsuspecting commander. "You can't do that." My jewel kept translating, projecting 3D images that flashed in front of me.

I was no longer hearing the commander prattle on. I picked up on the fact that Drak was still alive and the Dracos primary interest is research. As a human and daughter of a military commander, my primary directive was: Leave no man behind— especially not MY DRAK. Without thinking, before I could even consider the consequences, I volunteered to be a study subject. I asked the commander if he would be interested in observing and researching human behaviors in a rescue situation.

I argued that I was probably the first human to stumble through the portal. I may appear non-threatening but I am only one of billions. Mathematically the probability of encountering humans in the future was already high since I was standing right in front of him. I represented a rather rare opportunity to have a cooperative human subject to observe and study and prepare themselves for the possible future encounter. My reasoning was sound.

The commander appeared to be on the fence with my offer. In desperation and to top my offer I used the necklace and sent visual images of the last kiss shared with Drak. I hoped that the commander would concentrate on the electric charge and not the actual kiss because I wanted to pique his scientific curiosity in regards of the charge created between Drak and me and the scientific applications it implied, not get Drak into trouble. I convinced him that in studying me I could somehow provide scientific information that had eluded them to date. There was an obvious connection between Drak and me. Without Drak, there was no connection and no deal. I was fairly certain that the commander would not have understood the attraction part of the equation and I am not even sure that I could have explained it adequately. It was chemistry but not in any scientific way that I could explain. It was not clean and orderly. It was just there, unwavering, solid. This appealed to him because he promised to submit the request to the council.

Mission to save Drak

The commander went about his business, and I was left not knowing how much time I had to save Drak. The clock was ticking and nothing was happening. Just when I was about to do something drastic, and perhaps a little bit stupid, the commander turned to me and agreed to my proposal. His unit was at my disposal. He asked me what my orders were. I paused in the 'Ah-Ha' moment when I realized that the request and response had been telepathically communicated.

I froze in wake of his statement. Yes, what next indeed? This had all happened so quickly. I had only been awake for an hour and now I was in charge of a rescue mission. Where was my father when I needed him? My plan did not go beyond being given the opportunity to rescue Drak. Right now the details were eluding me. In an attempt to cover my ignorance, I proceeded to rattle off military mottos from memory while my mind coaxed a kernel of an idea and worked it until it grew into a full-fledged plan.

'We humans do not leave anybody behind... We try to rescue our own even if we know that the success rate is slim to none...' I wanted all the intelligence they had, no matter how inconsequential, about the situation. I already had all the resources I needed since he put his entire team at my disposal, which included the pilots and researchers, etc. Getting a quick 101 on their physiology was the first step.

I am not a scientist, but it was clear that the Dracos' physiology was not compatible with the worms. Their symbiotic existence with the nanites, especially the mechanical nanites, which surrounded their skin, was their Achilles' heel to the worms. The Dracos, nanites, worms and the portals used the same type of energy. While the Dracos shared their energy with the nanites the worms diverted all energy to themselves. This left the nanites and Dracos in contact with the worms, energy depleted and basically dead.

I did not want to risk worm exposure for Drak. After consulting the researchers through my necklace I learned that the sinking ship was stable until it was completely engulfed. Not being able to see past the worms, they had yet to learn if the ship was consumed by the worms or was transported somewhere. Either way, once a ship was lost to the worms, it was never seen again. We needed a way to get to the ship without exposing Drak or his unit to those elements. We had to get to the ship from the far end of the ocean since the other side was teaming with the Hexadoids.

The mission seemed impossible unless we got them out through a portal. I kept looking at the 3D image of the site and thinking that they could fly out of there. But flying would involve the nanites, and with the clouds above discharging massive energy and frying all circuits, any ship between the worms and the clouds, was at risk of being stranded. Suddenly I thought about marionettes. The Dracos, never having been exposed to entertainment, did not understand it; but I knew how to get them out.

All I needed was ropes made out of something similar to my wardrobe. Once it was constructed, the material did not contain any nanites. It would be immune to the effects of the clouds and therefore could be dropped down from a Draco ship, which would safely hover above the clouds. If my assumptions were correct, by dropping only the ropes through the clouds, the soldiers could be lifted out from the ship, unharmed. The challenge would be in getting the stranded soldiers off the damaged ship and onto the ropes. Staying positive, I was determined to find a quick way to attach the magnet to the soldier's outer shell so they could be lifted out of the ship.

Assuming Drak and his unit were at diminished capacity, leaving them alive but unable to move, time would be not on our side. In that case, the challenge was to find them quickly, attach the magnet on the end of the rope, signal to the ship to lift them and get out before the opening got an influx of worms. Anything beyond that was no longer a rescue mission. Someone would have to get them out. The thought was rhetorical. It had to be me. Everyone else was susceptible due to their makeup, but I was less so since I was mostly human, not needing external nanites for energy absorption.

But how would I get to the ship? I remembered that the worms did not harm me when I was lying on top of them on the first day. They were terribly disgusting, but not harmful to me. I assumed that although I was a hybrid, since I still needed to eat, it should work. The bio nanites within my body were not an issue. At least I hoped not. I vividly remembered the feel of the worms. I did not want to feel those ever again on my skin. I would need some kind of a suit to shield me from the worms and I needed a way to breathe if I were to sink underneath them. I asked the scientists if they could make me a very small portable air tank and breathing apparatus that I could take with me. I also asked them to modify the hard-shell suit, nanites free, to fit me. Slime and air supply taken care of, I focused on penetrating the ship for access. The ship had turned over as it was sinking and was now completely upside down. There were no access panels on the underside of the ship and once the ship was open to the elements, the influx of worms became an immediate threat to anyone on board. It was estimated that I had only minutes to extract the survivors. I would have to cut an opening as far up as possible.

The researchers supplied me with a torch the size of my lipstick case I had back home. I had great respect for their technology, but I had concerns. How could something so small cut into nanite-enhanced steel quickly without attracting unwanted attention? If the nanite technology was what attracted the worms, then exactly how much time would I have before being detected after I started cutting in? A brief demonstration led me to believe that the plan was coming together nicely and just might work.

As small as it was, I could carry the torch inside my suit or in my mouth if I had to shield it from the effects of the worms. The lab created two little gel tabs for me to swallow shortly before I would need oxygen. As I understood it, the gel tabs would line my lungs with an oxygen-enriched compound supplying me with air for fifteen minutes. Two of them should be more than enough I hoped. I improvised as I went along, wishing that I could ask my father for help. My methodology was weak but my reasoning was sound. In reality, a tactical commando would plan a more detailed operation using more reliable tools and come up with a million better ways to do this, but it was all I had in 5 minutes. I hoped I could convince them that I knew what I was doing. I did not want to over-think the operation or how each step would be performed. I was afraid that I would be paralyzed with fear and be unable to continue if I thought too much about what I was going to do. Then the what-ifs started. What if the ropes were too short? What if I could not cut through the hull of the ship? What if the worms attacked me? What if the oxygen pills did not work? What if I couldn't help them out? What if I was too late? That one got me moving!

I was hoping the ship was already touching the bottom and by walking on the bottom of the pool I could climb onto the top somehow. I did not want to think about the possibility of not finding the ship on the bottom. I planned to just aim towards it when I got to the edge of the worm pool and just keep going. I realize there was lots of optimism in my plan but there was no time for anything else. Since I was in charge, and my father's daughter, I was going for it. I crossed my fingers.

I did one final test before I suited up. I touched one of the worms in the lab to confirm my theory that they would not harm me. I figured their standard combat suit, which they modified for me, should protect me from the slime of the worms, and other surprises if needed. With my new gadgets and fully suited up, I was on the shuttle to the surface of the planet. As planned, we arrived at the far side of the worm ocean. I had forgotten how unnerving the worm pool was. Without waiting to analyze my situation, afraid I would back down, I exited the ship and advanced to the edge of the pool. Still not stopping to think, but concentrating on the task at hand, I touched the first worms with my foot.

Immediately they became aggressive, moving and bulging in front of me trying to keep me out. I could see Drak's ship on the horizon and desperately wanted to force my way through the swarm, but the more aggressive I got, the stronger the reaction of the worms against me. This was not the reaction I expected. The lab worm was dormant and unresponsive to my touch. Why would the worms act differently when separated from the group? I could not understand why these worms behaved differently than the worm in the lab.

I suspected that it might have something to do with the uniform. I had not been wearing the uniform when I touched the worm in the lab. I removed my glove and bravely submerged my hand between the worms on the shore. Like a charm they remained calm and stayed unaffected. It made my hair stand up thinking what that meant for me. I needed to go in without the uniform, between the slimy, nasty and moving worms. Ugh!

It was best not to think about it. Staring at the half submerged ship, I undressed quickly before I could change my mind. I kept looking at the ship while I got down to the fiber optics under-suit. My mind searched for a visualization that would steady my nerves and allow me to continue, and hopefully contain my gag reflex. I was repulsed by the worms but too afraid of what I would lose if I did not try. Now that I knew the worms were not going to push me back out, I had to plunge right in. There are two ways to jump into ice-cold water: slow and painful, or quick and painful. I was short on time and courage. I plunged in and did not look back.

When I was halfway in I chewed up one of the pills. I had to put the other pill and the torch in my mouth. With the removal of the suit, I did not have any way to hold my supplies and I wanted my hands free, ready for anything. Then I just closed my eyes and dove in or at least I tried. As much as I tried to submerge, hoping to walk along the bottom of the pool, I quickly realized that without the armor I was buoyant in the worm pool. I was suspended half way in the middle of the worm pool on the surface and just plain stuck. No traction between the worms.

Now what? How was I supposed to move forward? I was growing more and more agitated at my predicament and persistent bad luck. One obstacle after another was thrown at me, while Drak was out there dying. I tried to move, slow at first then faster and faster. It felt like I was trying to move through overcooked spaghetti noodles. Helplessness overcame me and I stopped moving all together.

I had been concentrating on the task at hand, trying to keep panic at bay, but when I stopped moving I became very aware of where I was. Feeling those slimy and slippery things moving all around me, I focused again on the ship and the tears came pouring down my cheek. The stupid worms were purring like cats. It was hypnotic and soothing with a rhythmic and infectious beat that ironically made me want to dance. With tears on my face and a swing in my hips, I had to acknowledge that my life was full of contradictions lately. Then I noticed that my rhythmic moves, so in tune with the worms, got me moving in the pool.

Those little slimy cuties had surprised me. Just when I thought I was finished, and I had resigned myself to the fact that there was no use fighting, they showed me a way. When I moved to their rhythm they moved too, propelling me forward. I was clumsy in the beginning as I tried to move towards the ship in the most direct angle possible, but the worms moved in an unpredictable manner, like waves on a stormy day, which had me flipping and losing direction. It was not until I slowed, focused on the ship and allowed the worms to create a path through them that I really started moving forward. It was difficult to trust my instincts, but somehow I knew that the worms were helping me to my destination. Still, I was repulsed by the slime. However, I learned fast which actions worked and which did not. Which movement agitated the worms and which sped me along. It was actually fun, which was hard to believe for my standards. I was moving much faster than if I had been walking on the pool's ground.

It did not take me long to arrive at the ship. But once again, my joy was short lived due to the realization that I had another obstacle before me that I had not anticipated. There was no way to climb onto the side of the ship. I was hoping for some nuts, bolts, or something I could hold on to and put my feet in, but there was nothing. It was completely smooth. I needed a break, or, better yet, Drak and his unit needed one.

I looked for something I could use, and I looked at the

worms. Maybe I could irritate them enough to lift me up like a giant wave. I had not agitated the worms when I swam with them to the ship; but remembering how they rejected the uniform, I was afraid of what they might do to me, and I was reluctant to piss them off. Pressed for time, I was forced to think outside the box. Flying would be nice, or I could just wait until the ship sank deep enough for me to get on top. But that would take more time than I had with the oxygen capsules. Not to mention I had to cut open the top and get 12 gigantic Dracos out of there. So close and yet so far. Their lives were in my hands, or in this case left to my planning and imagination. I felt crushed by this responsibility. They were dying in there!

I had come this far. That is farther than the Dracos had ever gone. Torn between my enthusiasm at having made it to the ship and cursing my inability to control my circumstances, again, I wanted to cry. I found myself desperate and looking for a way out. I was mentally and physically exhausted. My task was not completed. When I was able to think past the panic, I replayed the trip through the worms to the ship. How could I swim my way there? Dolphins! They jump out of the water. Could I? At this point it was worth a try. I needed to swim further away, and then accelerate fast enough to jump the right distance from the ship, out of the worms and land on the top.

It was the plan of a lunatic but was worth a shot. Without trying they were dead, so what did I have to lose? I swam away from the ship, and when I felt that I could get enough speed, I turned around. I dove in and started moving very energetically and quickly to the rhythm, swimming faster and faster. It was exhilarating to be able to move so freely in the worms. In my enthusiasm I got disoriented and wondered whether I was still swimming in the right direction; this was a bad idea from the beginning. What made me think that I could estimate something like that without any help or equipment? I deserve to crash into the ship; how could I be so stupid? Panic took over and I slowed down and wanted to swim up. Then I heard Drak's voice. It was as clear as an echo bouncing off a canyon. As I got closer to him, it became stronger. I adjusted my direction to swim towards this echo at top speed, hoping that I would not go crashing into the ship.

When I felt that I was almost in front of the ship, I swam straight up. And with even more determination, I shot out of the worms, landing, by some kind of miracle, on the highest end sticking out. I don't know how I heard Drak in my mind. Maybe it was because of the nanites we shared, or the necklace, or the connection we shared from the beginning, but without it, none of this was possible. With no time to lose I removed the laser from my mouth and set to work on cutting an opening into the ship.

The laser worked like a charm and without much effort I made an opening big enough for even a horizontal Draco. Grabbing the ropes, I rappelled into the ship. I did not stop to check vital signs, I just attached the soldiers to the ropes, as I found them, and gave a quick jerk, signaling the ship hovering above to lift them out. I was so relieved to find Drak that I gave him a quick kiss hoping to pass on some revitalizing energy and then sent him on his way.

As the last Draco was located, attached and lifted out of the ship, I attached myself, gave a quick tug and was on my way out. Then to my horror I noticed one rope hanging without a Draco on it and I realized that I was missing someone. In the stress of it all, I had lost count. Thunder was closing in on the hanging soldiers and, directing by instinct, I signaled them to move towards the shore without me. I went back inside the ship hoping that I was wrong. I started looking but could not find anybody.

Convinced that I just miscounted, I stopped my search. Then

a tap got my attention. I followed the sound and spotted a partial foot underneath a pile of equipment. I started digging. Some of the parts were heavier than others, but I managed to get all of them off. I recognized the Draco below. It was Snake Eyes. She was still alive, but barely breathing. I knew I could not pick her up by myself; she was bigger and much heavier than me. I was out of ropes and magnets, so I looked for something to create a pulley.

I felt the ship move and noticed the edge of the opening I cut in the hull had slipped below the surface. The worms started pouring in. Despite my quick thinking, I was going nowhere with my pulley idea and I was out of time. Then it came to me. If Snake Eyes were conscious and able to help, we could escape together.

I needed to recharge her. If she had just little bit more energy she could get herself out. Without delay I placed a gentle kiss on her lips and waited for the prickle feeling I had with Drak. Nothing happened. I reminded myself that with Dracos everything happens with images in the mind so I started thinking and imagining kissing Drak as I placed another kiss on her. And like a charm the prickle feeling crossed our lips. Relieved, I kept kissing her until I felt movement on her part. It did not take long before she gained consciousness and was able to follow me out of the ship.

Outside the ship, I was momentarily relieved only to realize that we were alone with no visible way to get to shore. Everyone was gone. We were standing on the last piece of ship untouched by worms watching the gelatinous mass flow in through the hole I had created. The horizon was empty and the ship was definitely sinking, becoming engulfed and consumed by the mass as it slipped lower. We were trapped. Without much thought I lifted the cut out lid from the ship and turned it around, creating a sort of surfboard with it. Placing it on the worms, counting on them to reject it as they did with my uniform, I hoped it would not sink.

Now I encouraged Snake Eyes to lie down on it. She had no idea where this would lead, but followed my instructions blindly. With her on top of the lid I did not have to worry about her touching the worms directly. She was insulated from the worms on the make shift surfboard. All she had to do was hang on, which without handles might be challenging, but I had my part to worry about and left her to manage as best she could, encouraging her through images of surfers from my world.

I was very comfortable with the worms. I was past the disgust and the fear. I might even admit that I liked them and actually felt, at moments, closer to them than to the Dracos. I could see the two ends of the spectrum these two species represented. The Dracos were cold, logical and distant. The worms were happy, playful and communal. Based on my observations, humans were spiritually closer to the worms and physically closer to the Dracos.

I swam underneath the surfboard pulling it towards the shore. The additional oxygen pill came in handy; otherwise this plan wouldn't have worked. This time I wasn't worried which direction to go. As long as I arrived on shore before the oxygen ran out and I got Snake Eyes out of there unharmed, anything was fine with me.

When we arrived on shore the unit was still waiting and I noted their surprise when they saw Snake Eyes. Dangerously low on energy, the rescue troops had brought all Dracos into the ship already, where portable pods were waiting for them. Not a standard equipment on their ship, but I had thought to add them. As I looked back at the planet, a sense of peace descended upon me, leaving me exhausted but happy. No one needed to die today. A giant weight was lifted off my shoulders and I noticed I could breathe again. I realized my muscles were sore and stiff and I was totally tense. I rotated my shoulders and rolled my head around my neck to help alleviate the tension and relax my body. I looked over at the saved Dracos, looking for Drak. Only then could I truly relax.

The rescued soldiers were staring at me. I returned their looks and smiled at a few, offering encouragement, but also recognizing that I would not get a thank you from a race that did not operate with human social graces. I imagined that I had won their respect and I felt marvelous about it, but when I reached out for Drak's hand he pulled away. I was no longer elated. Was he angry with me that I risked my life for him? What was his problem? I thought with some additional energy his chilly attitude would subside. But I was wrong. I waited impatiently until they were out of the pods. As soon as they got out, I ran into the armory to jump into Drak's arms once more. But when I got there his icy attitude had not changed.

Using the necklace he gave me I asked what was wrong, but he only walked away dragging his eyes along the floor, leaving me puzzled. To my surprise Snake Eyes stepped in. As the team leader, Drak had been issued new orders, and his orders were to report with his team to the recycling center. As harmless as this might sound, recycling meant that Drak and his entire unit would be humanly put to sleep and die. Recycled bio material would be used for the future clones. In their society the rules are relatively simple. You exist for your purpose, which in Drak's and his unit's case was to follow orders of the commander and help his research. She respectfully explained that since Drak's unit was already replaced, they no longer had a commander or a purpose. In order to not waste resources, they were therefore scheduled to be recycled.

"Why did they help me rescue your unit then?" I asked.

And as I could have predicted, the answer was as cold and

calculated as everything else Dracos do. I was the research subject. They wanted to observe me. Drak's unit was only a means to an end. To make matters worse, to die by recycling was dishonorable. In the battle you die with purpose and leave a useful memory. Current orders left the rescued Dracos disposed of like trash, waiting consciously for their end. There was no honor in that.

I was crushed. I was mad. I was screaming inside my skin with the outrageousness and unfairness of it all. I could remotely understand Drak's distance even if he thought he did it out of duty. What I could not accept was the disregard of their society for Drak's and the other's lives. All lives are valuable. How did this advanced race not get that? What I had imagined to be a heroic rescue mission had turned into a dishonorable euthanasia. Drak and his unit were already considered dead in their society. Rescued, they represented a dilemma for Dracos. Two clones could not occupy the same time frame. They were not set up for doubles. One had to leave. Instead of helping, I actually made it worse. I wanted to respect their rules and beliefs and be part of Draco's society but this went against everything I believed and everything I had just accomplished. I ran off to see the commander. I did not have a plan. I had no idea what to say, but I had nothing to lose and figured anything was better than just accepting it. I was prepared to fall on my knees and cry and beg for a second chance, but somehow I also knew that this would be a spectacle without appreciation.

I found the commander. I had decided that the best course of action was to emphasize my new understanding of the worms. It was unclear to me how much the Dracos had actually discovered about the worms during their semi-passive observations. I meant to base my points on the assumption that they did not know much since they had failed to mention that the worms were communal and fun loving creatures, not mindless ameba-like organisms as

I was led to believe. To the commander I offered an insight to the worms, which had, to date, been overlooked. I opened a door to possibilities. As I laid out the flaws in the Dracos observation tactics, I also, as dispassionately as I could, argued for the lives of Drak's unit. Logically, since the Dracos were already perfectly aligned in their purpose, they would have twice the manpower to pursue the flaws I pointed out. Arguably, the rescued Dracos, left without a purpose or need were expendable. With my brilliant idea they now had purpose again. What did the Dracos have to lose? It was a win-win.

I desperately wanted to convince the commander that Drak and his unit were not expendable but knew that in doing so directly, my emotions would be discounted and the merits of my plan diminished, if not outright dismissed. I thought about offering myself up to the exploration of the portals themselves but again, I did not want to overplay my hand. As it was, I was in unfamiliar territory. I did not know how much leeway a new cadet would have under these circumstances. The commander seemed to like the idea and again promised to forward the request. Based on the last time the commander and I had negotiated terms and how quickly the approval had come, I was confidant my request would be approved. Without waiting for a response, I ran to see Drak. He and his unit were safe now and I wanted to share the good news with him and hoped he would stop worrying so much. Based on what I knew about him, I could only imagine that he felt responsible for his unit. Now that they were safe from destruction we could move on and he could hold my hand again. Surely, he was only cold and distant to me to protect me, get me used to the idea that he would be gone soon, but there was no reason for this anymore.

Responsibility

I found Drak with his unit in the armory maintaining their gear. When I entered the room they turned as one and bowed deeply in my general direction. I was touched, at first, with this display of thanks but soon became uncomfortable when the entire group failed to rise after a reasonable amount of time had passed. Confused, I zeroed in on Drak hoping to get a response of some kind from him, or any indication of what was going on. I repeated my inquiry to Drak, but he kept ignoring me. Was our connection gone? At this point annoyed as I was, I wondered whether I had created some other catastrophe that I needed to fix. So instead of being triumphant and happy, I turned to the helpful Snake Eyes again and I asked her what I had done. But she also kept silent. Is it too much to ask for a thank you? I was confident they could be grateful, even though I had never seen it.

I kneeled in front of Drak to get him up, when I noticed a new emblem on his right shoulder where the dragon used to be. It was a representation of Earth. I loved it, but what was this all about? My stomach dropped and I suspected that their new purpose had to do with me and Earth. Were they going to help me to get back home? Did I even want to go home? What would that mean for me? Would they remove my bio nanites? Could they even do that? Would I die if they did? What about Drak?

I looked back at them; they were still bowing on one knee waiting for something. Frustrated and antsy I was jumping inside my skin begging them to get up and offer some kind of explanation. Anything at this point before I started developing more theories than there were answers in this world. To my surprise they got up. Following my inquiry they started explaining, I was sort of right, they had been repurposed and assigned to me. They were no longer part of the regular Draco mission. They were now part of my mission, at my disposal, literally. What mission? I was overwhelmed with the idea that I was now in charge and responsible for Drak and his unit. The repurposed Dracos were informed that my mission was to research the portals, while their mission was to assist me in any and all ways possible without violating their prime mission and without interfering with me.

After that explanation I thought I had underestimated their non-existent humor. I laughed. They could not be serious. The silly clunker Drak gave me was defective. It had to be. What did they mean I was their new commander? How do you become a commander? Don't you have to go to some military school or something? If our mission was to research the portals, what was the other commander doing? Then it hit me. This is no different than last time. They only allowed me to lead this team and do the hands on research because they still didn't want to risk themselves and we were now expendable. During the rescue mission, I had proven to be an interesting lab rat. A little entertainment for them. Be careful what you wish for. I had been longing for a purpose, but I never thought it would be entertainment. Was this what I had really wanted? Not really. I just wanted to belong to Drak. For crying out loud, I am just a teenager, barely responsible for myself. Now I was responsible for Drak and his unit? How did this happen? Ok, getting it together was now the next step. Trying to think of the silver lining. Could I see this as a promotion?

If I was their commander, would they follow my orders? This was of course my first thought. I needed to put this to the test. I asked them to line up. This way if they were joking I would know and could move on. But if they did listen, that would be so cool. They listened! In one move, like remotely controlled toy soldiers, they all were in a perfect line. Twelve, seven foot bio-robots moved into a line and all with one thought! My thought and order! This was amazing. Not wanting to lose the moment, I needed for them to do something else. So I asked them to aim their guns. Wow, that was fast, and comical since they all moved like one person. I had seen them many times before moving synchronized and fast like that, but this time, I caused it. I felt so powerful. Incredible, really.

I was conflicted by thoughts of how proud my father would be if he could see me now, and petrified of the responsibility I now had. I thought I was above looking for his approval but I was overwhelmed by the task and thrilled that I had been given the opportunity. The emotional highs and lows were exhausting. I could not settle on anything. I was jumping out of my skin with nowhere to go. I needed to focus on something before I disintegrated. The portals. I needed to research the portals. I had no clue about their Draco systems, no clue about their rules, and no clue about the science of the portals or the worms or the planet. Actually no clue what so ever. In attempt to be optimistic, I tried to convince myself that the advantage I had over the Dracos, where the portals and planet were concerned, was that I could not be limited by what I already knew, since I did not know anything and had no predetermined agenda or protocol. I could not do anything wrong since I didn't know what wrong was. Everything was open and an option. My father always said I would only get it right after I eliminated all the possible wrongs. It was time to start eliminating the wrongs.

Honestly I was still as clueless as I was before, but now I had a title. I am good at improvisation, and here I had a venue to prove it. I wanted Drak. He had the uncanny ability to calm my nerves. My skin was aching to touch him. I approached Drak and attempted to make contact but Drak deliberately avoided any type of connection again. I was frustrated and getting angry.

I just wanted a hug. Anything to steady my jumping skin and mind. The advance and repel of attempts became a dance, and it was starting to attract attention. I never realized how quick Drak's reflexes were until I felt them on my own skin. I was only subconsciously registering the fact I was determined to touch him. I stopped trying when I realized that I was about to cry. This was all wrong. I should be happy. He should be happy. I saved everyone. Why did I feel so rejected and alone? I walked out of the room before anyone could see my tears. Drak followed me out of the room. He had the decency to follow me but I was too frustrated and unhappy to feel better, only acknowledging Drak when he asked for orders. I wanted him to know that he had hurt me. I was stopped short by something in his face.

Drak looked hollow and lost to me. He explained to me that he wanted to be for me what I needed, my other half, but that I was the commander now in a class way above him and the others. With an unexpressed rule, no one below me was permitted to interact with me on a nonprofessional level. I argued that I did not fit any category or Draco rank. We were both in unchartered territory. How can there be rules regarding feelings? We were at a stalemate. I was exhausted. I was having trouble with the concept on a personal level. The Dracos did not interact on any emotional or physical level that I could discern so why did my advancement cause a problem?

I understood that this was meant to avoid attachment between the castes so they could be the most efficient and the soldiers disposable. But since they did not have any feelings this seemed to be a relic from the past ready for an overhaul. I was ready in this case to reject my new position, but Drak reminded me that with me as their new commander they had a purpose now and did not need to be discarded, which would change if I rejected the position. This was ridiculous, worse than a soap opera. One minute I have the boy and no job, the next I have an awesome job and no boy. I wanted the scenario where I get to keep the boy! My brain was working overtime and I did not sleep that night. However, I did come up with a solution.

As frustrating as my situation was, I loved and admired the Dracos and their way of life. I was not going to change them, nor did I want to. Their way of life was simple and uncomplicated and actually very innocent. Keeping it simple I realized that as the new leader of Drak's unit I was in sole control of a well-trained and highly skilled, heavily armed force. I was a little intimidated with the thought of all that power under my control. But I knew that if I did not follow through with my promise to observe, Drak and his unit would lose their purpose and be recycled. I was determined that, out of necessity, I would be the best subject they had ever observed. I had been operating, since I arrived on in this place, on instinct and adrenaline. It had worked for me so far. Now actions should include Drak and his unit. I took some comfort in knowing that they would heal quickly. I was not a Draco, and by saving them I already made them outcasts. Theoretically since I was the study subject too, I wanted to run the unit my way, for two reasons. One was very selfish, actually they both were. One was because I wanted to be with Drak, let's be honest. The other one was, because I was clueless. I thought this would help the other commander in his study of human behavior if I ran things the human way, or more precisely, my way. I mean he was obviously so impressed with my tactics, or luck, during the mission that now he was dedicating his entire team just to me. Should I be flattered or scared?

Of course I tried to keep the chain of command and run my new idea and the request by my commander before I informed my unit. Just so I did not screw something else up. And after I got the ok, I called in the entire unit, all 12 of them, for mission prep

71

and to introduce myself as their commander and to inform them about the planned changes. I did not want to force them to the new rules and structure; I hated when my father was ordering us around. Having a choice, they likely would go along given my new role. I hoped they might even enjoy it. I asked them to build pairs and for each pair to choose a function based on their interest: pilots, medics, research, coordination and unit leaders. I knew they were all excellent soldiers, but I needed them to step up and expand the scope of what they could do, just like my nanites did after they were introduced to my system for the first time. The nanites were not programmed to repair a human body, they were solely designed for a Draco physiology, yet they adapted their programming to do both. Wherever it was needed, they changed my DNA and used Draco DNA to maintain my health.

"I have to confess," I told them, "I do not know much about your roles, your abilities and limitations or what technology or resources we need to succeed. We don't have a full team of pilots, researchers, medics etc. When we go on missions, I need to be on the ground instead of in the command room, but I need someone to coordinate and trouble shoot if necessary from there. I cannot lose any of you. I am a human and we get attached like puppies to other living beings, in this case you. I need, therefore, medics to fix you or me on the ground not back at the station. And I also need you to speak up and treat me like an equal or more precisely like I don't know anything, because, unlike the other commander, I do not have centuries of experiences in missions. I need your experiences as well as your suggestions to make up for that shortfall among others."

Their faces were stoic and immune to my arguments, but I had a feeling that they understood. Laying out my logic, I actually got them to buy into it. Honestly, how could they not get it? I had told them that I was too dumb to be their leader. I continued with a warning: "You are already outcasts. By doing this my way, you will probably never fit into your society again. You might even become more like a human than a Draco, at least on the inside"

Over the next couple of days the Dracos in my unit divided the new roles among each other and started dutifully studying their new skills. I didn't know if it is as easy on Earth as it was here, but I did not need to do anything other than focus on the files sent to me by the other commander, at the central commander room. I had Drak and Skinny, another Draco. I named him this way because he was taller than the others and very skinny. Skinny and Drak were now the two new Unit Leaders. In the beginning, it was very difficult to sift through files, which were in movies, not in words. A very obscure way of absorbing information if there is no language to explain things. I was looking at things I had never seen before and did not even know how important one thing was over another. For example, there was a difference between reading the words 'massive vibration' and seeing it in the movie, which did not explain the importance of it in relation to the worms as the written word would have. I simply was not sure what I should pay attention to. I needed Drak and Skinny to pause the picture and shook my hand pointing at the worms so I knew that the vibration was relevant information to the worms.

But it was not all new just for me. The other Dracos had similar experiences. How do you learn to fly if there is no flight school? How do you become a medic if there is nobody you can learn from or practice on? How do you become a scientist in just a few weeks? This whole new approach would take time and lots of pitfalls but without trying we might as well give up.

The old commander's research was sound and very detailed, but all of it was done at a distance. I understood their indifference to the worms and perhaps their caution to get too close, resulting in lack of practical research, so I knew where my new focus must be. The commander's theory was that the portals had something to do with the combination of the worms' vibration and the clouds' energy. We needed to prove that. On Earth researchers use special designed probes positioned in predetermined locations on the tectonic folds, to measure and record micro tremors. We needed to do something similar. We needed to come up with some kind of probe which would record and monitor the vibration of the worms and the intensity of the clouds' energy spikes.

All of this sounded so grown up. If I just knew what the heck I was really doing I would feel so much better. As long as they did not notice that I was just improvising, I was golden. Anyway, the pilots were learning how to fly. The researchers had their hands full with inventing the new probes, which they did get help with from other scientists in the facility. The medics learned more everyday about Draco and human anatomy and I even offered myself as guinea pig for their little surgeries—just a little cut on my leg or arm to get a feel for real flesh. I did not feel anything and the real doctors were just around the corner so I did not worry. I would rather have them do it now than try to figure it out in the field without a safety net. It was not as easy as just cutting and stitching, or even replacing a damaged organ with a new cloned one, I discovered. Most of their surgeries were bio-nanite reconstruction. *All* they had to do was introduce new stimulated nanites to the problem area, like they did when I shot my leg. They also did genetic augmentations, where they introduced new programing to the nanites to change someone's anatomy like Drak did with me, if ever needed. So much could go wrong, mutations, disfigurement, even death. I wished they could just download the info into their brains, but now I knew even these super smart aliens had to learn things the old fashioned way, albeit at least a dozen times faster than humans. It took us a couple of weeks before we were ready to go.

I kept my distance from Drak and gave him as much space as I thought he needed. I wanted in the worst possible way to be with him. I was his commander and theoretically I could order him to be with me, but that would not have been real. Now since everything changed, I really did not get why he wouldn't take me in his arms. We needed to practice the whole charging thing just for the missions, but I was afraid that he would suggest to practice on other Dracos so I didn't suggest it at all.

All of us worked really hard on our new assigned duties and I could swear I felt enthusiasm from my Dracos. I kept myself busy learning about the planet, its life forms, the portals, the worms, the energy signature of the worms, Dracos and nanites—whatever I could find. All information was important no matter how trivial. I wanted to understand, with my limited technical background, why I was able to produce energy in my body and why I expelled it when experiencing emotions. I knew more trained minds were working on this mystery already, but maybe, with any luck, I would find it first. I hated not knowing so much about my body. Interestingly, all of the information they had, especially on the planet, was very intense but a little bit too limited on the worms. Not that I was complaining, it was way too much for my brain any way. I liked the fact that I could watch the Draco information library like a movie with my little jewel. This way of learning was much easier for me than the dry reading I did on Earth. Although it did seem that there were aspects of the information that could be open to interpretation. A particularly interesting but relatively limited section pertained to the planet's plant and animal life. I was enthusiastic to just see it in action and maybe get the feel for it. Time went by relatively quickly between the learning tracks and Drak deliberately avoiding me. I was ready for something new to do at this point.

After two weeks we had another team meeting where, after

many encouragements, I made sure all the Dracos knew they had an equal voice. Drak, Skinny and I presented to the team our findings and our suggestions. The scientists introduced the new gadgets they had come up with, like my new cortex stimulator, a little chip implanted onto my temporal bone, which would theoretically do the same thing as my jewel did, just inside my head not in front of my eyes. I wouldn't be a true telepath by any means, but I would not have to carry the display tool any more. I was so excited about it. Now I could send images to my crew remotely and they could send some to me. It would be very useful on the missions and I was happy they thought about me. The pilots worked out a flight plan, minimizing the contact with the Hexadoids or bad weather. Mission controllers introduced us to the modified monitoring stations they developed, enabling us to communicate in real time, including a new station in which they could remotely "drive" any of us. If there was an emergency, such as one of us passed out or became somehow vision impaired, the mission controllers would choose our brain pattern from the database catalogue and navigate our bodies out of the trouble by driving them like avatars.

All of this was so incredible. I never imagined that this could be developed in only couple of weeks. I was very proud of my team and feeling positive about the restructure of the unit. Watching everyone working together and the energy they had, proposing their new ideas and inventions, was so much fun. I felt like I had friends and we were working on a science project at school together.

One of the new inventions they wanted to introduce was in the shuttle hangar. It was a new propulsion system utilizing the worms' vibration. The demonstration was performed hovering over a bunch of worms in the hangar, with a modified ship. Instead of causing a wild frenzy among the worms as it usually would, the worms were calm and undisturbed. The applications for that were big. The ship and soldiers could now observe or fly over the worm pools undetected. We could not completely rule out that the worms would initiate lightning from the clouds, which they did when they were protecting themselves from a presumed threat from the overhead ship. This new ship would be able to fly between the worms and the clouds without having to worry about getting hit by the lightning.

Fire at the hangar

We were very excited. Well let's be honest, I was the only one visibly excited, but it appeared to me that my enthusiasm was rubbing off on some of my crew. As we were about to walk out of the hangar after the demonstration, Drak's attention was diverted to something behind us, and with a swift, strong push he threw me through the nearby observation window. Drak pushed me with such a force that I landed behind the navigation table. Deafening blasts roared above my head, and the smell of burning flesh filled my nose. I got up as soon as I could, just to witness the hangar destroyed and everyone in my unit badly burned on the floor. Drak had saved my life again and let himself be burned alive. With shaking hands, a whistling sound in my ears and out of my mind from worry, I called for help. It was pure chaos. I saw Dracos moving all around me including my unit. I could not split myself, so I ran from Draco to Draco to see who I could help and who was alive. With the help of arriving Dracos from all over the station to the accident site, I covered the burned bodies of my Dracos with a clear gel handed out by the researchers. This gel was designed to clean their bodies from all non-healthy bio tissue and any other materials stuck to their bodies by the blast. The gel kept the environment sterile for a rapid recovery. I was so scared for them. My entire team was burned and badly wounded lying right in front of me and there was nothing I could do.

I was so tremendously glad they were all alive but felt guilty for not being hurt myself. My priority was to keep them company and make sure nobody tried to recycle them. I could not sleep or eat and my face was wet with a constant flow of tears. I think there is a limit on how much you can cry, because after a while the tears stopped and the headache started. I sat on the floor in a corner of the room waiting for a diagnosis from the response team. Due to their incredible technology, the wounds, which on Earth would have been lethal, would be healed in three to four days. During the entire time they had to be stationary in the lab on the slabs. I decided to watch over them and using the new communication gadget they gave me, keep them entertained with my childhood stories. Since they did not have childhood themselves or if they did it was a few hundred years ago, they might enjoy a little tour through my childhood.

Searching for a beginning in my story, I remembered how often we moved due to my father's military carrier. At every new school we had to make new friends and prove our worth to the existing kids over and over again. It was exhausting. In one of the schools I wanted to be friends with a girl named Grace. I was convinced she did not like me and ironically she thought the same about me. We ended up best friends; one could even say soul mates, and had lots of fun together until we moved again. We kept in touch but it was just not the same.

Rambling about my childhood seemed like a good idea in the beginning but I could not keep it up for more than a few hours. As I pulled the phone out I glanced over the date and realized it was my birthday. I was happy I was able to spend it with my new family and sad they were in so much pain. I also wished I could have spent it on Earth with my Dad and sisters, or at least my sisters. I thought about how beautiful it would be to have a romantic birthday with Drak. It was then that I decided that my romantic birthday would happen, as soon as Drak was able, whether he liked it or not. I felt better having a plan, even one as frivolous as a romantic birthday. While playing music I was thinking about all the places we could go, when I finally realized that my fantasies were not private; I had witnesses. Whoops. Well at least I was thinking about something pretty and happy and not sad. I could not sleep as long as Drak and my Unit were in recovery. I was away from my unit for a few minutes each day to eat my chow chow and stay hydrated, but rushed back as soon as I could. I just did not trust the Council and worried that as soon as I passed out, they would find a reason to kill my people.

I woke up once again in Drak's arms as he was carrying me into the pod. I must have passed out towards the end. I was relieved to see him healthy and strong again. The rest of the Unit was walking beside him and I kept turning my head until I saw all of them healthy and accounted for. They were my family now.

Picnic

When I woke up in the pod, Drak was sitting beside me. It was nice to see him. The two of us in the pod once more and I did not have to ask him for it. I inquired about the rest of the team and was glad to hear that they were off doing their own thing. I asked Drak if he got my plans for my romantic birthday, on the planet surface and if he knew what that was about, but he did not seem interested. Instead Drak remained stiff and official as he asked me if I had plans for their next mission. From his attitude I could see he was bored and couldn't wait to get some action. I wanted to be the best commander they ever had and not to coup them up at the station. I also knew we did not know enough about the worms and they were the key to it all. Noticing how he changed the subject, I went with it and since he was all about business. I started asking about the progress researching our worm friends. As I suspected they did not have much new info about it. He promised to get right on it, but to my delight had to wait until the pod was finished with his cycle. Ignoring his cold disposition and aware of the fact that he carried me into his pod instead of putting me into my own, and that he did not need any charging, I curled myself to him and remained happy. I mean he might be all cold and business on the outside but clearly he was all fuzzy and warm on the inside. At the end of the recharge we got out of the pod and walked together to the hangar for a team meet. They were all there, dressed for a mission and ready to go, but where? I did not plan or order any mission. They also had my and Drak's combat armor waiting for us at the shuttle. For a second I was not sure what was going on until I saw the fake flower.

Happy birthday was written on what appeared to be a picnic

basket. My eyes filled with tears. A romantic picnic on the planet surface was waiting for me. What a surprise! I could not believe they knew what that meant to me. My heart was pumping out of my chest and my hands started to shake. I turned to Drak wondering if he knew about it and, based on the lack of surprise on his face, I realized he did. All the diversion in the pod was just an act to keep the surprise. I was not aware he was capable of keeping a secret.

With a fast, happy trot I entered the ship. Of course I made sure Drak was right behind me. It would be only half as wonderful without him there. Now with all of us on the ship, we took off and my OWN pilots were flying. It was so bizarre. I had my own pilots! The world was so perfect. What would my father say now if he could see me? I could not get the smile off my face nor did I try. I kept looking at Drak and squeezing his hand. The excitement was pouring out of my skin. We landed on the planet's surface. The spot they picked was nearly perfect it was on the top of a hill. The hill was covered with orange fluorescent moss surrounding a sort of upside down tree. The tree had a giant shell on top which narrowed down to a three-foot diameter stem that branched out on the ground to dozens of roots, which were sticking, for the most part, above the ground creating niches and hiding spaces. We left the ship taking just our basket and ear coms with us. The crew left us alone. That night all three moons were up in the sky at the same time. It was almost as bright as daylight.

If my calculation is right, this happens only once every revolution, which was equivalent to roughly two and a half Earth years. As our feet touched the moss, all went dark. The moss reacted to our touch. We climbed up the roots to a nice high platform, which gave us a view, with the picnic basket in between us. I started to speak but Drak stopped me by pointing at the moss. After a moment of silence the moss glowed with a vibrant pulsing orange, which created a beautiful orchestra of light. Apparently spore season coincides with the cycle of the three moons and millions of tiny spores were released into the air from the tree above. They looked like tiny fire flies swarming until they settled down. It was a marvelous show. I moved the basket away and leaned into Drak. He wrapped his arms around me and I rested my head on his shoulder. He was so different. No trace of the cold distant treatment, giving me the illusion of a perfect date. I hoped that this beautiful night would never end.

I got up and started climbing all the branches. Drak followed me everywhere always ready to catch me if I fell. I told him to relax, knowing that this word or the principal of it was foreign to him. It was lots of fun teasing him by pretending to fall and making him jump. I ran and climbed faster hoping to outrun him but I was no match for him. I swear I could tell he was enjoying it.

The perfect moment was interrupted by a laser fire. By now I knew the difference between that and thunder. I tried to spot where it had come from when I noticed that Drak stopped following me and had in fact disappeared. The sounds also made the moss dark, which did not help me find Drak or the shooter. I heard a cracking sound and realized that it came from the spot where Drak was standing. I followed the noise and saw Drak below lying on one of the bigger branches. I wasn't sure if it was the site of Drak lying helplessly on the bottom or something else, but I also did not feel all that well. I was sweating and I must have spilled something because I could feel it dripping down my arm. To my surprise it was coming from my chest. I was hit and bleeding heavily.

I went cold when I realized that this must have also happened to Drak. Ignoring my own injury, and as quickly as I could, I climbed down the tree roots to check on Drak. He was not moving. The hole in his chest was huge. I put my hands on it trying to slow the bleeding but they were almost not big enough for that hole. I used the ear coms to call my unit for help. I knew it would take them few minutes to get to us. I was getting light headed myself and worried what would happen to Drak if I passed out and let go of his wound. So I decided to lie down on top of him, using my body's weight to apply pressure. At least, if I did pass out there would still be pressure on the wound. Barely conscious, I saw the ship's arrival. More shots were fired as my team tried to pick us up. Leaning over the both of us and looking at our injuries, something must have happened because they stopped the rescue and asked me whether I wanted to save myself and let Drak die or try to save both of us. There was no question what my choice would be, but they give me one anyway. They enclosed the two of us, positioned as we were, in the transparent medical gel and brought us on board. The rough transport kept me wake for the most part but the gel kept me from moving. Strange that I have to admit, by now I was used to getting shot and hurt, and that the presence of my unit made me feel rather safe, even in this circumstance. I realized how much my life had changed since my accidental fall through the portal, when I imagined that few months ago I still was scared walking by myself in the dark on Earth.

We arrived at the lab and my medics showed me images of the injuries Drak and I had, which perplexed them a bit. Apparently when I laid down on Drak to prevent him from bleeding to death, gravity filled his body with my blood including my somewhat creative nanites. His heart was badly damaged and shortly after it stopped working, my nanites, being originally designed for Drak, found a solution to the problem by rerouting his arteries to my heart. Essentially, those little buggers were making my heart pump for the both of us. It was freaky but ingenious really. None of us would have thought the nanites could do that. So until his heart got either replaced or repaired, whichever the medics would be able to do, we would be conjoined. That was certainly one way of ending a perfect date I thought. Hmmm when I was craving contact, this is not what I had in mind. And to be connected at the heart! It was an ongoing cruel joke. Again, careful what you wish for. Nothing here heals forever; even the fire that burned them was fixed in only few days. I was willing to do whatever it took to save Drak, so I wrapped my arms around him and asked them to wrap us in gel once again until we both were safe. All I wanted in this minute was to be with him in any way and go to sleep. I was very tired. I loved every minute of it, because no matter how I looked at it, I had to admit to myself, I loved him.

I knew it would take more than a few days for us to be released from our gel cocoon but I never imagined what it would really mean. When I woke up I noticed that the nanites had removed all non-bio and non-sterile substances to avoid infection. If I had really thought about it, it made sense, but it left me without a stitch of clothes to separate me from Drak. We were skin to skin with me on top. Not an altogether unpleasant situation but certainly one that put me at a disadvantage. Not how I envisioned our first encounter, this was very weird. My thoughts wanted to go to places that I wasn't sure Drak wanted to see. Whatever kept him from being with me, after I became the new commander, was still there. My fantasies might have been fun for me, but I thought they would be an intrusion for him and I wanted to spare him that, especially since he seemed to make progress in our relationship with the picnic idea. So I kept myself occupied by thinking about the worms and how to integrate them into the Draco's society in a symbiotic relationship. The unit should share their ideas daily with each other so they could inspire one another and maybe help solve each other's problems.

All my thinking was interrupted with images of us back at

the planet. We were chasing each other happy, as I hid in one of the trees roots. Drak was looking for me, and when he found me, he offered me his hand to pull me out, but instead I pulled him in. He landed on top of me. After a brief moment of silence and looking deep into each other's eyes we kissed. It was an intense kiss. Skin on skin in the lab, I felt Drak's reaction to my fantasy about the kiss. It felt like a memory, but it could not be a memory because it never happened. An unexpected thought descended upon me. What if that was not my fantasy? The nanites could have changed my mind as well to match Dracos' physiology or psychology and I could be becoming a telepath. Looking back I remember hearing Drak calling out to me during the rescue mission. Otherwise, I never would have found the ship and I would never have been able to succeed at the rescue mission. That would be pleasant news, if he indeed was fantasizing about us together as well. That would be my dream come true. I could not be sure, so I decided to wait and see if more memories, not of my making, were revealed to me, before I even entertained the idea.

Efficient as always and unknown to me at the time, Drak had read my mind regarding the mission, but not the part of my new discovery. He conveyed my mission thoughts to the unit, who already started working on the preparation and my new ideas, getting us closer to be ready when we woke up. The nanites worked fast, and my unit's medics helped by cloning Drak's heart and replacing his shattered one with it. Together they got us healthy and up and running in only a few days. Itching to see some action, the unit worked tirelessly during our recovery.

Using our newly acquired information, my unit's scientists came up with a protective gel to use under the armor, which allowed the Dracos and worms to share energy, rather than feed the worms with their own life force. Lightning is initially absorbed by the worms and its energy is sent to nearby Dracos. It also works between Dracos. They can through this gel, share energy between each other unlike before. So if I could load Drak, he could than send the overcharge to members of our unit if needed.

I loved the inventions. They were so original and unlike anything the Dracos would have come up with before. But I had nothing to contribute myself, and honestly I felt a bit useless, so I came out and suggested practicing charging with Drak. I needed another Draco for that practice so Drak did not feel like I was using this as an excuse to make another move on him. But I did not feel comfortable practicing charging on any other member from my unit, other than Snake Eyes, since the rescue mission on the ship. I wanted to be able to effectively load anybody from my unit in the future and had to start somewhere, so I asked her to participate with the exercise. During our practice I kept getting fragments of Drak's thoughts. I tried desperately to hide the effect it had on me but it was distracting. I don't know how the Dracos managed to have their own thoughts and hear someone else's all at the same time. It's like having two conversations at once.

In the beginning charging Snake Eyes was very hard. I held her hands and thought about Drak and our times together, very careful not to think about any embarrassing or too private moments. He was standing next to us and he could read my mind. I half wished he was not there, but during our missions he would be there. I needed to practice with him there. I was very aware that the charge process was regulated by my emotions and is stronger if my feelings are stronger, but since I avoided personal memories and emotions, the charge was weak and failed each time. Frustrated, I had to come up with a new strategy. I tried to think about the times I spent with my last boy toy. The memories were free of Drak and I did not have to worry. The theory was sound but I had not contemplated how that would affect Drak. As soon as the images of me with my ex came into focus they were interrupted by Drak's thoughts, which I could see now. And he did not like what he saw. Not at all. For someone who was not supposed to feel, he felt very strongly about these images. Of all feelings, why did they leave jealousy off their elimination list when they genetically altered the Draco minds to not feel anything? Of course I could not let him see that I noticed what he was thinking about. Somehow I have to keep part of my brain shielded from him. At the same time I was having trouble thinking about my encounters with my exes now. I couldn't think one thought without seeing his objections, making charging completely impossible. This entire situation was so complicated and confusing. I was at a loss I did not know what to do. If I thought about him and our moments, I became too embarrassed and worried that I was imposing on him and if I thought about someone else, he became confused and upset and I could see he did not know how to handle it. Unfortunately, the charging was directly linked to emotions. I wished I could channel his, because right now, ironically he had enough for the both of us.

During my rest time I had an idea. It would be little bit hard for me, but not impossible. I could imagine myself with Snake Eyes. I liked her now. She had become the second closest person to me. Would Drak be jealous? Since Dracos do not distinguish between the sexes, would Drak see her as competition and react the same way he did with my exes, or would he be like any other guy on Earth, and like it or at least not mind it? I did not have to worry about her. She couldn't read me, and if Drak would not object, I knew I had to try it at least. I was holding her hands again and I closed my eyes. I remembered the rescue mission where I had to kiss her and I tried to remember what her lips felt like, what the kiss and her response to it felt like. I paused to check with Drak and my suspicion was correct, he reacted just like any human boy would. He was very curious about it.

Don't get me wrong, he was as surprised by these feelings as he was by the jealousy, but he wasn't adverse to it. I have to admit I loved seeing his perplexed face. Now I was hungry, after the little woman on woman experiment and left to get some sustenance in me. Drak came with me to keep me company. As always he was very quiet and still but this time I kept getting fragments of his thoughts. And they were speaking volumes. He was trying to make sense out of the feelings he had discovered in the last few days. Desperately, he was trying to suppress them. He failed, fortunately for me, each and every time. I also noticed that he was fighting his urge to pin me to the wall and kiss me. It was a primal biological urge and not logical, so naturally new to him and it was driving him out of his mind.

I had to fight really hard not to show how much I wanted him to give in to those urges. I wanted him to know that despite their strange nature they were good urges. It was strange to be a telepath. I did not just see his thoughts, I felt what he felt. I felt his attraction to me, leaving the both of us short of breath and dazed, as well as his persistent self-control. I also felt his fear; in fact he was terrified to open his heart to what he was feeling. He was confused about what to do with his new emotions and was not sure he liked what it was doing to his mind but did not want it to stop. I knew he felt how much I cared about him each time I was next to him. My hands would sweat and I would blush. I could barely stay focused when he was in the same room and when I looked at his face I wanted to lose myself in his eyes.

The pressure to demonstrate the new charging system was mounting. After practicing with Snake Eyes I knew I was ready for the demonstration, but in order to show how important feelings were for charging, I knew I had to show the previous commander the difference between charging with Drak, Snake Eyes and Dracos I didn't know. I needed to show him I was not a machine, who could charge any Draco. I needed him to understand why it was important to keep my unit alive at any cost. I felt like their lives depended on it. But what would be the right venue for the demonstration?

I decided to use the protective gel to demonstrate the charge with Drak and Snake Eyes but I had trouble starting the demonstration. The gel was a perfect addition to the combat suit. It was transparent like petroleum jelly. It did not interfere with the nanites already on their skin but it protected them from the worms. Dracos covered in this solution were able to interact with the worms without losing energy. Furthermore, when the worms received a charge from the clouds with Dracos in the vicinity, the charge would spread to Dracos covered in this gel. I knew the commander was already impressed with the research progress. My charging of Dracos was just a follow up on the promise I made to him. I also chose the gel because I wanted to show what happened without the gel if I overcharged a Draco. Last time we blew the safeties in the lab.

A hologram floated over Drak which displayed his energy saturation. We started him at half energy and had him touch a worm. This nearly depleted him. I felt it was hard for him to allow the worm to deplete his charge. His natural instinct was always to avoid those creatures but he did it anyway. After the worm was fully charged it was placed next to Drak. Now I needed to apply the gel on Drak. The theory was simple, but with Drak lying in front of me on the table looking straight into my eyes, it was another story. Suddenly I was afraid. I was afraid I would lose control, reveal my deepest most secret thoughts and generally embarrass myself.

Drak knew I was under a lot of pressure and helped me overcome my hesitation by catching my hand and placing it on his chest over his heart. All my reservations dissolved with this one simple act. I continued with the demonstration as planned. I made sure Drak was fully covered in gel. To generate enough energy to load Drak, I imagined being with him in the pod. Our eyes locked and I think I made Drak blush, but I could not worry about that. I needed to charge, and overload, Drak fast, and this was the only way I knew to guarantee success. His energy saturation was spiking fast. I could see the commander's skepticism and curiosity at the same time. What he did not know was that my entire unit was already covered in the gel. When Drak's capacity was reached, and the incoming charge no longer had a place to go, the commander was prepared for a blow, but the charge went dispersed to my team in a bright lightning arc. The beautiful light show had the desired effect on the commander. He was more than pleased, but as I suspected he wanted me to show how I could charge other Dracos. I failed at that attempt as I knew I would, proving that the charge is directly linked to my emotions to the Dracos and would fail with a Draco strange to me.

I continued the demonstration, using the overcharged worms as conduits, to reroute the overcharge from Drak back to the grid. As a final demonstration thanks to my wonderful unit, we showed that by adding worms as passengers to the ships outer hall, we could reroute lightning from the clouds into the ships power grid. I was so proud of my team! We succeeded in proposing a symbiotic relationship with the worms, similar to what the Dracos had already done with the nanites. Now we had the means to get to the portals without risking lives, or more precisely my team's lives. The next step was to plan a mission utilizing analytical nanites on my portal. We had to find a way of using Draco technology to design protection for the nanites, so they also were safe from the energy drain of the worms and the clouds or the Hexadoids.

Planning for our first mission

While the team jumped into the research first and execution later approach, I saw Drak had difficulty with it. He was burning to go on a mission and I suspected it had something to do with me, and his confusion about his reaction to me. To ease his restlessness, I laid out a rough plan to distract Drak and get him refocused on the mission.

We tended to congregate as a group as my team now found themselves separated from their own. They were starting to change. It was not obvious at first. But gradually I noticed that my team surrounded me all the time, and it felt right. After the demonstrations, we set out strategizing our first mission. We already knew we needed to study the worms, but we did not know how to go about it. Brainstorming was new to the Dracos, but with a little prompting I got some helpful ideas from my team. Eventually we came up with a plausible plan in which we attached nanites to the worms using gel. The nanites would do their thing and create a symbiotic relationship with the worm allowing the Dracos to monitor the relationship between the clouds and worms without interfering with the worms. Not to get ahead of myself, but I was hoping the monitoring would expose the relationship between the worms and the portals. Were they dependent on one another? Or was their location a coincidence? Could the portals be studied independently of the worms? How do we measure success? So many questions. The beauty of that plan was that the worms could be studied in their natural habitat, without disturbing them in any way. If we used the gel on the research nanites, the power received by the worms could be diverted to the nanites. That way they could stay active indefinitely.

It would be also interesting to know whether the portals are doors to another time or dimension, whether the portals could be closed, how and what effects that would have. This planet was covered with portals ripping through space and possibly time as the Dracos suspected.

This planet appeared to be a point of convergence. The only place in the known cosmos where the portals were in mass quantities leading from places unknown throughout the universe. The Dracos believed that those portals might be the very fabric holding the universe together, and that is why they were so fascinated with them. We did not know if new portals were created over time or what was at the opposite end. There were too many unknowns. The Dracos were confident that the portals were stable on this end, but they did not know whether the portals were static and stayed open on the other end, So many questions and until now, no new methods to get closer to the portals for in depth exploration.

I wanted to further explore the avatar idea I lost consciousness in this place countless times, so it was not that farfetched to think that it could happen to me again, or to anybody else during a mission. The chairs they designed for avatar-driving Dracos were very ergonomic and very comfortable. I wanted to sit in one but, apparently, I did not have the brain to drive anybody, as I was told. I didn't think they appreciated how difficult it was to drive me! And I was doing it on a daily basis. Anybody else's mind should be a cakewalk for me. I reasoned that since they were the experts, I should trust that they knew what they were doing. It bothered me to be just the observer, so I offered myself up for practice. I was willing to be driven by my teammates. Again the idea was simple. I would be injected with a solution, which would knock me out. One of my Dracos, Skinny volunteered, would download my brain patterns into his mind allowing him to control my unconscious body functions. I insisted that the event be recorded. I was curious. I wanted to know what happened while I was not myself and how Skinny handled the operation. I lay on a mat and took the injection. It worked almost instantly. I do not remember much after the sting of the needle. When I woke up, I felt like a truck had hit me. I hurt in places I never knew existed even with the pain meds and my nanites.

I vaguely wondered how I would I have felt without the Draco self-made pain solution. What would happen? Would everybody feel like that after they were driven? Everybody around me was very concerned with my wellbeing, and the medics were there as well. They also were helping Skinny and Drak. I wanted to know if anything went wrong. And I was right, there were problems. As planned, Skinny downloaded my brain pattern and submerged his mind into mine. For some reason, with all the info they had about me and my anatomy, they did not anticipate the problems he encountered shortly after. Instead of driving me, he got lost inside my brain. He was confused and panicked. This was totally unlike anything they could have anticipated. Emotion is not something the Dracos knew how to handle, and as soon as he was exposed to my emotions, it acted like a virus, and totally overcame him. In the wake of that, there was not much he could do. Virtually, he crawled into a corner of my brain, like an infant, paralyzed, scared and lost. Skinny was unable to get out.

Drak had been in my head exposed to my emotions and feelings now for a while. The logical choice was for him to go in and retrieve Skinny out of my head, before any permanent neuro-damage would be inflicted on me or Skinny. As a result of Skinny's brain overloading mine, I started bleeding out of my eyes and nose. Apparently Dracos have a much larger brain capacity than humans and my brain could not handle him for much longer. What a nightmare! Drak went in, and did not need long to find the confused Skinny in there, but he could not get him out. Paralyzed with panic, Skinny attached himself to a version of me and did not want to let go. It was difficult to understand exactly how Drak did it, but in a nutshell he convinced me, or a version of me, in my head to push Skinny out. I was surprised that Drak did not suffer the same emotional overload as Skinny. In fact, he had the wherewithal to stay behind after releasing Skinny to repair the virtual damage without any additional harm to himself or me. Maybe because we shared nanites and he had been snooping in my head for that long, he was the only one compatible to me and my funny brain. I was more than OK with that. The problem was, it would be difficult on missions. He would never want to be at the central command to drive me from there. But maybe we could come up with a mobile version of the avatar chair and still make it work.

After this disaster, my researchers were a little bit reluctant to experiment with me and the avatar chair. They had to admit that they did not understand enough about emotions and didn't know where to start to account for it as a risk factor. With everybody busy in their new roles, I could either learn more from the database, which I was so bored with, or find a new thing I could do. Let's face it, the scientists or mission operators were so much better suited to do the database thing than me. I dragged my feet. I decided to check on my team to see what they were doing and if they needed help. It all reminded me of Earth with a spattering of weird as I walked by the lab and saw my two researchers looking at a very detailed hologram of the worms' interior, exchanging thoughts and ideas telepathically. It was all so quiet and dry. It was the same when I walked by the infirmary and saw my two medics studying a giant holographic of my brain with their hands virtually inside it. Again no talking or smiling made it seem very robotic and mechanical. Even the pilots stood facing each other quietly while they telepathically navigated a holographic mini shuttle between planets and asteroids. I was missing fun! A good day on Earth was skimming, lies, deception and apologies, and now look at my menu.

Bored I fingered the hem of my fabric uniform and wondered if the scientist could make a nanite suit, similar to the suits worn by my team. They were made out of enough nanites to cover their body three times over. The excess was used to stimulate the muscle groups with little surges during recharge. I needed one too. How else could I keep up with them? The nanites feed off of the Dracos skin to receive the energy they need and respond to their psychological need for form and protection. Unlike my fabric suit, it could take any form, any color and any texture or density the Dracos would like. They of course kept it kind of black-greenish and tight with slots for their weapons. I would be able to change the style and have fun with it. They proposed skin grafts from clones, but then I couldn't load them anymore and I wouldn't be special. With nothing else to do I decided to see what it would take for me to have my very own nanite suit without the skin grafting.

I walked with newfound purpose into the lab and presented them with the challenge. I was determined to know my options and any obstacles. If it proved to be impossible due to my physiological makeup, then that would be fine, but I needed to at least explore the possibility. Controlling the nanite suit would take intense concentration—difficult but not impossible. The challenge was providing enough charge to sustain the nanite activity, since the nanites simply could not take charge from my skin. The only way to share my energy was by being with Drak and loading it. I was convinced I could somehow power my own suit by just thinking about Drak every now and then. His energy should transfer to my suit. It would be easy enough since I thought about Drak quite often.

When it was time to test my theory, I asked the scientists for a full set of nanites and replaced my fabric uniform with them. It was very awkward to have only thick jelly paint covering my body. I wanted to keep some fabric on my private parts underneath the nanites, but they had to hold on to my skin. I simply decided not to walk around with it. Instead I went into a secluded part of the station and experimented with controlling the nanites. The Dracos made it look easy. Each and every time I thought about changing the color or form of the original setting, I lost coverage somewhere. Pockets on my hips caused me to lose half of the top covering my breasts. The color pink changed the pants into a loincloth. I simply did not have the right brainpower-concentration to change part of the program and keep the stability and integrity of the suit.

Now I understood why they all had the same boring color and design. It was easy to control, or rather not control at all, and just let the nanites decide what to do. Never the less, I was determined to rock the design. I practiced until the entire suit fell off of me like sand. Not having any fabric underneath suddenly became more of an issue than just comfort. I could not possibly return naked back to the lab and the dust suit just did not want to go back on me! It was depleted of energy. I completely forgot that the scientists had advised me to return before the nanites' energy was gone.

Trying to fix it I started thinking about Drak, hoping I could load the now sand suit and make it active again. I was glad nobody could see me. Even though they would never judge me or make fun of me, it was more than enough for me to feel embarrassed. Sitting in my god given suit on the ground I closed my eyes, tilted my head and imagined being with Drak in the pod. That was the last time I knew the nanite suit followed my direction even if it was unintentional. I slowly submerged my hands into the dust next to me, hoping the charge would travel right through my fingers and into the depleted nanites. And it worked! I was so happy! The nanites flew back onto my skin covering me up.

I waited until I felt the nanite suit settle to open my eyes again. I felt triumphant. Then I realized that the suit was back to just one layer. The entire programming was gone; there were no pockets for storage. Nothing. Even the color was very uneven and random. Whatever programming the nanites had left they retained and the rest was now up to me. I looked like a drunken chameleon without a plan. It was funny looking but a definite improvement over being naked. Now I just needed to concentrate to get them back to some sort of order.

I was so busy experimenting with the suit I totally forgot it was time for my chow chow and that the team meeting had already taken place without me. Drak, being connected to me, of course knew what was going on and he left me to my experiments during the meeting; but he was not going to let me go without food for long without showing up and getting me to the lab for it. He was concerned for my health. I liked to think he genuinely was worried about me like a boyfriend would, but I was not sure that was it.

So here I was playing with the suit and going from completely naked to sort of clothed, when he showed up in my little private place to pick me up without any warning. Of course with my luck I was naked when he showed up. Standing like Eve in front of him, while he was trying to get me to go with him, was quite shocking for both of us. For a second we both froze like deer in headlights. He got my thoughts and knew it was something significant to see me like that. He did not know how to react, other than to close his eyes and turn around. I could feel he wished that he had announced himself before showing up. Or was it something else?

I swear, I could see a smirk in the corner of his mouth. Those were precisely the moments where he confused me, and I did not know how much he was like a human and how much he was like a machine.

Respecting my need for privacy, he went down to my nanites on the floor and used his hand to collect them all. They charged themselves on his skin and were ready to be applied back onto my body. For someone without empathy this was quite impressive and kind of him I thought. I made sure all the nanites were in fact covering all the right places and went with him for my chow chow. Feeling better now, after I collected my dignity back and for this little display of caring, I grabbed his hand as we walked down the corridor. I smiled and thought about his smirk and what that could mean for us. He either reflected my emotion or started developing some of his own, because the little smirk on my lips was also on his. We kept looking at each other like that for the entire remainder of the evening.

After I ate, both of us had to go to the pod for recharge. I had the option to either go to my own and practice with the nanites or just give it a rest for the night, and let Drak handle the recharge of my nanites with his skin. Sooner or later I would have to involve him in my little experiment any way, why not now. Having made up my mind about which way to go, the two of us went to his pod and I cuddled myself back onto his shoulder, hoping the nanites would not have to leave my body to take energy from his skin on his hands while they were wrapped around me.

It felt different to have my nanites against his nanites than when I had on clothing. It was just little bit thicker than paint and I knew he could feel my pulse just as I felt his heartbeat match mine. The nanites amplified the pressure sensation of our contact. My leg was over his thighs, and my chest was tight against his. I could feel his skin almost as if there was literally nothing between us. It was more exciting than I expected. I felt the scars on the side of his chin. How much pain he must have gone through, I wanted save him from any more. How could this solid soldier seem so vulnerable to me? How could his touch have such an effect on me?

My heart beat faster and I could see he felt everything. He knew what I was thinking, feeling and how much I was holding back. Why did I even bother to hold back? I should just accept that there were no boundaries between us. I looked into his eyes, which opened instantly as my head elevated. The eye contact was intense and all I could think about was what I wanted to do next. Energy automatically started leaving my body and flowing right into the nanites. They were not meant to receive so much of it and naturally started shorting out one by one like little firecrackers. In order to not lose the entire suit, Drak put his hand onto my arm making them all leave my body and flow onto his. The entire time he was looking into my eyes and for some reason knowing that it was just to save the nanites did not help. I still had butterflies flowing throughout my entire body.

It was dark in the pod, for which I was grateful; but with our Draco eyes we still had our night vision. By keeping eye contact I was preserving some of my privacy. Right now I was at a junction where I either could go ahead and seal our relationship or choose to preserve our friendship and divert my thoughts to something else. I knew what my body wanted but different from my usual self, my mind wanted so much more than just this. So I decided to wait. I closed my eyes and started thinking about the next mission.

As usual he respected my decision and closed his eyes as well, tightening his arms around me. It took a while for me not to be toxic to my nanites and be able to coax them back onto my skin, but I managed. From that point on I used any chance I had to practice changing color, texture, form and feel on my new uniform without losing the safety or integrity of it. There were lots of obstacles in the beginning but after few days I was in the control of my own suit. I had known the right amount of focus to keep my uniform in the right form and just the right amount focus on Drak for him to load it on a regular basis. The perfect time was before my chow chow and after I got out of the pod. Not understanding why I need this fancy uniform anyways, Drak observed my practice with skepticism. For him all this extra energy was spent on something trivial. But it made me feel better and I proved to myself that I could do things.

A week after our last team meeting we were ready for the mission. We had practiced all of the possible scenarios with all devices, existing, new and modified. We were ready to move. For better or for worse I wanted to introduce my new ability to change my suit. With their great ideas I thought they would appreciate it. However, with a dry unimpressed motion they dismissed my idea instantly. I would have appreciated some kind of acknowledgment about my suit. I did not understand why my ideas were so quickly discarded. In the spirit of being their commander I insisted that Skinny and Snake Eyes try to modify their suits. Following orders they did as I asked, even though they thought it was waste of their precious time. And we ran into our first problem. Trying to change the color, Snake Eyes had trouble with the image. Apparently Dracos lack imagination. How could I help them be creative? I stewed over this for a while before I had another great idea. Of course another one of my great ideas got an eye roll from Snake Eyes.

But she had to do it anyway. I wanted to try to feed their suits my design and then return the suits back to them. I figured the nanites had proven in the past to develop a mind on their own anyways. I wanted to make this phenomenon work for me as well. They didn't understand any of my ideas. Why tinker with the suit? It was perfectly functional and efficient as it was. So again to indulge me and get rid of me they agreed. Skinny and Snake Eyes lent me their suit for the day. To save time I decided to put both of them on me at the same time. The idea of loading their suits with my ideas was a great one. But I spoke before I knew whether it would work. Now I had no choice but make it work. I thought if I made their suits change for different scenarios, it would be quite useful and efficient. So I hid once more, closed my eyes, and went for it.

I went through all the colors and embellishments I could possibly imagine. It was exhausting. I don't know when but it made me so tired I fell asleep. Drak knew better this time than to look for me so he just left me to my own devices. When I woke up the two suits were barely powered. I had forgotten to load them. I remembered that last time I let a suit go totally empty of power; it lost its basic programing stranding me with a chameleon suit. While it would have been funny to see Skinny and Snake Eyes in spots and barely covered, I knew I had to fix this. With Snake Eyes' lack of humor she would have shot me on sight for that. I was sure of that. I did not want to risk it. So I started imagining Drak and me the last time in the pod again thought about how close we came to changing our status from friends to more. This time I controlled how long I was thinking about him in order to not overload the suits. And it worked. Fully loaded, and I hoped with the entire spectrum of fashion, they were ready to be returned to their original owners. Now I was hoping nothing would go wrong. Snake eyes and Skinny took their suits and added a pocket and changed the color from green-black to green with tiger stripes. The thought was what counted for me. Baby steps I thought.

Now all parts in place, I personally could not wait until we finally put some boots on the ground, as my father would call it. We had our new gel armor, which felt a little slippery but very comfortable, and we had our sandy gel chunks with nanites, which we could spread under the portal and over the worms. After Drak's presence in my head during the avatar disaster, I was waiting for him to confront me about my new ability to read his mind; but as I discovered, oddly the secret was still mine to keep. The bad part was that I now had to keep my thoughts to myself and not mix them up with Drak's. Part of me wanted the secret to come out and be done with it. In the beginning I could hear and feel fragments of Drak's thoughts; then the fragments became chunks, and now all I could hear was him mixed with my own thoughts. Sometimes I didn't know where he stopped and I started. I imagined that this was similar to people with split personality, hearing multiple thoughts yapping all at once. And how did he not notice all of this going on in my head? I started suspecting that perhaps he stopped intruding in on my thoughts. Was he giving me privacy?

Very confusing. I wondered how Dracos managed to separate their personal thoughts from others. How do they not go nuts? I was about to go on my first mission with my team. This time no more seeing Drak and his unit take off and wait until they came back. I was about to go with them. I was so excited. Drak's anxiety about the mission, contemplating all that could go wrong, was so loud, I wanted to tell him to take a chill pill, but hoped that after we took off it would quiet down. It did not occur to me until much later that it was unusual for Drak to be anxious about anything. It was no longer business as usual. He had something to lose. I was feeling so lucky, my team needed little to no instructions from me. Actually what was I saying? They had to make sure I was where I was supposed to be, like a cadet. They dragged me along, and watched me like a mascot, not like a commander. I was happy with that. Who would want all this responsibility anyway?

When you jump into the ocean you swim or die. Destiny found a sick way of making me grow up, I thought. Not long ago I was barely responsible for myself yet new and strange circumstances had put me in charge of others' lives, of my "family's" lives! A heavy burden, and I was not about to fail. Not on this mission or any other. So what was I forgetting? It felt like something was missing. My father would say, "A great leader is defined not by how many follow him or her but how many he or she can keep alive." Would we encounter the Hexadoids? I was determined to be the best leader ever, and none of my unit would die.

Hovering several meters over the drop off zone, the Dracos jumped off the ship in a rehearsed, predetermined and coordinated order, already armed and searching for the enemy while still midair. As soon as the first two touched the surface, they took a knee; making themselves smaller to the enemy and scouting further into the forest area, while covering 360 degrees around the site and prompting the next pair to jump until all of us were out, leaving the pilots behind. Just as I've seen them do at the OC. No matter how many times I saw this, I never got used to the beauty of it. I was of course going down with the last pair like a precious cargo.

On the ground all was very quiet and dark, nothing unusual there. Thanks to my Draco eyesight the visibility was the same in either darkness or light. The drop off zone was very close to the portal. Since the portal was only accessible from the Hexadoids' hotspot, we found ourselves surrounded by an ocean of worms behind us and with the Hexadoid patrols in front of us. The plan was to retrace the route we took out of here when I arrived my first day. We would then drop off the research nanites right under the portals at the pool's edge. Precisely where my body went through if possible. To get there, we had to pass grass the size of trees, dark bluish and shaped like Japanese fans, and patches of midsize hills covered in illumination moss, scattered throughout the territory. We had to be very quiet not to ignite the moss. But luck was not on our side. A few moments later we were discovered and surrounded by Hexadoids shooting and crawling all over us. A full out confrontation was leaving us the only option to retreat and hide. The only safe shelter we could find was the cave where Drak gave me his nanites. The cave was inside one of the hills, well hidden between the bluish grasses and mainly underground with only one way in and out. It was our only option if we wanted to survive. We waited for the patrols to stop searching for us in this area before we tried to go back, but they were very persistent. They swept the area again and again, it was almost obsessive. Luckily the nanites kept me hydrated but I was very hungry, and physically as well as mentally exhausted. The bigger worry was my Draco friends. They were hurt and low on power, which would be increasingly needed for their healing. I looked at Drak and he grabbed my hand and directed his eyes towards the low energy levels on his calf display. With his hand tightly inside my, he looked me deep into my eyes and I instantly knew what I needed to do. It would be embarrassing to kiss Drak but my unit members were desperate.

I was never happier that I could load my unit than in this minute. With my remaining strength I moved myself closer to Drak and placed my lips on his. One gentle lasting kiss, few thoughts and a little bit of time. That was all it took to recharge Drak and my unit but we needed a plan B for the future. I thought that when we get back we should add belts to our suits with reserve power. A secondary energy source was never needed before, since they were considered expendable. But now they were my family so it was different. We were so close to completing our mission. I could not believe that we would just turn around and go back.

I tried to think of an out-of-the-box plan, but Drak's thoughts were getting louder with each minute we were cooped up. He wasn't very patient and was trying to come up with ideas on his own. I tried to close my ears to get a minute to focus but it did not help. His thoughts kept yapping. With all the pressure I think I actually yelled "Shut up!" out loud, even though we were hiding from the Hexadoids and could have been discovered relatively easily if they just followed the screaming lunatic, which was me. There was no better time than now to come clean with Drak, and ask him for help. I was useless if I could not think straight, and this was not the time to keep secrets and be vulnerable. He was a bit surprised at first but also relieved. He took my hands and squeezed so hard that he hurt my fingers. Confused, I asked him to help me to focus and told him he was hurting me. But it worked. With the pain came clarity. My brain was focusing on my pain and my thoughts instead of Drak's. It was strange. A human's basic instinct is to survive, and I just had to focus on the most important thing when faced with pain or danger.

As soon as I was alone in there, I had an idea. Since Drak and I could communicate and I was not impaired by the worms nor was he with his new gel suit, we should advance alone. The team would draw the fire and the two of us then had a much better chance to slip by the Hexadoids defenses if we used the worm pools for cover. The decision was made and my plan was accepted. I always could rely on logic when I wanted my unit to agree to something.

As we were leaving our safety, there was heavy exchange of fire. It was difficult to see where it was coming from, everywhere I think! Drak jumped on top of me to protect me with his body from an incoming blast, cradling my head with his hands. I whispered "air" as he did not realize he was crashing me. Apologetic he pushed himself a little bit off me giving me space. Our eyes met again, stretching the brief moment and reminding me that he once more chose my life over his. He kept saving me and risking his life in the process as if it did not mean anything to him. Or was it rather that I meant so much to him? Either way I could not lose him, so I had to start being more careful.

Separation from the Unit

As our Unit moved away, drawing the fire with them and leaving us behind unnoticed, we continued with the mission. Under the cover of darkness, Drak and I crawled along the worm ocean towards the portal site. The Hexadoids knew about the deadly effects the worms had on Dracos so it was the last place they expected to find us. We were able to deliver the nanites beneath the portal right under their noses. They never saw us coming. The plan worked and that part at least was easier than anticipated. Now we had to get back somehow. Moving away from the portal site, we hid behind a tubules bush. These bushes are about three feet tall and are similar to Earth's coral, but hollow in the middle. Tentacles swivel in all directions catching prey. Its natural defense mechanism is to hide those soft tentacles inside the hard tube branches if needed. As long as this bush had its tentacles out, the Hexadoids did not think to look near it for us or anything else. Our research gave us the advantage. As long as we didn't make rapid movements or noise, this bush would ignore us. Between the bush and the worm ocean, the Hexadoids would never find us and we could wait there until they gave up their search. Patiently hidden away, we listened to the Hexadoids commander strategizing the search.

The Hexadoids had dark scaly skin, black round pop-out eyes and two holes where we had noses. The mouth looked like a big tongue which went from the bottom up to those two holes. They had no visible neck and many hands. From their shoulders, antler-like spikes branched out, forming a basket-like net all the way to the front, a little bit like a tumbleweed in a desert. They didn't run, instead they rolled themselves up like armadillos. The antlers kept them safe from injury during the roll. Their fronts

108

were soft and the skin on the back was hard like armor. When rolled into a ball, between the armor skin and spiky antlers, they appeared virtually invincible. But when they rolled they could not shut. So their strategy involved mainly ambush. Their commander looked to be the tallest of them and had the biggest antlers; he looked intimidating and relatively majestic.

Instinctively, I knew the commanding figure would not give up his search for us easily. Somehow the Hexadoids knew we were in the area. The commander reminded me a lot of my father, whose name was Colonel Rogers, so I decided to name this Hexadoid commander Rogers. He was huge. Maybe larger than Drak. After couple of hours observing him with his people, I started wondering about the Hexadoids and their motivations. Assuming the commander was like my father, why would he find it so important to find and fight us? My father would only do it if he had direct orders, which was unlikely for this commander, since from all we knew about them, he was the top dog on this planet. The other reason would be if he felt threatened. In that case, why would Rogers possibly be threatened? Was there a side to the Dracos I didn't know about? Were they possibly not the peaceful, protective, research race, I perceived them to be?

Could the Dracos be the aggressor in this case? I forgot totally that Drak could hear my thoughts and he objected strongly to my assumptions as they developed. But this whole scenario did not make any sense to me. I'd seen enough dictators and tyrants on our news and in history books to be relatively certain that Rogers was not one of them. I could tell through his body language that the way he communicated with his people was strong and decisive, yet patient and understanding. He was clearly frustrated with not finding us, but he did not take it out on his subordinates. He listened to their reports, retrieved and regrouped just like my father would. So if neither side was the enemy, why was everyone fighting? This question was really bugging me.

My body rebelled at the lack of nourishment, and I wondered how Drak's power supply was doing. The Hexadoids displayed an impressive persistence and patience in our pursuit. Not being able to do much about it, I logically started to worry about Drak. Our location was perfect as long as we were not moving or making noise, but if I wanted to load Drak and start sparking all over the place, all bets would be off. I knew that Drak would not tell me if he was running low on power because there was nothing we could do about it anyway. Or so he thought. I checked his levels, relying on my intuition. As I suspected he was almost out and running on fumes. In moments like that I could hear my Dad's maddening rational to collect all the info to come up with a plan. I looked around and there was no chance the enemy would give up their search anytime soon. There was also no way we could move past them. The only way I could safely load him was to carefully retreat into the worm ocean. I asked Drak to trust me and take his uniform off, planning to test the gel he was covered in and hide during the recharge between the worms. He was covered in the new gel, so he was safe from the worms and the lightning, but we never tested whether he would survive a full body dip. Since loading him would definitely cause some bright sparks, there was no way we would not be discovered unless we were inside that pool. And if we managed to get in, I hoped that to the Hexadoids, the power discharge would look like any other worm activity.

Another problem was that the gel only worked, if the worms surrounding Drak were saturated with energy. I couldn't recall the last lightening episode that would have done that. There was a good chance they were as empty as Drak. I looked deep into Drak's eyes right after I asked him to trust me, and knew I was gambling with his life. So did he. And yet, he took off his uniform to make the transition into the worms, knowing that the uniform would cause an angry outburst to hard services. Giving each other privacy, we started shedding the protective layers and the only thing keeping us safe from the enemy. The situation was less than perfect, lots of unknown factors. Still, I could not help my curiosity, as Drak was getting undressed. In the corner of my eyes I gazed at him and noticed that he did too at me. I went through so much with him and yet at this moment I was bashful.

Regaining our focus we quietly tossed the gear into the worms, to hide it from any Hexadoids passing by. Now it was time for the real test of the gel Drak was covered in. Embracing the moment of truth, he grabbed my hand and bravely started walking into the pit. With his strong hand in mine I had to restrain myself from loading him right there. Controlling my feelings was never my strong suits, and I was so scared for him. As low as his energy was, I knew that if the gel failed I would have to abandon all caution from the Hexadoids and rapidly start a massive load to counteract the drainage by the worms. We were half way into the pool and the worms remained calm, Drak was still walking and I didn't send lightning in panic. Overall it looked like our luck had changed and we were going to make it. But as my father would say, "If all seems to go well, you obviously overlooked something." So what was it?

I did not have to wait long. Drak was shoulders deep into the worms and I could not feel the ground under my feet anymore, but I could feel Drak's life slipping away. The gel had a gap somewhere. This strong man was getting weak in his knees and going down. I wrapped my arms around his neck and started kissing him while submerging the both of us completely under. With my arms wrapped around his neck and my legs around his hips, I was holding tightly to him and his hands were holding me tightly against this body. Would the massive surge I was prepared to deliver look normal to the Hexadoids? The ocean was big and since the worms would certainly take their share, my flow would have to stay constant. My fear was that I wasn't sure how much energy I would have or be able to give, to save him.

So I gave it all and held nothing back. I kissed him and opened my heart entirely to him, while feeling for his pulse for improvement. It wasn't enough. He was growing weaker by the second because he wasn't reciprocating. Every worm, that was now saturated with Drak's energy, felt like a deep stabbing dagger to him. I tried to find the spot where he was exposed to the worms, and cover it with my body, but quickly realized I was just wasting time we did not have. Instead I swung myself around and started kissing him more intensely. I needed to refill his energy faster than the worms could drain it out of him. I had to do better. I opened my mind to his. Now merging both of our minds and hearts, I could feel the burst of energy increasing. It was still not enough. My sharing with him was powerful but only one sided. Drak was holding back. With his life on the line, he was still not willing to open up to me. That really pissed me off. What was he so afraid of? I needed to convince him that I needed him alive or I would perish. I started imagining what the Hexadoids or Rogers would do to me if I were to be captured.

I could see in his eyes, his life was slipping away. No! He could not leave me! He could not do this to me! I refused to give up or let him give up! Not really knowing what Hexadoids do to their prisoners, all I had to do was to imagine what my father would do if capturing an unknown alien. The images were growing more gruesome by the minute. It was terrifying and I could feel Drak's reaction. It was exactly what he needed. A little push, or a big one in this case. Under the duress, that my capture would happen soon, he opened up. Talk about last second. I would do anything to save his life just as he did so many times before. Why didn't he get this? When he finally opened up I could understand his persistent hesitation. The only feelings he had ever known were obedience and duty. No traces of self-preservation until now. In addition, he was hit with this overwhelming feeling of desire, and it was terrifying to him. This strong, giant man was forced to his knees by love. How biblical. His uncertainty if I would grow bored with him and move on, drove him crazy. He could not imagine he would ever feel anything like it for anybody else. He also was afraid that he would be unable to stop having feelings for me once he allowed himself to acknowledge them. He'd rather forfeit it all together than risk the fallout.

Given the choice, he had to give in. Not to preserve himself but me again. His kiss was soft, warm and increasingly intense. I had to admit, what he lacked in expression he most certainly made up in passion. The flow of energy increased massively as he completely opened up. I felt every cell of my body was pouring energy into Drak. Wrapped in a blanket of his warmth, surrounded by the worms purring like a cat, and being rocked in a cradle of waves, we fell into a rhythmic trance. I felt so soothed and relaxed; I almost forgot the danger outside the pool and the mission. I could have stayed there forever. Subconsciously, I found myself opening up, body and mind, not just to Drak, but also to the worms. I fed them with the same heartfelt energy that I fed Drak. They devoured it all in a feeding frenzy, connecting with my mind, understanding now what we were going through. Consequentially, they created a sort of bubble around us, supplying us with oxygen and space. Saturated, they also stopped draining Drak, enabling me to nurture him back. For a brief moment, free of care, Drak wrapped both of his arms around me and kissed the back of my neck, while hugging me from behind. Never in a million years would I have thought that the two of us, would be saved and protected by the conscious choice of the worms. In the pool among the worms, in Drak's arms waiting for the danger to subside, while the worms were rocking us, it felt like I was on the porch swing with my boyfriend. How bizarre my life had become to make this kind of comparison.

Seeing Drak with the worms I could not believe that the two species, which by nature could never coexist, could work together like that. I also did not know that the worms could do the bubble thing or choose not to drain a Draco and they preferred to feed from me directly and on top of that connect to my mind. So there was more to the worms than just pure instinct and primitive behavior. They were in fact capable of complex thoughts. If this impossible thing could happen maybe and only maybe, peace between the Hexadoids and Dracos was also possible. I needed to find a way to communicate with the Hexadoids. My dream now was a peaceful world in which I did not have to worry about Drak or any of my unit members' lives.

Momentarily safe my mind went to the Hexadoids and how we could communicate with the Hexadoids or at least with the large leader. If I surrendered myself to them in an act of good will, if they were anything like my people, which I strongly believed they were, it would be met with suspicion and mistrust. Counterproductive to my purpose. In addition, I probably would get badly hurt in the process. If we were to capture one of them and bring him to the Draco station as they did with me, we would be allowed to do it only as a prisoner. The only way they allowed me to wander free was because Drak shared his nanites with me and could read my mind. What if we could inject one of the Hexadoids with the nanites? Well first of all, we didn't know how this would change them, whether it would harm them or not. The only reason why Drak did it to me was because I was dying and he had nothing to lose. I remembered how drastically it changed my physiology. Given the history of violence between the two species and no means to communicate, we couldn't really ask for a volunteer to participate in this reckless experiment. We were

114

right where we started. But I did not give up hope. I knew an opportunity would present itself; I just had to recognize it and take it when it did.

Something about us opening up and melting with body and mind for this brief moment had changed him. Drak and I we were so in tune with each other that it was hard to determine where his inner struggle started and mine ended. It stripped him from his reservations and inhibitions. He was different and I did not know how to take it, but I liked it. He even attempted humor as he tickled me to get me to turn around during our hugging moment. As I turned around he placed a gentle kiss on my lips. Energy continued streaming out of me. Since Drak was saturated, instead of blowing a fuse, thanks to his gel, he started passing the energy along to the worms that needed it. Drak's sharing was creating a wave of energy, spreading throughout the worm ocean, causing a feeding feast among the still hungry worms. From the surface it must have looked like a giant stone was dropped into a pond causing a ripple effect. Without lightning I knew it definitely was noticed by the Hexadoids. I was perfectly happy with Drak's new and changed disposition, but I was afraid he would change as soon as we got back. I was not by any means set in my ways. Arriving on this planet less than a cycle, or what counts here for a year, ago, in light of recent events, things were changing fast for Drak and his people and I couldn't help but wonder whether it was due to me. Could a little human girl have so much force of nature?

Finally, there it was! I don't know how it was possible but I could see in my mind the Hexadoids retreating. Was I getting the images from the worms on the surface? Were the worms watching out for us the entire time? Was this even possible? We did not know enough about them in that regard. Even Drak was completely surprised. We got out of the pool and were on our way home, dressed only in our under armor, having tossed the hard-shells into the worm pool! Not just that. Aside from the embarrassment of having only paint on, we also were without any protection. There was nothing between us and laser fire, if we were to be exposed to it.

Out of the pool and into the fire! The Hexadoid search party had disbursed but every now and then we encountered singular patrols. For the most part we were successful evading them but there were a few exceptions. We could not avoid being shot at. With Drak serving as my personal guard and saving my butt once more, we arrived at the rendezvous point battered, bruised and exhausted, but relatively unharmed. Rogers left Drak with a leg injury to remember him by, although we did not really need any other memories than the ones we made our selves in the worm pool. The sight of us at the rendezvous point surprised our team even more than our lack of protective armor, which was my main concern. Without much trust in my ingenuity, they actually believed we were lost forever or dead. Faith in my abilities increased when they learned that we had succeeded in placing the nanites under the portal. We had much to report and share with the high council, but my stomach took absolute priority and I still needed sleep. Since Drak was fully energized and did not need sleep, I left Drak to his Draco duties and went my own way.

The Draco researchers reviewed the influx of information from the nanite probes. The revelation that the worms had a collective mind was a huge surprise to the Dracos. Needless to say, our mission impressed the high council and warranted some favors for the future. I wanted to follow up on the belt idea as a secondary power source. I could not believe they never thought to have one. Frankly I did not care, whether it was on a belt or on the shoulder as Skinny suggested. But I insisted on adding this to our regular armor. Seeing how little regard they had for self-preservation, I asked Skinny and Snake Eyes to show me their prior deaths. I thought if I knew what could kill them, I could get them to focus on how to prevent future incidences. And so they did. After the first dozen deaths they showed me using my necklace, my stomach could not take anymore.

I understood why the Dracos recorded and did not deem it necessary to transfer their final thoughts to their new clone. This information would have just prevented them from being able to go forward with life. How can you see yourself dying violently so many times and not go crazy or numb like a psychopath? No matter how I felt about it, my initial idea that I couldn't prevent what I don't know was still valid. I would have to find a way to review those records, maybe a dozen a day, but not more. Over the next few weeks, I religiously played the deaths of my family over and over again like a horror show. Filled with sorrow, tears and a broken heart, my view of my family gradually changed. I fell in love with all of them. How could I not? The suffering they went through, and their commitment, was more than admirable. On the plus side, watching gave me the insight and inspiration I had been looking for when I started this endeavor. Each day I came up with a new challenge for my support team. Researchers, medics, central coordinators, pilots and the weapons specialists were all involved. I was incorporating safety measures whether they liked it or not.

A few days into the data flow from the nanites, the Dracos finally understood the portals and how they were created. Somehow the combination of the vibrating worms and the enormous energy from the clouds created a massive disturbance in the time-space fabric. It was just mumbo jumbo to me. The thing I did understand was that we could disturb the ripple effect and close the portal, at least from our side. In a nutshell, we had the ability to close the portal and stop the influx of the Hexadoids from wherever they came from. That would solve the alien migration problem. But what about sending them in the other direction? Could we send them back? If not, was there a plan for the Hexadoids already here?

And what about me? Had anyone thought about my situation? Could we send me back? Could I travel between here and Earth, in my time? Would the council be ok with that? I grew restless and uneasy, totally forgetting that Drak was now part of me and could feel my turmoil. I felt him withdraw; the walls he had dropped in order to connect to me in the pool were up again. Now he was as closed to me as he was before the pool. I had half expected this to happen, so I was not too surprised. I took comfort in the knowledge that I had gotten through to him once. I was almost positive that I could do it again.

Before his defenses were in place I caught a glimpse of Drak's internal struggle. Would I leave? Would he go with me? Would I want him to go with me? What would he do without me? There were too many unanswered questions about portals to be able to make any type of decision. As far as I knew, opening a portal back to Earth was not even an option. At this juncture I would rather stay with Drak. There was nothing for Drak on Earth. I swore a long time ago to protect him with my life and I was not about to risk it just to see my family again.

Watching my Dracos die and die over again was torture. My resolve of protecting all of them by any means was growing stronger with each virtual death. My requests for safety started bearing some fruit. The medics put their heads together with the scientists and the weapon specialists and come up with a marvelous new invention. Skinny actually originated this idea after I forced him to wear my modified nanites suit and requested a belt back up power. What I imagined as a belt around the waist, my practical and fashion ignorant Dracos translated into a spine protector in case of an accident, impact or laser fire, the most common cause of death. They put in multiple functions like battery backup and memory chips and a few more gadgets I did not particularly care for. It was black, of course, with flexible interconnected hard-plated segments, running along a Draco spine and attached by reverse polarity.

The spinal belt was not part of their body, nor was it powered by any means, that way it could not be drained by the worms. The backup battery was for the Dracos as well as their bio and mechanical nanites. In the event a Draco fell into a worm pool and their gel was impaired for whatever reason, the nanites would be sustained by the spinal belt, with just enough power for the bio-nanites to keep the Draco brain from expiring. The Dracos never cloned a brain before, but I knew we could do that, the same way we cloned Drak's heart. The memory chip would constantly download the Draco's brain pattern including emotions. If the Draco ever got completely depleted, including the brain, the Draco would die in the traditional way. I was hoping we could download this stored information into the new cloned brain. Of course we could never test that; I was grateful for that. I was thrilled. I could not believe they had the technology and had never seen the need for this type of invention. It was easier for them in the past to just clone a new body than to protect the one they had.

Having all this info from the nanites, our next mission seemed at this point to be clear, at least to them. "We need to close the Hexadoids portal." The problem was that my consciousness did not see it so simply. For me the issue remained that we could not communicate with them. I knew that the Dracos' only responsibility was towards the worms and their planet. Their prime directive did not include any other species they perceived as intruders and foreigners to this planet. But with this logic, this included me as well! I was an accidental intruder. I had not planned to arrive on this planet nor had I planned to stay here. I had not intended to alter or harm this planet or its inhabitants. So I kept wondering if the Hexadoids were there under the same circumstances. What if closing the portal harmed them in some way or took away their only ticket home? I just thought we needed to know more before making such a decision. Sadly I was the only one with these concerns.

The advanced race I now called mine, the Dracos, did not consider it worth their time. Even Drak knowing all of my arguments was not willing to wait. I think mainly because he did not see a way we could learn to communicate with them. Apparently the Dracos studied the physiology of the Hexadoids and found no base for telepathic development, therefore no common ground for negotiations. But what about me? I could communicate verbally. Heck I could even learn sign language if it would be helpful. Besides, there was no base in my genetics for telepathic development either and here we were and I was talking and communicating just fine. But nobody was listening! I was feeling ignored and frustrated. Human history is full of wars because neither side tried to see the merit of the other. Why would it be different in this advanced alien society? Further tests and research revealed that the portals only went one way. Evidently since there were no worms on the other side of the portal, i.e. Earth or the Hexadoids planet, the transfer of the body would not be supported.

Mission to close the Hexadoid portal

The mission to close the portal to the Hexadoid planet was still on. We suited up and brought the equipment and weapons needed for the mission onto the ship. Everybody was very tense and seemed nervous. I did not know what to expect, since I should have been more prepared for the last mission. Reviewing that mission, I had to admit I was pretty useless in regards to protecting my team and myself. I couldn't, nor was I prepared to, fire when needed. If not for my out-of-the-box thinking, we would have failed at the mission. To be a bigger part of the team, I spent weeks in the simulation or OC to train my body and mind to react when needed instead of thinking. I also spent time polishing up my weapons skills, concentrating on improving my aim with deadly accuracy and bringing my body to optimal performance with the nanites enhancement. The OC had live shots and I got injured each and every time I made a mistake, just as I would on a real mission, but my gut feeling told me this was different. I couldn't explain it but I was not afraid of getting hurt, I was not scared I would screw up, but I was anxious. I thought watching them bring the gear onto the ship would distract me, but instead it just made it worse. Each minute we were closer to take off my stomach felt more of a squeeze. The minute the ship's ramp closed, I threw up. They all looked at me and then at each other, completely unaffected by the display. They continued the take-off looking stoically ahead like plastic soldiers.

The flight itself was smooth and uneventful. It took only 30 minutes or so to get to the planet. I couldn't tell exactly since the ship had no windows. Their technology allowed them to fly the ship using holographic images, transferred into their minds directly. So from my point of view it looked like two Dracos with closed eyes strapped to the wall sleeping. I could feel the change of gravity and only saw the surface of the planet when the cargo door opened. I wished that the ride to the surface was more like a plane ride on Earth so I could have watched the landscape upon approach. Briefly, I envied those lucky Dracos who were all linked with their minds and could see what the pilots were viewing, leaving me, the only blind soldier on board, wishing more than ever to be a telepath like my friends.

They began jumping off the ship in pairs. They lowered the hover vehicle, with the impulse emitter between me and the last two Dracos. The device was designed to disrupt the vibration of the worms by digging under the surface and producing vibrations to disrupt the frequency of the worms. The transportation vehicle hovered about a foot over the ground. Once we were on the ground, the ship took off and we were on our own. The Dracos had 360 degree artillery coverage at all times and we were ready to move towards the Hexadoid portal.

Upon arrival at the portal, I hesitated. Delivering the device felt deeply wrong. I needed more information and I had to delay. But I was an open book for my unit and Drak. I tried to rationalize that the idea wasn't without merit. As far as I knew, we did not perform the recon Dracos would normally do before any other mission. Our mission was to get to the portal without being noticed, and only then assess the situation.

Does this sound like a Draco mission or like one of my own? With all due respect for Draco mission planning my whack-a-doodle style did not have, in my opinion, the necessary finesse. Subsequently I begged them to just wait a minute and take it slow. As expected, I was unsuccessful in my plea. We went ahead as planned. I don't know if the Hexadoids left the site virtually unprotected because they did not expect the Dracos to come so close to their portal, or if it was just hope and luck, but we made it. They didn't see an entire unit with a giant ground vehicle? Was it luck or something else? We positioned ourselves as close as we could, and to appease me, we took the time to observe the portal.

Satisfying my curiosity, how the Hexadoids came to this planet, we witnessed a Hexadoid falling through the portal landing unceremoniously onto the ground among the existing Hexadoids. They ignored him at first as the confused and disoriented accidental intruder looked around. There was no attempt to communicate. Once he assessed the situation, the newcomer simply started a fight with the biggest Hexadoid in the area. Depending on the winner the hierarchy was adjusted and reformed. The newcomer seemed to be confused and unhappy about his arrival. It did not look like he planned to invade, as I had suspected. It was not looking like an elaborate invasion but rather like a mistake they had to adapt to and deal with, just as I did. Closing the portal did seem like we would be doing them a favor. However, at least it would spare this fate to other Hexadoids. Or at least that is what I wanted to believe.

Since the mission was based on hope, luck and assumption it quickly became a disaster. We found ourselves surrounded by Hexadoids. Seemingly surprised by our presence and not happy about our ambush, they expected the worst and responded accordingly. They opened fire and did not hold back.

We split into two teams. Team one would create a diversion to attract the Hexadoids' attention, and lead the majority of them away from the immediate area. Team two would deal with the remaining Hexadoids and deliver the emitter. Based on our plan B, unit one started shooting and drawing the Hexadoids attention away. Most of the Hexadoids took the bait, but not Rogers or his unit. Of course he saw through our plan, and was waiting for us. We never stood a chance. In the past when casualties were acceptable, we might have, but not anymore. I was not willing to sacrifice even one of my Unit members, especially for a mission I did not believe in.

There were a lot of Hexadoids, but the Dracos were perfect killing machines. Almost every shot was accurate and hit its target. Although their military precision made me feel safe, I was struck by how cold and robotic Drak's shooting was after observing him for a moment. There was no hesitation or regret in his aim. Drak and the others shoot with the confidence and skill that I had always admired, but suddenly I was uncomfortable watching others cut down with the emotional indifference. Despite my training, I could not fire a single shot and I could not explain why. We were close to the portal. Closing it was the mission. This was supposed to help the unintentional immigration of Hexadoids! They were like me! Weren't they?

Suddenly Drak's efficiency seemed brutal and scary and this entire mission looked to me like a bloodbath. He was killing them! Despite all my training and my battle proficiency, I wasn't paying any attention to the battle; instead I was watching Drak. I could not believe what little regard Drak was showing for life. Focusing, I distracted Drak with my thoughts and got him to stop firing. Too late, I realized stopping Drak was a mistake. A Hexadoid saw Drak's hesitation and attacked from behind. It was sure to be a kill shot. My training kicked in and I delivered a perfect shot hitting the Hexadoid mid strike, dropping him to the ground. Drak whirled at the movement and stared down at the Hexadoid expecting to deliver the final kill blow, but instead he paused, watching the Hexadoid's final breath and my part in it. This was a game changer.

As I was reliving the moment, I had to come to terms with

the fact that I wasn't thinking, I acted. Just as my training taught me. My dwelling was interrupted as I watched the Hexadoid's body roll down the hill. It stopped abruptly at the bottom where the hand that had been clutching something, fell open, revealing a white stone. It did not look like a weapon. In fact it did not look like anything one would bring to a battle. Yet he had been holding it with everything he had up until his last breath. I ran down the hill to his body and picked up the stone, whatever it was. With all of this blood and destruction on my hands I started at the stone with awe. Was this stone valuable or precious with sentimental value? Did it invoke memories of his home, like my iPhone did for me? On closer inspection I wondered if it was an egg. Was it his egg? My heart broke and my head spun. I did not know anything about those creatures or about their reproductive ways.

Horrified, I dropped my gun and started to shake. Drak had been a witness to my distress while looking into my mind. With the battle still going on around us, he did not know how to help me. Wrapping his strong arms around me, he tried to calm me down, by assuring me that the white stone was not an egg, but the damage was done. I was a murderer and I did not know how to undo this mistake that was still happening. They were still shooting and killing each other! I was suddenly not only worried about my team but also about the Hexadoids. This entire situation was out of control and needed to stop. There were too many of them, we did not stand a chance in succeeding at the mission unless we killed all the Hexadoids, and I was not willing to do that! When I gathered my courage to face the battle again, I saw that Drak was not shooting to kill, but only to wound the next Hexadoid. To my heartfelt surprise the rest of the unit followed Drak's lead. No more killing! At least not by the Dracos. The Hexadoids were still intent on eliminating the opponent. Now we would have to be more careful.

With the change in the mission's direction we were left with no other choice but to abort. Shots were exchanged while we were retreating and I saw the Hexadoid commander, or Rogers as I like to call him, follow us. It was obvious that he would not stop in his obsessive pursuit. Looking over my shoulder, cautiously avoiding injury, I saw him go down. He was injured and it appeared to be serious. Drak was a serious marksman and made all of his shots hit their mark. Given the severity of the wound, I think Drak had a bit of resentment towards Rogers from our last mission. After all, Rogers was the one who had shot him in his leg. Let's just say I do not think they would ever be best friends. As we were hiding in a grove of trees, feeling remorseful and in need of a miracle, I decided to go back for Rogers.

We just killed so many and I did not want to have one more on my conscience. I could see behavioral similarities between the Hexadoids and humans but I could not see any emotional connection. There was no effort or concern regarding their injured leader, Rogers. 'Leave no man behind' didn't appear to be a consideration on their part. Every man was for himself practicing survival of the fittest. The biggest and strongest animal is automatically the leader. Too bad for Rogers. He was hurt and no longer had strength, therefore he was left behind. Oddly the Dracos, who are all about following orders, questioned my request, to go back for Rogers. I mean it was a new idea for them just to save their own, never mind the enemy. Justifying my need to save Rogers and ease the guilt I felt, I continued with my idea. Rogers was not just any enemy. He was their leader, at least until Drak took him out of the game, Additionally, Rogers reminded me of my father. That meant given the right incentive and opportunity, I believed, Rogers would be willing to listen and do the right thing. "I prefer the enemy I know over the enemy I don't know," whistled through my mind as I went about changing the Draco directive. We had Rogers in hand; we did not know who his replacement would be or what wacky decisions he would make. On top of everything else, Rogers was dying and the opportunity I was looking for presented itself. Since he was dying he had nothing to lose, so I could inject him with the nanites.

Assuming he would have to share his nanites with Rogers, Drak protested heavily. Saving me was one thing but having to share thoughts and experiences with Rogers was not going to happen. However, the nanites did not have to come from Drak. This was all on me. Drak saved me because of a connection we had and because I didn't represent a threat. I could not ask the Dracos to share their mind and body with an enemy.

Introducing nanites into a Hexadoid was only theoretically possible. Apparently I was the first non-Draco to be injected with them successfully. But there was no reason to assume that nanites couldn't adapt to any other life form. I felt like I owed the Hexadoids a life. Additionally, in theory, once Rogers was injected with my nanites, we could read each other's mind. If we had a connection, maybe we could reach an understanding.

I swore I would end this stupid war and now was my chance. I could feel Drak's disapproval. I assumed he was not willing to share me with Rogers. I could feel how strongly he would object to it, and how far he would go to prevent it, so I asked Snake Eyes and Skinny to hold Drak back while I went to Rogers. Clouded with blind conviction, I promised myself, this was the one time I would pull rank on him forcibly. Crawling on my stomach, I slowly advanced alone towards the dying Rogers, second-guessing my decision to restrain Drak. But as I argued the salient points of my determination, I just did not see any other way I could have handled it.

When I arrived, Rogers immediately grabbed his gun and pointed it towards me. Once again I had underestimated the situation. Rogers could have ended it for me right then and honestly I probably would have deserved it, but what followed I could not have anticipated. Instead of shooting Rogers kept pointing the gun at me, steady, sure, ominous and waiting. Our eyes locked on to each other, time passed, and still no action, just that hard unwavering stare. I did not know how to explain to him that I was there to help. Honestly I was there to experiment on him, inject him with nanites, and use him for my benefit. My ignorance saved me. Since I had forgotten to pull my gun, I puzzled him, and he was curious to see what I would do next. Very slowly I advanced towards him on the lookout for any other danger in the vicinity. There was a slight chance one of his comrades would come to actually help him. But there was no evidence that the Hexadoids cared for one another so the chances of being interrupted were slim. I must have seemed harmless to the wounded Hexadoid since he let me come close to him but kept the gun pointing at my face. I've seen this situation in the movies where a gun is pointed in the victims face and it always looked very heroic but in my case I think I nearly peed myself from fear. I was afraid to touch my gun. Wherever I moved this stupid gun followed me, pointed at my head. I covered my eyes. I knew that only a stupid move like that would get me to relax and I was hoping it would do the same for him.

I stayed like that, motion-less, for a few seconds, which seemed like forever, and when I took my hands off my face Rogers had placed the gun on the ground next to him. I had two things going for me that day. One, I was small and non-threatening. I must have seemed like an amusing pet and not a serious threat. The other, I had the audacity to approach a wounded foe unarmed. He must have thought I was too stupid to be dangerous. I was willing to play the innocent fool to get close enough to inject him with my nanites as long as he did not kill me in the process. I needed him off guard and open to my approach. I could not help but notice that although mortally wounded he was still a formidable presence, large and foreboding with a confident air of indifference. He still seemed able to crush my neck if he desired. I had spent the last few months witness to countless acts of violence with 'game over' results. I tried not to think about what it would feel like to be on the receiving end of Rogers's defense attack.

I was helpless to defend myself against his strength, even in his weakened state. The nanites needed to be injected into the spine. I doubted that Rogers would allow me unrestricted access to his exposed back, if that was where indeed his central nervous system could be found. This could be tricky. I only had one shot to inject Rogers. I knew where my spine is but where do I find it on this sort of reptile? Even if I find Rogers spine, would my needle penetrate his reptilian armor? I was near enough that I could reach out and feel my way around his back, hoping I could feel a soft spot or opening in his outer shell. Rogers saw my hands going towards his neck and started pulling away. I paused, looked at him, and decided to mimic Drak when he came to my rescue those many months ago. I slowly reached out to one of Rogers's hands with my own, never breaking eye contact, hoping it would have the same effect on him as it had on me in this situation.

To my surprise he allowed me to advance, enter his personal space, and encouraged me to move closer to his neck with my other hand. His facial features were contorted in, what I imagined as, pain, distrust and curiosity but there was a hard edge to him that could never be described as weakness. I did not have to be a Hexadoid to know that any wrong move on my part would result in my death. I slid my fingers along what I assumed was the spine. I remembered that when Hexadoids roll into a ball, the hard shell had to stretch or bend somehow. And there it was. If I had been moving any faster over the scales I would have missed it. Very slowly, still not breaking eye contact I removed my hand from his and fished for the syringe in my handy suit pocket. Was there a limit to how much luck a single person had before it ran out? How much luck did I think I had? It was too late to turn back now. Rogers must have been losing lots of blood because his attention was fading.

I was able to move with the syringe towards his neck and surprisingly he did not stop me when I forced the needle blindly between the scales hoping it would find his central nervous system. He instinctively lashed out at me and I flew a few meters, before landing hard against a nearby tree. The blow knocked the wind out of me and surely would have broken me in two if my bones were not reinforced with fiber optics, making me much more robust. While I was catching my breath I watched Rogers, ready to flee if he had the energy to attack. I may be indestructible by Earth's standards, but Rogers, even mortally wounded, was still stronger than me. I was immediately sympathetic when the convulsions set in the same way I remember they did with me. I withdrew a second syringe with the pain medication Drak had given me but Rogers's facial expression looked like he was in a killing rage so I decided to wait. I had a feeling he would shoot me, before he would allow me to come closer again.

I waited. I made sure I remained motionless, as unthreatening as possible, and that nobody else came any closer to us. It seemed like hours before Rogers stopped shaking, screeching and convulsing. It was unbearable to listen and I was itching to help but he was so stubborn, he would not let me come any closer to give him the pain injection. When he finally stopped screeching and passed out from pain, I cautiously crawled back to him and injected the syringe. I knew from experience the pain was by far not over and I really did feel sorry for him. Now having accomplished what I had set out to do, inject Rogers, I had two choices. I could either take him back with us, making him our prisoner, which would forfeit any chance we had to negotiate since there was no way he was going to trust me after torturing him with the nanites, or leave him where he was. Both options seemed a cruel and unusual punishment but what alternative did I have?

I decided the latter and crawled back to my unit leaving Rogers behind. Upon arrival I was able to convey to Drak and the others what I had done. Not surprisingly, they did not understand any of it. They looked at me like I imagined the villagers looked upon Dr. Frankenstein, making me feel unsure and ashamed of myself and my actions, for the first time in my life. That disapproval stung and grew the closer we got to home. There would be no keeping secrets from the council.

The council had rationalized Drak's decision to save me from assured death upon arrival by injecting me with his nanites, but the same understanding did not extend to my actions. The council knew my true motivation for injecting Rogers, which had nothing to do with compassion and everything to do with my egocentric and deluded plan of linking my mind to the enemy and convincing everybody of peace. As reckless as I've proven to be, they made it clear that I was to be stripped of rank and unlikely to ever have any responsibility again. The hardest to bear was Drak's disappointment and judgment. While he did not abandon me, as I would have expected, knowing his thoughts was more than I could bear. I was back to being a pet. Actually it was worse than being a pet. Not only was I tethered to my unit again, but the council saw me as some kind of a misguided, ignorant monster that had no regard for life. I was ashamed and saddened that my indiscretions were laid before me so coldly. I found it hard to look into their eyes. I wished I could go home and forget this place. I was so deeply hurt. What had seemed like a good idea at the time was now a horrendous, unforgivable mistake. After closer self-reflection, I had to admit I could not possibly know what the nanites would do to Rogers. I coerced Rogers into trusting me then cursed him possibly with disfigurement and pain. What would his own people do to him once he changed? Light downs on marble head. It slowly seeped in! What have I done?

Time dragged on, as night after night I woke up in a full sweat, reliving my encounter with Rogers over and over in my mind. I could not face Drak's disappointment. He was kind enough not to dwell on my mistakes but I knew he was careful around me. Not wanting to see myself through Drak's eyes, I avoided all contact with Drak and my crew, spending most of my time alone and escaping to my pod whenever possible. I could no longer find comfort in the pod or Drak's arms. I was finding it hard to focus from lack of sleep and everything was slightly fuzzy. Everything about the Dracos seemed foreign to me and I started to question not only my actions but the actions of those around me.

I attended the next few Unit meetings, numbed with anger. I barely noticed that I was not included in their conversations. I could not hear or see their thoughts and was not surprised when I realized that I did not even care. Nothing made sense anymore. My mind was filled with black thoughts, nothing was good, and all seemed lost. I never asked for any of this. All I wanted was to save them and this is how they treated me.

I was stuck in a cycle, hating and feeling sorry for myself, then hating and despising Dracos for beating my humanity out of me. My routine became monotonous, predetermined and predictable and I found myself more often than not sitting in a dark corner just listening to my music, and suppressing the memories of that awful day. I wanted to go back home. Dracos and their routines were getting on my nerves and starting to tick me off. Especially irritating was Drak. He kept looking at me and trying to connect to me, but I just could not allow him in. I was deeply withdrawn and he was not able to read my mind anymore. I could see it made them all uneasy. I took a crazy kind of comfort knowing that my withdrawal made them uneasy. Let's just face it. They had trouble controlling my crazy ideas when they were monitoring me inside my head, now all by myself in there, who knew what crazy thing I would come up with next. I was past the point of caring what they thought.

Once I became aware that all my thoughts were shielded from the Dracos, I was surprised. I had not thought it possible and vaguely wondered if Drak and the others had the same ability. They had centuries of perfecting and developing telepathy and I figured the Dracos could expose selected pieces of themselves to each other and leave other parts of themselves hidden and private. I had a glimpse into a new ability and I needed to learn fast how to switch part of my brain on and off from them. I had no time for a learning curve. I did not want any other Draco to see my thoughts anymore. Not even Drak. I was damaged and not innocent anymore. I imagine my innocence was what Drak was so attracted to, but that was not me anymore and I questioned now whether he would like what I became.

Drak finally broke in. Seeing me shutting down and isolating myself, he focused on distracting me. Given his past experiences with my emotional ups and downs he had discovered that introducing me to something new, challenging, unusual or humanly impossible, I would discover my new limits. For better or for worse I would obsess over it until I mastered it. He literally dragged me towards my new project.

Drak found me hidden away in a dark corridor and he knew I was not about to open up or talk to anybody so he purposely sat down next to me and grabbed my hand. As much as I wanted to lean into Drak and feel his protection, I was so wrapped up in my own misery I found his touch difficult to tolerate. I pushed him away and got up to leave, wanting to get as far from him as I could. Surprisingly, Drak gently refused to let go of my hand. I pulled and twisted, feeling childish but finding I could not help myself. He simply stood up and led me across the station. Resigned, I dumbly followed, barely noticing where we were going and not really caring. Finally I realized we were in the shuttle hangar.

As I stubbornly held on to my depression, I failed to notice my unit plotting to get me out of my funk. In the shuttle hangar two of my pilots were practicing flight on a mini version of a shuttle. The shuttle flew right above my head almost hitting me with its wing. My two pilots had their eyes closed and they were connected to the main flying conduit, but in my self-pity I saw this as a slap in the face. Just another thing that separated me from my host family. I was convinced they taunted me because they thought I could not fly those things. After all, I was a "dumb human."

A spark of irritation ignited. I wanted to fly. Hesitantly, but obsessed now with proving those Dracos wrong, I wondered if Drak would help me. I knew he was busy doing my job as the commander now, since I was no longer in charge. Momentarily forgetting my resolve to avoid contact with anybody, I looked at Drak, opened my mind and asked him. I did not know what restrictions were placed on me and I really did not care to find out, but I found my head clearing as I became determined to fly. I was not sure I was ready to mind connect again with Drak and what it meant for the two of us working together again, but I knew I had to try. Seeing what it meant to me, he agreed. I mean how difficult can it be to fly those toys?

As we approached the conduit, still not realizing their convoluted plot, I saw what I imagined to be skepticism in the faces of all the Dracos within the room. Everyone's eyes were on me. In my mind they were all very doubtful about my baby human brain being able to handle the flight simulator. In order to show me how the conduit worked, Drak went in first. He closed his eyes and one side of the flight conduit activated immediately. As if putting a chip into a computer, his brain started the mainframe download of the schematics of the shuttle, followed by the star-charts. It was daunting to see his brain absorbing tons of info with a few clicks. Now I understood what I perceived as the skepticism by the other Dracos. This computer downloaded a huge amount of information into his brain. Could my puny human alien brain handle the download? I imagined I would make contact and after just a fraction of the information was downloaded, my brain would fry like an old generator. Could the nanites fix this kind of damage to my brain? Or would they just give up on me and my infantile attempts at crazy?

I hesitated. I was having second thoughts. Maybe this wasn't such a great idea. Trying to talk my way out of this situation, I argued that an alternative approach should be considered. I didn't need to fly the ship telepathically. I could fly the human way! It didn't look so fun anymore. My pilots made it look so easy. I felt tricked. I stared at Drak with my mouth open but the effort was wasted on him. He was still connected to the main frame with his eyes closed, receiving a ton of info. The information just kept flooding into his brain.

How much did we have to know? It's just a shuttle we needed to fly. I started wondering how much brain capacity could possibly be available in Drak's brain, and how much more of a download he could take. If I thought of his brain as a hard drive, I wondered if his brain, after accepting all of the flying algorithms,

135

was at 100% capacity. What if that capacity was maxed out and would there no longer be any space for new information? I was so confused and about to just turn around and run. At that moment, Drak, still connected with his eyes closed, grabbed my hand and pulled me closer. My burden was lightened when Drak sent me visions of me flying. I don't know why, but he seemed to think I could do this. He knew me better than anybody. I was beginning to think he knew me better than I did myself. Right now, I hoped, for my sake, he was right.

To further prevent thoughts of fleeing the scene, he disconnected himself from the conduit so he could assist me with my connection. I felt the presence and pressure of everyone watching and waiting. I already knew I had the capacity to embarrass myself even without the added pressure of everyone's eyes on me. I knew better, than to accuse the Draco's of having even one judgmental bone in their body, and realized they were just deadly curious, wondering what I would do next. There was always the possibility of getting seriously hurt, yet with all of this unspoken support I was more afraid to fail. Directing me like a puppeteer holding a marionette, Drak placed me in front of the conduit. My defenses were down and I was ready to connect to anybody and anything. Somehow, Drak let me know he knew exactly what was going on with me, and that he had no doubt about my success. Was it that he knew I had a rebound time of approximately 5 minutes and if it was not this crazy activity, which occupied my time, I would come up with another crazy activity in 5 clicks or under? Either way, my mental state was in his hands. He was determined to plug me in; however, there was nothing to connect to! The purpose of the conduit was to keep the pilot from falling down while they occupied with the download. I discovered it kept the muscles in my body active in the environment without distracting my mind from the main purpose. In order for me to start the download and the resulting connection to the ship, or in this case the simulation, I had to allow it into my mind.

My wonderful imagination had no trouble imagining exploding hard drives, I was afraid this would happen to my head. It was not easy to relax and let the information flow in. Drak saw me resisting as I looked around at the staring Dracos. I was about to call it a day,–and just walk out mumbling some unintelligible excuse hoping to pass it off as another brilliantly hair-brained idea, when Drak took my face into both of his hands. He forced eye contact and did not let me break it until I focused all of my attention on him and lost my train of thought, along with myself, in his eyes. With his calm nature and forceful grip, he virtually pulled my mind out of panic, allowing me to accept the transfer of information without shutting down. I found that as long as I stayed focused on Drak, I could ignore the onslaught of information. It was odd. I knew the information was foreign and new to me but it intertwined with my thoughts allowing my memories to coexist. I found myself accepting the downloaded information as if it had always been accessible to me and I always knew the schematics of the ship. It was all right there. I did not have to struggle to access it or even to look it up, I just had to think about it, and I knew that it was accurate. I knew every inch of every part of the ship and understood the controls and how the ship would react to every command. I knew the limitations of the ship and how those limitations were discovered. It was amazing how simple and orderly it all was.

I found myself hungry for more information. The inflow of the data went from a trickle to a river as I hungrily accepted the data. I also became aware of an increasing pain in my head. For now the pain was bearable since I had no intention of stopping the flow. Access was not as simple as Drak made it look, but I was happy it was working at all. I let the data flow continue. It was so fast. I could not tell what I had just downloaded into my memories but I trusted that if I needed it in the future, it would be available to me. The pain had increased and became excruciating but I was determined to manage. I knew this process came with a price. I also knew that this would not be as fun and easy as Drak made it look. Never the less, I was prepared to pay the piper. Pain I could handle. Mainly because I trusted the nanites and I knew that they would be able to fix whatever caused the pain. Drak's download was completed in about a half a day. It looked like my download would be at least ten or twenty times longer.

I returned each day for additional downloads only stopping when my pain-receptors were overwhelmed. I retired to the pod right after to recover from the ginormous migraine I was inevitably left with. I admit that there were times when I failed to see the fun of it, which was what I was going for. I was determined to show the, skeptical Dracos that I, "the human," was able to do it. There was no going back, if not for the fun than for my pride. Each and every time I ventured to the pod, Drak was waiting to see me in. I knew he was fully charged, waiting for me in the pod, he must have waited to keep me company. Hesitant at first, I only went in because I knew I could keep myself and my thoughts shielded from him. I was still determined to protect myself and to keep my guard up but it seemed rude to rebuff him since he was helping me and I would not abandon common human courtesy, or distance myself completely from him. On the other hand, this type of attention was out of character for Dracos, and definitely meant progress in his emotional development. But I was in too much pain to fully appreciate it. I was making notes for later though. Paranoid and tired, after many days of this exhausting ordeal, I was convinced they were downloading more than just flight simulation data. I would not be surprised to find they had downloaded all the data from central command. When the download was finally completed, it was so abrupt that I thought I had somehow broken the machine. I plugged myself in again and again, waiting for the download to continue and the pain associated with the download to split my brain, but nothing came. I screamed at the top of my lungs, to the detriment of my already chronic migraine,

"I DID IT!"

The last time I felt this exhilarated was when I fired my gun for the first time. I looked around to see if all the doubting Dracos had seen it. There were no limits to what humans could do if we literally put our mind to it. I hope I'd proven that. My father would have been so proud of me right now, and I was not surprised that I especially wanted Drak to acknowledge my success. He was standing next to me and I could not help myself and leaped triumphantly onto his neck with a small "Yippee!" He gave me a supportive hug and he gently plucked me off his neck and placed me back in front of the conduit. Having provided the required support, Drak indicated that I was not done, and this was just the beginning. Just possessing the data about, the universe, dimensions, space and time jumps, worms, black-holes, portal travel, slipstreams and hyper-drives was not enough. I had to learn how to use the information, which was scattered all over my brain. Not in a theoretical way but for real. I had all the know-how; it was time to practice. The machine needed the two of us. I looked over at Drak, encouraging him to get started. I wanted to fly that baby! I did not remember ever wanting anything more. As much as I was itching to continue, I was losing concentration and I had a splitting headache. Pain won out and I got out of the conduit and marched into the pod, and slept for three days.

Fully refreshed with no sign of migraines and fully invigorated with the thought of utilizing all the newfound uploads, I was ready for some flying! When I was connected inside the conduit to Drak and the shuttle, I felt like the three of us were one. The ship felt like part of me, or me and Drak in this case. Being part of the ship, I stretched out my arms as if I was in the air and I could see the ship actually assuming that form. The nanites, out of which the ship was built, were just an extension of our brains, so whatever we thought actually happened. We were literally one. We could reshape the ship to anything. The bubble we usually sat in during all previous flights was just a pro-form the pilots chose. It was not actually how the ship had to look. Since there was no fixed structure to the ship, not counting the cargo, we could change form, speed, direction, and polarity all in an instant. The natural laws of physics did not apply. I discovered that two brains were better than one and we could fly through, around and next to a black hole completely unaffected!

Concepts once foreign to me were now understood. I knew that the black hole gravity was directly proportional to the mass and since the little nanites individually had virtually no mass, all we had to do was get them to act collectively to escape the gravitational pull. Using a self-modified and powered gravity field, the mass of the object was equivalent to the cargo we were carrying and could be reduced further, if required. I felt as if I was flying solo, unencumbered by the ship and its crew. I could feel, see and move as if the ship, Drak and I were one. I had a surreal moment when I fought to distinguish where I stopped and the ship started. It was simultaneously thrilling and unnerving. I felt confident and in control as I flew the ship even knowing that I had never left the hangar.

No matter how awesome we were and how easy it felt for me to fly, for some reason we kept crashing. Or, more accurately, I kept crashing. Two Draco minds working together equally as one, could easily calculate in a fraction of time how to escape the pull of a planet or the radiation of a star, but while Drak was calculating, my mind was searching for information. I did not have the practical experience shared by the Dracos to inherently deal with this massively complex amount of data! The download of knowledge was simple compared to applying it. First, I needed to retrieve the information instinctively and not waste time searching for it. I rationalized my shortcomings and clumsily explained that on Earth, humans learn things by associating new information with time and practice. Human memory is tied to our five senses, emotions, and pictures. The Draco information was downloaded rather than learned and I had trouble accessing it.

Desperate to succeed I went inward, to organize the download. Knowing what was coming, maybe I could inventory what was in my brain. If I could compare my situation with what I knew maybe I would find a clue how to make this work for me. The only comparison I could make was to Olympic athletes. For example, synchronized swimmers, ice skaters, or so many more, they don't calculate what degree they have to turn for the perfect dive or jump. They practice for years until muscle memory takes over.

I tried the Draco way, now it was time to do it as a human. Maybe I needed to start using Drak's brain as my own internal computer or somehow connect to his references and let his system guide and retrieve for me. Let me use him as an extension of myself. But how would I go about it? Until I knew how to use his brain, I decided to get familiar with my own. Once again I went to my dark corner, but this time to be alone with my thoughts. I imagined I was at the conduit, flying out in space. I had seen enough science fiction space movies to imagine quite a few catastrophic events. Each time I staged a different scenario I mentally timed my reaction. I was getting frustrated with the effort. I was too slow. I needed muscle memory but did not have the luxury of time to acquire it.

I returned to the conduit where Drak was waiting patiently for me. Drak stood in front of me. I focused on his logo instead of his face as I mentally connected to the conduit. With an effort to relax I loosened my grip on the conduit, only then realizing my fingers were cramped from the effort of digging in. He took my hand and released the tension in it. The telepathic mind works like a hologram, at least for me. If I close my eyes and imagine Drak as my virtual connection to the shuttle then I can use his mind to retrieve and borrow his muscle memory to direct my hands to fly. This would leave my mind free to oversee other obstacles or situations. Could I let him take over like that? All I would have to do is imagine stepping into his holographic body and become one.

As I worked my way through the downloads and became engrossed with this new project, I was surprised to realize that once again I was happy. With all the new info downloaded into my brain I was too preoccupied to dwell on what had happened in the past. Too exhausted to do more than sleep, I passed out each night. The nightmares were gone. It took me awhile to realize what Drak and my crew had done for me. Looking back I recognized their clumsy attempts were quite obvious. If I had not been in such a low state, I would have seen right through their attempts to pull me from my funk. I was touched. But Drak had done more than that. He knew I would take the challenge and get redirected and obsessed. Was Drak changing? Or are the Dracos more like humans than I gave them credit for?

Although I never managed to fly with Drak I decided to spend more time with him. Knowing he would enjoy it in his own way I went with him to the obstacle course for mission simulation. I was blocked. I was afraid that I would freeze while under laser fire, that I would get someone killed on the next mission. I suspected this invitation was staged by him to get me mission ready. As long I wanted it too, why fight him?

The first chamber was dark and quiet and I could feel my heart beating in my chest. My palms were sweating, my legs heavy, I had to sit down and get some air. I noticed that my lungs were refusing to supply me with air and I looked at Drak with tears in my eyes. There was no way I would be able to move. All I wanted to do was to run out of there and go back to my dark corner. He grabbed my hand and stared down at me. Over his shoulders a laser shot bounced right in and separated a large portion of the simulated ship away from its main body.

Flooded with adrenaline and half aware of what was going on, I grabbed my gun and pushed Drak out of my way while firing on the origin of the shot. It was an instinct that took over my body as if remote controlled. Clearly it was not a human reaction. I pushed more forcefully than I should have been able to, and my emotions suddenly were non-existent. Drak looked at me and tilted his head in a surprisingly humanlike manner. He read my mind and he did not feel the same "ME" I was a few seconds ago. Was I able to separate the part of my brain controlled by emotion when needed? Was this a new ability I now possessed? Was I becoming more like a Draco? In my pursuit of getting Drak to be more like a human by exposing him more and more to myself, I neglected to foresee the effect this deep and constant connection would have on me. I was stupid to believe that this exposure was one way. Yes I was proud to say that Drak was more and more like a human. Ironically, it appeared that I was becoming more like a Draco at the same time.

Faced with danger, the logical part of my brain took control. I shook off the distraction of where my thoughts were going and hefted myself up, stood in front of Drak, and gave him all the time he needed to deal with his emotions. Shooting at targets and getting us through to the next level of practice was suddenly as easy as crossing the street. Action without emotional baggage was clear and enlightening. I did not have to be that pathetic little girl anymore, always second guessing decisions based on emotional turmoil and regret. It was cut and dry—clean. I had a new understanding of the Dracos' culture and was trying to decide what was better for me. I was not completely sure I wanted to switch back to my human standards when it hit me. What if I can't? What if accepting Draco standards meant abandoning my human qualities? As my mind struggled with these questions I continued to operate with Draco-like efficiency coordinating movements from target to target. I looked at Drak and wondered whether it was worth having feelings at all. Just as the thought ripped through my consciousness, a new thought shot through my mind. 'Then you would not be you and you would not need me.'

Cold and concentrated multi-tasking without being compromised. It was great. After I got us past the first level Drak got his confusion sorted out and started participating in the practice. I noticed he was shooting the targets to wound not to kill. It seemed ironic to me, where before I insisted on shooting to wound, now I found his efforts inefficient and not practical. The enemy would definitely shoot to kill, rather than give the enemy another chance to kill.

After the practice was over I connected to Drak with no reservations. Not even to protect his image of me. Our score was more than perfect. A dry acknowledgment of completion and plan for our next move was all I could think about. We were an efficient team now that I no longer had my emotions clouding my judgment. The down side of my emotional detachment became evident as soon as the danger subsided. I was hit with all of my emotions, all at once and it hurt. No different than a hit from a sledge hammer. For a second, I was overwhelmed as a wave of conscious ripped through me, left me wheeling, and then was gone, leaving me slightly dizzy and off balance, but whole. Mission accomplished,

I was out of my funk and functioning again. This time minus the emotional turmoil I had thrust upon the Dracos.

Months went by in awkward silence and avoidance. I was still considered persona non grata for sharing nanites with Rogers. The biggest pain I felt when looking at Drak was that he was torn. I showed him my deepest self, but he had such strong values and beliefs into his directive, he did not know how to deal with what I had done to Rogers and what I had done to him. I could see clearly, he still wanted to connect with me and have us be as before all of this, but this was just something he had to sort out for himself. This whole, 'one mind one body' thing had seemed so romantic, but trust me, it is HELL. Opening up means exposing yourself, completely, with no reservation, because frankly there is nothing to hide, they see it all, my motivations and selfish thoughts, hang-ups, and weaknesses. How am I supposed to protect myself? I might have been able to forgive myself and move on, if I was not constantly reminded of his point of view and my influence on his view of his world.

The mission to close the Hexadoids portal was priority for the high council and aside the obvious distrust they had for me, I was still an asset to them. They decided to include me on the mission, but under guard. Drak and Snake Eyes were my appointed watchdogs. They were responsible for me and any harebrained stunt I got involved in.

That meant that when I screwed up, they would get punished. I get it, my actions have consequences and to deter me and my judgment they made me responsible for people I care about. It really sucks to be me! I wanted to say, forget it. Almost. My judgment was obviously not to be trusted. I was afraid the alternative was to be recycled. Their policy regarding the purpose of people within the society, overshadowing individual objectives

145

and emotions, was stronger and was proving to be more efficient than my clumsy attempts to fit in.

Still invested in protecting me, Drak could not get over my reckless behavior. He was trying but at the end of the day, we were still one. Additionally seeing Drak's and the unit's activated replacement clones, reminded me about their redundancy, and that my future was entwined with theirs. So I sucked it up, and did my best to behave and protect them. I loved my Unit and I considered them my family. I considered all Dracos my people and that is why it hurt so much, that they saw me as a reckless primitive being. In the words of Shrek, "Just because everyone perceives me as a monster does not mean that I have to become one. I can be what I want to be." Centered again, I remind myself that I am human, not an alien and not a monster. I can feel good about the events and situations that I choose to mold and change me. I may no longer be totally human but I can hang on to those traits that I feel keep me human.

Nightmares were now my constant companion. I learned to accept them as I learned to accept my mistakes and they did not wake me up anymore. Now I woke up in the morning tired but no longer sweating, so I guess I was making progress in my recovery. I also think that it helped knowing that if I had enough I could always just shut off my feelings and be like a true Draco. I practiced shutting out my emotions a little bit here and there. Of course I did not want Drak to notice what I was doing. I did it when I thought he was distracted. Prior to the mission prep, Drak and I went by the hangar and I just missed running into the ground vehicle for the next mission. That is when I realized I was not getting enough sleep. If I could not get it together, I would be putting everyone at risk on this mission.

I loved the new suit they came up with to protect the

Draco's from the Hexadoid fire. This would come in handy since the new orders were 'shoot to wound' not 'kill'. The new suit was created using images from my head. It was fitted and worn like an exoskeleton. Nanites reinforced the outer shell. Other nanites beneath the exoskeleton shell were within the gel they used after massive skin damage for repairs. This gel was modified similar to the gel for the worms. After impact from a hard object or laser it instantly turned hard. Furthermore, when under pressure it turned solid. This allowed the Dracos to pick up ten times their own weight, like ants. Instead of the hard-shell units they now were all soft, mobile, and cozy until otherwise needed. I took great pride in knowing that if Dracos knew how to be grateful, they would thank me for it.

We flew to the planet's surface to test all of the new toys. All of us were wearing the exoskeleton suits and it was time to see what they could do and how they would perform on the planet. The Dracos simulated battle games. I was not invited to participate in the practice battle and found myself leaning against the hover vehicle, bored. I watched as long as I could, when I decided to take the supplies off of it and do some testing on my own. I climbed onto the thing and did some experimental jumps to see if it would drop under my weight. It did not. Incrementally I increased my weight but the craft remained stable proving it would also repel the gravity pool as it increased.

I laid down on the empty vehicle, on my back, looking at the stars, listening to my music and with all my weight on the right side of the vehicle. It moved to the right. I moved to the left and it moved as expected. The only thing missing was forward momentum. There was no resistance on the surface and the new suit would allow me to handle objects much heavier than I was. Better yet, I could shoot my gun. I had under estimated the effect. With a small pulse of my gun the hovercraft countered the blast with forward momentum and then took off with lightning speed. My earphones were ripped right out of my ears. I immediately flipped over, facing front and gripping whatever handholds I could find on top of the craft to anchor me to the moving projectile. I screamed as the landscape whizzed past me and I hurtled away from the battle games and my unit.

The sound and pitch emitting from me was less like human sound and more like a bat. With my unused vocal chords, modified by the nanites, the sound was so high my ears could not hear it anymore. I realized my eyes were shut tight but I could see shadows in front of me even with my eyes closed. When I moved to the right or left I could avoid hitting the objects in front of me. I opened my eyes but I was overwhelmed and it was more difficult to avoid objects. The first obstacle was a little bit too close and I skimmed it with the corner of the vehicle. With the speed of a bullet I carved a one-inch hole into the tree. It was amazing. I was flying!

And it was fun. I used my voice to avoid hitting things, especially since my eyes were useless any way. Boy was it fun and exhilarating. I flew for a while before I returned to the practice battlefield. I had not been missed. The battle was still in play and I was returned to my spot and continued to guard the gear. I decided to keep this little flying excursion to myself. It was fun having a secret. It did not have any practical application and fun is considered a waste of time. No harm no foul. No one needed to know but me.

Second mission to close the Hexadoid portal

Gathered at the team mission meeting, I was happy to note that all of the protocols I had established were in place with the exception of my involvement. I was slightly hurt that I was summarily ignored. I knew that my presence was a courtesy and any insight I offered would be dismissed. Mentally I understood, but emotionally I was irritated. They went over the details of the mission and treated me more like, a necessary evil than a member of their team. Snake Eyes, the most intuitive of the group, kept looking at me during the meeting with pity and at times I had a feeling she wanted to give me a hug. Clearly she could feel it was what I needed but definitely not what I wanted. To his credit, knowing how torn he was about my situation, Drak tried to offer his support. I never felt so alone among so many people. I could hear everyone clearly inside my mind as my heart sank knowing this was only the beginning. Dutifully I followed my team to the drop off point where we quickly advanced towards the Hexadoid portal. This time the Hexadoids knew our objective. The portal was heavily guarded. The Dracos had anticipated this and they were ready. Disregarding their safety they were willing to die for their cause. It drove me out of my mind knowing that some of them could actually die before I got the chance to make amends. Determined I was ready to jump in front of any fire to protect my family.

There was heavy fire on the ground but it wasn't directed at us. I saw Rogers, completely unharmed, running towards us, blasting fire at something huge behind him. I was about to shoot him when he jumped at me and cradled my head to protect it from incoming laser fire. What the heck just happened? Had I completely lost my mind? My unit was stunned by what was happening. Rogers was still on top of me and more of his people were running towards us, firing at the shadow behind them. My unit ceased firing on the Hexadoids. Who were the Hexadoids firing at? Who was firing at them? Why?

At the Hexadoid camp

We all agreed Hexadoids were not a threat, therefore closing the Hexadoid portal could wait and communication was now a viable option in our mission strategy. The Dracos council was desperate to know what was going on. What were we dealing with? If the Hexadoids were not attacking us then who or what was? Hidden away beyond a very large hill, we were temporarily safe from whatever threat was after the Hexadoids. The two groups were very uneasy with each other and the tension was so thick you could cut it with a knife. The battlefield alliance was too new to be comfortable. Guns were visible but not pointed at anyone or anything in particular. I walked between the two groups trying to ignore the threat and testosterone buildup. I suggested learning the Hexadoids language the way I was taught languages, the human way and no cutting corners this time. I appealed to Drak knowing that if he bought into my idea the rest of my unit would also.

Instinctively I felt no danger from Rogers. I backed towards him with my gun pointing to the ground, trusting my gut and displaying no aggression to his trigger-happy Hexadoids friends.

I was nervous, but I couldn't let anyone see my hesitation. I moved slowly, acknowledging and trying to decipher the Hexadoids' emotional state. Standing alone with my back to Rogers I reasoned my way around any arguments I could imagine and focused on the positive attributes. We needed to communicate with the Hexadoids and the quickest way was through immersion and the only candidate available would be me. I already had a connection to Rogers. He protected me. I would be safe. I was earnestly babbling in my enthusiasm to get started. I wanted to rectify my mistake with Rogers and this was the only way I thought I could do it. The idea of handing me over to our recent enemy was not sitting well with Drak. While being bombarded with heavy objections I approached Rogers, I turned around and looked up into his face. I wasn't even sure if I could convince Rogers to teach me their language never mind take me with them back, but I could only worry about one problem at a time. Thinking positively I deduced that Rogers would not have saved me if he had wanted to kill me.

I searched his face for understanding; I wanted to find a way to express my plan. In a giant leap of faith, I reached out for one of Rogers' hands. Where I had expected aggression at my touch, Rogers seemed to accept it. Looking into his eyes, something inside me told me he would take me back to their camp. Was it really that easy? It seemed like gloat as he displayed an almost perverted satisfaction seeing how uneasy Drak was. I felt a little uneasy picturing myself as a willing pawn in his game. Could it be that he knew what Drak and I were thinking? With an effort born of self-control and restraint, Drak watched Rogers raise his hand-like stinger and inject my neck with some kind of venom. My body seemed to absorb it and quickly, my muscles and bones went from solid to jelly in just under a minute. As a result, I dropped to the ground in a puddle of human flesh.

Rogers engulfed me inside his body and rolled away. I could hear his men following in the same way and I could feel the distress of my unit as I collapsed and disappeared. I tried to convey positive thoughts to Drak to calm everyone, after all I had asked for this. Whatever this was. Traveling in this manner was like being inside a washer's spin cycle. As we rolled to our destination point I lost any sense of orientation, but was surprised that I did not get motion sickness. It was unsettling to roll around with a stranger and alien wrapped around you, totally formless, but I was used to funny by now.

I trusted that Rogers would not hurt me, but I wasn't entirely convinced, he understood the purpose of my going with them. Nothing I could do now, except to enjoy the ride. It felt weird being formless. Would I reform back to myself when the venom wore off, or would I have to get used to this state? Could the Dracos fix me if something went wrong? Odd, but I seemed to have lost my sense of touch and smell. My hearing seemed to be more acute. I heard a heartbeat. Is that mine or Rogers?

Finally the rolling stopped. Rogers released me from his form but I remained a lump for a while until the venom wore off. I still had my senses, as I noticed we arrived at a cave with orange luminescent pixy dust, flowing like a river with no beginning and no end. I was entranced by the ebb and flow of the dust and thought of infinity. The other Hexadoids opened up as they arrived, and without hesitation jumped right into the Pixy River, happily exposing their interior towards it in the process. They relaxed inside the swirling dust and let the current drift them away. They looked like they were in a trance while the river turned them around and around. Rogers did not go in, but stayed behind with me. He turned towards me, and started, what I presumed was, teaching me.

He touched my heart, then his belly and my heart again. What was he trying to do? He repeated it again all the while he kept making snorting sounds and swinging his lower disgusting lip from one nose hole/nostril to the other. I knew why I wanted to join Rogers's group and what my mission was and this looked a lot like him trying to communicate with me. Call me suspicious, but what are the odds he knew what I wanted to do there? I was starting to feel foolish, having second thoughts. I also was having trouble looking at his ugly face without thinking about the many times he or his people attempted to kill me and Drak and those times he had actually succeeded in killing Dracos. I thought I could look beyond our differences, that it was all about the bigger picture, but being here with them and seeing how happy and careless they were made me angry. It seemed to me that they had no remorse or reasoning for shooting at us. However, I reminded myself that I did not have to like them; I just had to find a way to stop this craziness.

Rogers continued with his repetitive motions, trying to convey something to me. He repeated them so many times, touching my heart and his stomach, I wanted to shout out, stop and give me a minute to think. His movements paused. As I took a moment to thank the high heavens, it dawned on me that he had read my mind. I had wanted him to stop and he did. Every reaction he had to me appeared to be deliberate. A direct response to what I was thinking and not because of any action I was able to mimic. Frankly I had no idea what I was doing and all of my physical attempts were clumsy and obviously wrong based on his reactions. But, when I wanted to shout at him to stop and give me a chance to think, he paused. He understood me. Shifting my focus back on the lesson, I started thinking. If I wanted to teach someone a word, I would repeatedly say the word and point until the connection was made. This is exactly what Rogers was doing but what could he possibly be trying to teach me by pointing at my heart and stomach. It was unlikely that he wanted to eat my heart. Perhaps, he was trying to show me where his heart was located? And what's with the snorting sounds and licking of his nose? It was quite disgusting. I wanted to be polite so I made an effort not show how appalled I was by him. Rogers went back to pointing at his heart and stomach and I started nodding my head and tried saying 'heart' aloud hoping I was getting closer to some kind of understanding. Unfortunately that was not what he was after. He lost his patience and smacked me so hard that I fell to the ground with a bloody nose. He was incredibly strong.

Now that was uncalled for, I was trying. I was thankful for my nanites because that hit broke at least one or two of my ribs. Based on his outburst, I realized Rogers was not a natural teacher. He did not have patience for it and he was not going to be gentle during these lessons at all. My situation took on a whole new dimension, learn or die. I was a prisoner, not a guest. It would appear that this was not going to be as much fun as I had anticipated. I really wished I could just leave! I wanted to be anywhere but here. I started worrying that Rogers only pretended to be nice so I would go with him and now that he had me all to himself, he was going to pay me back for the torture I had put him through. I resented Rogers and his people. Who knew how long Rogers had been battling the Dracos? How much anger and retribution were the Hexadoids capable of? I had to pull it together, find out more and not freak out.

I got off the ground and the lessons continued one "bloody" word after another. I discovered that as long as I tried and repeated the awkward snorting sounds and stupid body movements, exactly as he wanted me to, he seemed satisfied with my progress and refrained from physical assaults. If l lost focus, showed signs of fatigue, failed to mimic exactly or somehow did not meet his standards, he smacked me to the ground again. Each assault to my body, had every fiber of my being screaming to retaliate, but I rationalized that he was so huge I would just hurt myself. That first day was long, painful and frustrating. Between the pain from his blows, the humiliation that each blow was a personal failure, growing hunger and the understanding that I had volunteered for this torture which may leave me dead and abandoned before we were through. I was just about done. He seemed to understand this. The lesson stopped and Rogers brought me what I thought at first was food, but it turned out to be SLUGS! Oh boy, I did not think this through.

'Hell No!' I would rather starve to death. Before I could finish my thought, my face kissed the ground once more! My stomach retched as it became clear that I would be eating a slug. Resigned, I got myself up and took the slug from him. I was scared, revolted, retching, dizzy with hunger and wishing I were anywhere else. What if they were poisonous to humans and made me sick or worse, killed me? Rogers was standing before me insisting, making it clear I did not have a choice. I picked up the smallest slug I could find shut my eyes and I put it into my mouth, desperately trying to ignore its movement on my tongue. I threw up immediately. Ignoring my reaction to the slug, Rogers presented a new slug and insisted I eat it. I refused to eat any of the slugs. At each refusal I was hit, again and again. The pounding seemed preferable to the slugs. The hits kept coming and I kept refusing.

When I was too tired, hungry and could no longer recover from the beating Rogers decided to take a break. The nanites would not allow me to die, but this torture could potentially go on forever. The nanites were my saviors, lessening my pain and keeping me whole but at the same time, this never-ending cycle of crushing blows was wearing thin on my psyche. Beyond my delirium I noticed that Rogers was getting exhausted from the beatings too. I hoped that he had satisfied his need for revenge and that he would get bored with me and, let me go. There it was again, my stupid human hope! I hated myself for my constant reliance on hope Close to passing out, I resolved to resist tomorrow. Maybe I could gain his respect and he would be so impressed he would stop this insane torture.

Throughout my beatings, I kept reminding myself, it's not about the days or even months I spent here suffering, if I could prevent them from going to war with the Dracos that would be ideal. To keep my spirits up, I kept thinking about Drak. How proud he would be, seeing me not giving up. Each time I took a hit, it made me angrier, but oddly not at Rogers, I could feel myself getting physically and mentally stronger. As drained as I was, I was determined that this would not break me.

Rough wake up

I woke up to heavy kicking of my side. I did not feel rested, and it did not feel like I got a good night's sleep. I had no way of telling how much time had passed but felt that it could not have been more than a few hours. I opened my eyes to see Rogers standing above me with more of those awful slugs, making noises with his throat and tilting his head repeatedly. Remembering my resolve to take a stand, I obediently repeated the noise and movement but pushed the slugs away. Not one to give partial credit Rogers hit me again We were in a never ending loop with Rogers offering slugs with each clicking motion, losing patience at every fifth request or so and knocking me to the ground. Me repeating every gesture and sound yet refusing the slugs then dragging myself up after every request only to start over again. After two days I grew noticeably weaker. Rogers kept teaching me new words, interspersed with a request to consume a slug. I knew I was being stubborn and this was a battle of wills, but I was all about to pass out with hunger and knew that sooner or later I was going to have to give in or die. The Draco nanites were designed to keep me hydrated, but I wished now more than ever they also were designed to keep me fed. I saw Rogers eating the slugs so I suspected he sincerely wanted to feed me, but how could he know whether they were poisonous to humans? With that in mind, I was solid in my resolve not to eat them. Almost instantly, seemingly having an inside to my dilemma, he grabbed my hand and rolled me inside him, tumbling us into a secluded chamber nearby. As soon as we were out of sight Rogers backed away from me and started twisting and stretching, until his whole physical appearance changed into a human man! The fog I had been under from the repetitious beatings was lifted as I stared transfixed. Rogers is a shape shifter? Wow. Can all Hexadoids change shape? Probably not since we were hiding from the other Hexadoids in a corner.

As speechless as I was now watching him shape shift into a human, I had to watch him spaghetti these disgusting slugs down his throat, right in front of me. Ugh. Instantly, a thought crossed my mind, did he change to a human to show me that the slugs were safe for me to eat? Ok maybe the slugs were not poisonous to humans. But, ugh once more!! I was disgusted just thinking about what that meant. Defeated and lacking any further arguments, I accepted the slug from Rogers and decided to take another stab at the slug-eating thing. Quickly I swallowed two of them, bypassing my tongue as much as possible. Rogers was pleased with this but confused about something else. He tilted his head and approached me. With one push I was against the wall and trapped with some kind of tentacles catching me from behind and holding tight to the wall. He appeared to be comparing my body to his in a curiously calculating manner. It became clear that his confusion was centered on our gender differences. Not having the means to explain or the desire to let his examination go beyond his sense of sight, I was relieved to see that all he did was observe and not try anything else. Curiosity sated, Rogers quickly became bored with his inquiry, and turned himself back into a Hexadoid.

So he could turn to a human and back to a Hexadoid at will? Thinking about it a little, I was convinced that the other hex could not do what he could. That was definitely the handiwork of my little friends the nanites, and totally my fault. It also looked as if Rogers was keeping it a secret from the other Hexadoids. That would explain the hasty trip for privacy. If he felt in need of such a deceit, it would mean the Hexadoids were not open-minded to hybrids. I understood his need to keep his newfound ability a secret and I would keep it to myself. It only takes a moment of understanding for things to change and In this brief moment I learned more about Rogers and his motivations than I could have hoped for. This insight was the reason he was not my enemy anymore and on some basic level I felt I could trust him with my life. He probably felt connected to me, just the way I felt with Drak. I may be jumping ahead of myself but this could be the missing link we were looking for to create a bridge between the Dracos and Hexadoids, Maybe I did not screw up as much I thought.

It was frustrating and at times painful, and it took me seven or eight weeks, but I finally learned the basics of their language. It was a combination of sounds and movements similar to the under lip from nostril to nostril motions from the first day. Without the movement the sounds did not really mean much. Once I stopped refusing the slugs Rogers stopped beating me up. Fed and pain free I was able to concentrate on my surroundings and able to open up my mind to see Rogers for so much more than just an alien, an enemy or even, my personal torturer. Truth be told, I ended up liking him. I learned how to eat the slugs without gagging and if I swallowed them quickly, I did not feel the need to throw up. Although not my choice of food they did keep me nourished.

During the seven to eight weeks we stayed in the cave, I had been curious about the pixie-dust river. I had been too preoccupied to give it much thought while being acclimated to Hexadoid culture, but now I wondered why the pixie-dust-river kept flowing. The dust seemed to drug the Hexadoids and make them compliant and drowsy. The floors and walls were different from anything I had seen on the planet. The floor in this cave was hard, and patterned like the hard shell of a turtle. Nothing soft, smooth or solid like stone or grass at all. Since I was sort of speaking the language, it was time to take it for a test drive, and I dared to ask Rogers a few questions. I did not want to start with the most obvious and burning questions, like where they came from and how they ended up on this planet, which might be too personal for the Hexadoids and totally self-serving to me. My first questions were meant to be ice breaking or relatively irrelevant. I asked about the cave and why it was the way it was. The question seemed to amuse Rogers and I just had to know why. He kept shaking his head and pointing at one of his nostrils again. This must have been a word I had not learned yet. He kept repeating it anyway. After maybe three times, he moved closer. My first thought was that he was going to hit me again, but instead he touched my nose and his stomach. Or his heart since this is where it was located. So heart could mean love, feelings, life.

Open my mind

I was guessing. Love? No response. Feelings? No response. Life? He agreed. OK, so life is in my nose? No, that was not it. Life and…. Nose…. Were we inside a life nose? Were we inside another being? Rogers did not object. Of course, Earth has millions of different life forms, so why would this planet have only the worms? We knew so little about this planet. The Dracos and their research! Their focus had been directed only at the worms and the portals, but nothing else. I was really beginning to wonder about the Dracos. Since my arrival, we encountered glowing moss, upside-down trees, and a bush with tentacles that hunted bugs. There was so much diversity, why didn't they study all of it? I felt pretty stupid and had to agree with Rogers laughing criticism. We (the Dracos) were relatively narrow-minded.

This discovery opened so many doors and brought new perspectives and possibilities for everyone! Rogers could see my dawning understanding and I must have looked excited, or, as previously suspected, he could read my mind, because he nodded in understanding. I interpreted his demeanor as happy. He seemed to be proud of me. Here I was thinking I was only there to learn the language.

I was surprised that I responded to Rogers pride and I was feeling pretty good about myself when it dawned on me that Rogers was adaptive and appreciative of his situation. The Hexadoids had assimilated to the planet in a way that the Draco never had. Did Rogers plan on enlightening me to his way of thinking about the Dracos? Was he planning on showing me his point of view during the conflict? The question posed itself immediately after this revelation. If Rogers was as appreciative about life as the Dracos were and there was a good chance that all Hexadoids were not completely oblivious to this appreciation, why didn't the two species work together? Why were they fighting?

Now it seemed that Rogers wanted to ask me a question. Not one to beat around the bush but obviously new to asking anyone anything he wanted to know why he and I were different. At first I did not understand his gesturing but then I remembered his curiosity in the cave. Of course! I suspected that the Hexadoids were asexual and therefore might not understand the finer points of a two-gender system. My turn to chuckle, I explained to him as best I could, that for reproduction humans needed two, a male and female. I was female, and he was obviously male. Without missing a beat, he responded that I was 'a half' searching for the other half with no hope of ever finding it. He seemed to pity me. It was so sad and odd to look at it that way, I guess because I always had Drak. What if he was right and I didn't really have Drak? This was a very unsettling thought and I did not want to dwell on it any further. I decided it was time to change the subject and asked for more information about this nose of life we seemed to inhabit.

Rogers accompanied me while I explored the outside of the life forms nose, learning new words and Hexadoid insights in the process. The bonding transformed our relationship from teacher/ student into a sharing of new discoveries. The initial mistrust turned into friendship and an appreciation for each other's differences. The Hexadoids, under Rogers command, all seemed to accept and share his trust in me. I had to admit I liked them and almost forgot why I was there. As time passed I had to admit that my mission to communicate was complete, and reluctantly I had to go back. I was totally invested in finding the right solution to the Hexadoid— Draco problem. Bolder, I started asking Rogers the hard questions. Why did the Hexadoids come to this planet? Why didn't they go back home? Based on answers to those two questions, I might be able to ask about their intentions with the worms.

Hexadoids arrival on the planet

Once Rogers understood what I was looking for he was able to convey the story of his arrival on the planet without any objection. Rogers was answering one question after another. As I already suspected, their arrival on this planet was accidental, just like it was with me. A few were deliberately tossed into the portal by their elders as punishment. As for going back, they all wished they could, but they were stranded on this planet, just like I was. Rogers shared with me that for the most part being stranded was bearable but the most painful aspect of their isolation is that they had to go back to their planet to reproduce. I was right that their species had a single gender. Once in their lifetime, each organism produces a single egg containing all their genetic coding to pass on to the next generation. The timing is out of their control and their only opportunity for continuing their existence. Without having to explain further, I understood that it was very important to them. Before I could ask the obvious questions, Rogers went on to explain that planetary conditions were integral to the reproductive process of their species. In order for the eggs to hatch the Hexadoids waited for the two moons orbiting their planet to cross paths. This happened once a cycle, and conditions were such that they provided the needed heat, radiation and gravity to complete the process. The ceremony, for this is how I now pictured it, always happened above the same crater. The Hexadoids who were carrying an egg knew to drop their egg into the crater and wait in the nearby cave.

Conditions needed to hatch the egg were lethal to all other living creatures on the planet. Once the two moons completed their circuit it became safe again for all to return to the planet surface. The expectant Hexadoid parents came together around

164

the crater and collectively raised the hatchlings for the next five years, They raised their offspring communally since there was almost no way to distinguish between the hatchlings. There were always a few eggs that did not hatch, but the parents were spared the pain of knowing if it was their offspring that didn't hatch. Since the hatchlings were raised together in a community with their own societal rules. Parental love was also foreign to them but they had an indelible sense of loyalty to a group. The adults were able to adapt to the environment but if they released an egg, there was no way to replicate the hatching conditions and the egg would die within a cycle, ending their genetic line. No Hexadoid would ever choose to get himself into this situation, and they would do all they could to get back.

I dared not ask but Rogers volunteered that every Hexadoid accepted the end of their genetic line and unless they found another planet they could go to, this planet was now their home. They felt they had more rights to it than the Dracos. As they saw it, the Dracos had a choice and could go back to where they came from. I could not disagree. This opened more questions about the Dracos. Where were the Dracos really from? Would I be allowed to go back with them when they went back? I suspected they would not let me go back to Earth with the nanites in my system unless they could remove them. And why did they feel so entitled to this planet and the worms. I knew more about their so-called enemy than I knew about my own people! All my discoveries and the following conclusions seemed to please Rogers. I could see it in his smug face! At this point I was convinced that he could read my mind. There was no other way to explain the expression on his bug face. With Drak, I was oblivious to the mind reading possibility, but with Rogers I knew better than to underestimate the nanites and what they could do. I was puzzled that the nanites didn't give me the ability to read Rogers mind. Why was I forced to learn to communicate the hard way? I just did not understand those little buggers at all. I injected Rogers with nanites so we could communicate, not to make him a shape shifter!

I could see Rogers was enjoying my confusion. With all I had learned, I now felt it was time to go back to the Dracos with the valuable intelligence they were hoping for. I just had to make sure Rogers approved. I wanted him to trust me. This war broke so much on both sides, and created a large rift between the two species. For better or worse, I was confident I could resolve some of the misunderstanding and open relations. Now I found myself worried about Rogers and his people. The new enemy they were running from and shooting at when I arrived for this mission was still a mystery. Every time I asked Rogers about them he squashed the dirt underneath his hands and drew in the air an image of the worms. I was beginning to wonder if he was trying to tell me that there was another race on this planet with guns. I did not understand him and I figured that unless I actually faced the new enemy, I probably never would. I let it go for the time being.

As the end of my stay with the Hexadoids approached, we went to meet my Unit; we came upon what Rogers called "dirt." Dirt was a massive energy-based lifeform made out of ground particles or simply dirt. This lifeform could change its shape into anything; I equated their 'form at will' capabilities to the nanites we had our symbiotic relationship with. The new lifeform did not acknowledge us or the Dracos because it was busy squashing the worms in the nearby pool. Although the pool was small, I could hear the painful sounds of worms in distress. The dirt creature was killing them! Squishing and eradicating an entire pool of worms at a time! When the dirt creature was finished with the worms in the pool we stood transfixed as it sucked all of the energy from the clouds above, until those too disappeared. Leaving the worms dead, the nearby portal closed, and the creature was temporarily satisfied. We suspected that this sated state would last long enough for it to move on to the next pool.

We were witnessing the destruction of this eco system unwillingly and unprepared. Say what you want about their limitations in expression, but I could see on Drak and Rogers' faces how stunned they were and deeply disturbed by this. Just like towards the worms here, this creature displayed a hostile and destructive demeanor towards the Hexadoids and Dracos alike. Suddenly we had a common enemy. I could feel it from both sides. Not one to let an opportunity slip away I used my new linguistic knowledge to suggest a common mission. Inject the last research nanites package into the resting dirt creature. That way we had a vehicle to collect data about the creature to understand it better. Neither party objected. I volunteered to help contain and distract the creature. Rogers proposed to position himself with his people at the opposite side of my approach ready to distract the monster if necessary. The Dracos would cover me as a shield and Drak insisted on going with me as my wingman. Life was perfect again in my twisted reality, at least for now. A quick plan was born.

Drak and I crawled towards the resting blob of dirt. It seemed to pulse in place a little, not paying attention to its surroundings. We had to get closer to deliver the nanites. Not knowing how much intelligence it possessed or how it would react to our presence, we wanted to complete the mission without being noticed. As we were creeping towards the creature, I could sense Drak had a million questions about my time with Rogers but was holding back. I suspected that he missed me, and was surprised about the void he felt while I was gone. I was happy to discover, without a doubt that, I knew the feeling was mutual. Since the telepathy thing only worked when we were relatively close I was surprised to find that Drak was extremely jealous of Rogers. Did he really think it was all fun and games or that Rogers was someone to be jealous of?

His insecurity was starting to annoy me. Admittedly his jealousy could have been wishful thinking on my part. Never the less, if he was really jealous, I had to give him some slack. I had years learning to deal with all sorts of emotions and this one is a tough one to deal with for anybody. Even though this whole situation was driving him out of his mind, I could see that he still managed to think about the mission and the prime directive. He was completely focused and cool. As soon as the research nanites were injected, information started streaming into HQ. It was beautiful to watch, the teamwork, the precision, the smooth wrap up, all accomplished using a team of former enemies, with no leader, I might add. I felt compelled to fill this gap. I was pumped, it worked. I was back in the game. Once we regrouped I asked Rogers to shadow the creature. I wanted to know whether it was alone or part of a larger group. Did it come from a portal or was it indigenous to this planet? If it had come through a portal, I wanted to know if more were coming and from which portal. This was information that could not be obtained from the nanites currently offloading information to Draco headquarters but I felt sure it would be needed.

To display our contribution to the partnership, especially to the other Hexadoids who still harbored doubts regarding the need of a partnership with the Dracos, I explained via Rogers how the Dracos would collect the data from the nanites and analyze it. I stressed our commitment to defeat a common enemy and our desire to share possible plans, strategies and resources with the Hexadoids. I was on a roll checking off points while simultaneously checking with Drak to make sure I did not overstep my authority again. I was fairly confident the Dracos would keep my promises and agreements, as long as Drak did not object to anything. Negotiations completed, we watched the Hexadoids leave to monitor the creature. Tired, elated and looking forward to getting back to life on the station, we boarded our ship and took off. The entire flight back, my unit, including Drak, stared at me. They all were very impressed that I had mastered the Hexadoid's language and managed the situation on hand. However, I had trouble understanding why they were so impressed given all their technological and social advances. They had by now all seen from Drak the past weeks I spent with the Hexadoids and the beating I took. I guess in their eyes it took extraordinary commitment and endurance. They especially did not expect me to go through with it. If they only knew that much of the bleeding was because of my resistance and stubbornness, I don't think they would have been so impressed. But I took their admiration and loved it!

100 Foot Monster

Of course my moment of glory was short-lived. But after takeoff, while still enjoying the glow of success, as the shuttle was skimming the surface, a hundred-foot monster grabbed us and brought the shuttle down into the worm pool below. The monster was just about to start feasting on the energy from the overhead clouds when our shuttle appeared and was seen as a threat. Luckily nobody was injured. YET! Twelve Dracos, including Drak and myself, were submerged in the soon to be exterminated pool. My first concern was for the gel covered Dracos. This would be the first real test of their protective gel coating, I prayed to the stars everyone would be safe but then I quickly realized that the worms were in as much, if not more danger than we were.

The Dracos, managed to get out of the pool, but I was still in among the worms when the attack on them began. I guess when Drak and I hid in one of the pools, I accidently made a connection to them as well. Immediately I felt the pain and loss of each and every one of them. The pain was excruciating. Overwhelmed with it, I screamed and squirmed and twisted as the worms did. As connected as they were to each other, as each worm was massacred their pain and energy was transferred among those remaining in the pool. The pressure was paralyzing with every death pressed upon me like a concrete weight. I felt like I was going to pop.

Trying to protect themselves and reacting to the massive transference of pain the worms stiffened up on their tails. No longer malleable and squishy, they were ridged like an ice pick, and started making jerky stabbing motions trying to ward off or impale their attackers. The worms were blindly jabbing at any foreign body around them. Unfortunately I was it.

I felt each and every stab-wound. Not a single inch of my body was left unscathed, they jabbed me in my eyes, ears and stomach. There was not a place on my skin left undamaged. As a human I would have had the luxury of dying. But as a hybrid, the nanites covered my organs with the same protective fiber optics layer as my bones and muscles, making me literally indestructible and a perfect pincushion. My body may have been able to sustain destruction but it could not protect me from the pressure, pain and mental anguish that I had to endure. Finally, self-preservation yanked me out of this nightmare and into sweet oblivion and the pain stopped. There was only so much my brain could handle. The Dracos wanted to help me, but what could they do? Getting in was not an option. They would die instantly if jabbed by even one of the worms and the worms made it impossible for any new foreign body to enter anyway.

I acted instinctively, knowing I was fading fast. Before I was no help to anyone, including myself, I stretched my hand out for Drak to pull me out. I was covered in blood and could not see anymore. Rogers, who had seen the shuttle go down, arrived just as Drak was reacting to my cries for help. Rogers assessed the situation and using his stinger, immobilized Drak, rendering him unconscious. The thing about Rogers was that he had human like emotions and wanted to help me in the worst possible way, but he was first and foremost a practical being seeing the situation for what it was—a lost cause. Drak, who was always so superior, representing perfect control, was always thinking, ten moves ahead, but in this situation he was lost. Blinded by his newly emerging emotions, he was about to charge in against better judgment. I slipped out of sight in the pool, completely understanding both sides, happy with the fact that Drak would risk all for me, disappointed he was unable to rescue me, but

171

equally understanding of Rogers, realizing that he had saved Drak and not at all surprised to realize that this was probably the end for me and that I was ready for it.

I passed out but not before the worms felt my anger, determination and the unprecedented human will to live. This primal and strong instinct was just what the worms understood. While adrenalin flowed through my veins and my muscles contracted ready to fight, the worms sent their own signal across the pool. Between my unbeatable human survival instinct and the worms' unity, they connected and used my muscle memory to function as one. Instead of stabbing me, the worms attached themselves to me. One by one they created a chain reaction soon resulting in the entire pool being connected into one entity and one mind. MY MIND! I may have been unconscious but the worms communicated on the subconscious level. Apparently I was just as much trouble passed out as I was awake. With my unconscious body in the middle of the pool, a domestic, self-made new creature started forming, and it was pissed! This form started to take complex shapes using my imagination and experiences, and attacked the creature.

The Dracos and Hexadoids were stunned to see the worms mounting an attack like that, but quickly followed their lead and joined forces against the monster. Little by little the worms began covering parts of the creature, draining its energy and dismembering it in the process. The Dracos, working together with the Hexadoids, were shooting at the main body of the creature not yet covered by the worms. This united assault proved to be too much for the monster, which fell to the ground in smaller und weaker pieces. And it continued getting smaller until the entire creature was completely unrecognizable and melted into the planet surface. Once the danger was gone, the worms also separated into individuals. They moved my bloody body to the edge of the pool as their final act. I don't remember much and cannot really take credit for the victory, but together we defeated the monster, before it could eradicate the pool and the surrounding eco system. The next thing I remembered I was waking up, once again in a Draco lab. This lab was different from the others I had been in. Apparently I was the lab rat. They were probing and studying me, driven by their curiosity about how all of this was even possible. They had never seen the worms working together as a unit. They had always assumed that worms were on the same level as Earth's insects, operating instinctively as nature intended but not capable of thought. It never occurred to them that it was even possible. I was the anomaly in the equation but it was unclear what the connection was, if any. The Dracos were obviously more than curious about me based on the latest events and wanted to figure out how this happened and more importantly if it could be repeated.

I was in the lab about to be experimented on. I was scared because I didn't know what this meant for me. If I were on Earth, I would know what to expect and also knew it would not turn out well for me, but the Dracos were different. I had to think of something else before I mentally tortured myself so I concentrated on Drak and Rogers. It was not much better but at least it was not my drama. After Rogers stunned Drak at the pool, any trust between them was gone. Even though it was for Drak's own good and it saved his life, Drak's ego, self-esteem or whatever the Dracos have was chipped. He felt like he grew soft, letting Rogers surprise him like that. Filled with mistrust Drak vowed he would keep an eye on Rogers. I knew this was not good for the peace or for us working together. We have already proven that united, the 100 foot monster could be defeated. Granted Drak was weakened by Rogers but couldn't he see what they accomplished? I hoped he could get past Rogers' action and focus on the end result. I wanted to do something to help them get past that, but how could

I explain to Drak, who is straight as an arrow, that in this case the end does justify the means.

The scientists were hurting me, but it was nothing I couldn't handle. I was irritated that I had not been consulted prior to the work being performed but sucked it up and hoped that their intentions were noble. I did not expect them to be gentle but hoped that they remembered that there was only one of me. I didn't have a clone and I was not expendable. So I quietly took it for the team and mentally drifted away, concentrating on Drak and his emotional turmoil, to distract me from my own ordeal.

I discovered I could find Drak's mind if he was not too far away. It was comforting to know that he was relatively close by. I wanted to see what really went on between the two of them so I went to Drak's mind and retrieved the memory. I could feel Drak was not happy with my intrusion but also felt a sense of relief that I was conscious enough to even try. He understood my need to understand it so he let me in. I could feel the anger, sadness and frustration through Drak as I saw my body emerge from the worm pool and lie bloody and limp at its edge. It seemed like eons passed while Drak struggled to take control of his body as he watched helplessly. The ship had sent a new shuttle to retrieve the unit and my broken body but by then Drak had his mobility back. He had stood still with rigid anger waiting for the right time to attack Rogers. Honoring the peace treaty and without using deadly force, he hit Rogers so hard I could feel the memory of its force as it charged up his arm and sent Rogers sprawling. Rogers seemed to be smiling as he got off the ground and advanced towards Drak. Apparently they both wanted this to happen. They fought like titans. Rogers put all of his frustration, anger and resentment, accumulated over time, into the fight. Drak used all of his skill, experience and strength to make a point and send a message. Do not cross the Dracos! It was bloody, violent and merciless. I had never seen a fight that brutal. The Draco's as well as the Hexadoids, watched intensely. As bad as it got, neither side interfered with the one-on-one battle. There were hoots and hollers and egging from the Hexadoids. The Dracos silently watched as each blow echoed like a shot, drawing blood, cracking body parts. The fight reflected the mood of the spectators. That neither Drak nor Rogers ended up dead was a miracle. Given the time those two had been mortal enemies, this encounter was long overdue and needed to take place. I only hoped that this would help them get past the hostility and find a way to work together without suppressing their resentment or suspicions too much.

Back at the Station

Back at the lab the scientists wanted to recreate and study the circumstances which led to the worms' behavior. For what seemed like days, they kept me awake and repeatedly stabbed to duplicate the pain and reawaken my self-preservation. I was fully aware during the transition, in and out of consciousness, and felt everything. I felt like I deserved every invasive stab for what I had done to Rogers. How scared he must have been, hurting and alone, feeling like a lab rat, thanks to me. Thinking about what I'd done to him helped me to hold onto my sanity.

All I wanted was to sleep. I did not care about anything else and wanted to be put out of my misery. I did not care if I died and left them my body to study. I knew how important it was to find out how and why. In between my screams, I could suddenly hear laser fire. The scientist got distracted and stopped torturing me for a second. I was so grateful for that break. Their attention was drawn towards the door and they seemed to be confused. A very loud blast forced the door open, and Drak with Rogers at his side, barged in. They kept shooting at the walls not injuring the scientists but keeping them at bay with the lasers. While Rogers pointed both of his guns at the scientist, Drak picked me up from the lab table, and carried me out. Rogers followed him, keeping the remaining Dracos at gunpoint. In a rapid retreat they moved towards the shuttle hangar on the other side of the station. I could feel Drak close to me, but I couldn't hear his mind.

I was hurt, tired scared, and confused. Had I lost the ability to connect with Drak? Drak was my constant, my reason to live. I could not lose him. I was starting to panic. I trusted him. Seeing him working with Rogers, to rescue me, was very out of character but reassuring. What was disturbing was that Drak was acting without authorization. He would never disobey orders. He would never put any person before the collective need. Why now? I was too tired to question him so I just wrapped my hands around his neck and held on tight. My eyes were closing and I could feel myself slipping away again. My vision was getting blurry until it all went dark.

When I opened my eyes I was in the shuttle hangar, beside the force field to the stars. Drak had slid along the wall beside me, supporting my head on his lap while brushing my hair away from my face, as Rogers stood guard. I felt safe and happy. For a brief moment I forgot my situation and pain. I could feel Drak's love with each stroke. Was he able to do that? I looked into his eyes and smiled. I could feel and taste blood dripping out of the side of my mouth, down my cheek and into my ear. But it did not matter. I was perfectly happy and did not want Drak to stop stroking my hair and hugging me. I looked at Rogers and also felt at peace knowing he was with me. Rogers was the big brother I never had but always wanted. Rogers had my back. He was standing beside us, waiting and watching for danger. He made me feel safe and I was glad he was on our side. I looked out of the hangar to the stars. It was so quiet and peaceful. Deep space seemed endless with possibilities. I dreamed of taking a ship and going away, somewhere, and all of this would be over. Drak's arms were wrapped around me tightly. This was just what I needed. It was dreamy and romantic, if I ignored all the circumstances around it. But my curiosity yanked me out of my oblivious bliss and right back into reality.

Hearing nothing from Drak, not knowing how else to communicate with him without my implant translator, and assuming that I was no longer able to communicate with him telepathically, I turned to Rogers and asked him what was going on, and why was he at the Draco Station. Rogers seemed confused at my question. I looked back at Drak in some hope that he had heard my question and would be able to answer, but he also looked confused. Why were they so confused? I was about to press the question, when I started coughing blood and my abdomen felt like it still had knives in it, My chest was burning and I had trouble breathing. The injuries from the lab had not healed and my body was just too weak to have this conversation.

I wanted to sleep. I did not have the strength to deal with their confusion. I was frustrated that I did not know what was going on. I knew I was being ungrateful but I was irritated that they had put themselves in danger just to save me. Drak disobeyed orders, which justified recycling and Rogers was still the enemy in the Council's eyes, until they approved my peace negotiations with the Hexadoids, Or at least as far as I knew being sidetracked with alien attacks and lab rat participation. Please, would somebody tell me why all of my plans were falling apart, and why my torture at the lab was not over yet?

Why didn't those super smart scientists figure out yet how I did it? They had enough time and my cooperation to do it. I was growing anxious and about to get up when I realized I was in no condition to do so. Following my thoughts Rogers and Drak finally understood my questions. Rogers explained how Drak smuggled him onto the base after he insisted on getting me out of the lab. Rogers had no trouble convincing Drak and my Unit to join him on this rescue. As interesting as this new development was, how did Drak and Rogers communicate? And how in hell did Rogers convince Drak of anything? As it turned out, while I was unconscious, Drak was roaming free in my head trying to support me in any way he could. This is where he virtually ran into Rogers, who was also in my head. Huh, virtual meeting room. Who would have thought?

And that is how they communicated. Similar to how Drak pulled Skinny out, after the avatar chair accident. This whole telepathy thing was getting beyond my understanding, but totally cool. At least I knew now that those two could converse with each other, using me of course. Furthermore and most importantly, they could work together and even listen to each other's ideas. All of this was fascinating but did not change the fact that even by my standards it was an irrational act and a stupid idea to rescue me. Why would Drak ever go along with it?

I attempted to get up, but my legs were giving out. Drak caught me and carried me out of the hangar. Without questioning my motives and not having a clue as to what I was up to, Drak let me point the way. Rogers close behind us. Outside the hangar I was surprised to find my entire unit guarding the hangar entry, presumably to allow me to rest after my ordeal in the lab. I looked at all of them and I was trying to be brave but tears deserted my eyes and ran down my cheeks. They had all worked together, against their orders. Never in a million years could I have imagined this happening. I was convinced they worked hard pretending they didn't care about me but at this minute I knew they loved me. What else would move them to do that? They were surprised to see us getting out of the hangar. I think they expected us to escape to the planet surface, or anywhere else. The last thing they expected was for me to go marching right back to the lab. Or being carried, in my case. Perplexed, they looked at each other searching for clues; why I would want to go back? It was simple for me. Risking Drak's, Rogers and my unit's lives was not an option. Additionally, we had unfinished business; we had to defeat the giants before they killed off the worms and those worms were my only hope to get back home. We did not know how many of those monsters were out there or how many times I would have to get into a pool of worms.

The idea alone that I would have to go into another pool while the worms were being killed, to recreate the same circumstances as the last time, and repeat that as many times as there were monsters out there, was even more terrifying than the thought of going back to the lab. I was brave but not that brave. I was afraid that I would freeze up and not be able to get into another worm pool under attack. I just couldn't. If the scientists had to poke and hurt me some more to figure out another way to do it, what choice did I have? Believe me, a huge part of me wanted to take off and run, but it was time to go back to the lab and continue with the research! I must say for beings without feelings, I could see the surprise and shock on all of their faces.

They could not understand why I chose to return to the lab from which they just saved me. I must have changed, because all they knew about the old me was that survival for humans came above all other needs. With the exception of my family needed to survive and they would not be able to survive this latest threat unless the scientist discovered how I was able to unify the worms in their hour of need. So my place was back in the lab. I was choosing to go back into the lab, fully accepting the fact that I most likely would not come back alive. I did it for them, because they saved me and I loved them. I hope they would understand. This rescue mission exposed Rogers, who was technically a hostile intruder and implicated Drak as an assessor. If caught, my unit would definitely be recycled since they participated in acts against the direct orders from the council. I felt responsible for them and I did not want them to be all killed. Anyway, where would we go? My head was not fully clear yet, but one thing made perfect sense to me, this was where I belonged and running away was not the answer. Hopeful I was putting my life back into the council's hands, counting on that they valued my life enough to forgive them. Besides, if I died they would never be able to replicate it anyway.

I also knew that if we did not figure out how to stop the monsters or blobs as I liked to call them, from eradicating the worms all the portals would be gone including mine With it my last chance of going back to Earth and seeing my family again. Following all my logic, escorted by my rescuers, I dragged my bleeding body back to the lab.

As soon as I arrived at the lab the scientists continued as if nothing happened. I was mentally preparing myself for the painful prodding and experiments to continue. To my surprise they placed me into a pool of nice, calm worms and left me there. After a few minutes, they played the music from my iPhone. This was different. I began to relax. My mind began to wonder and I was beginning to think that the experiments were over but all they really tried was to experiment with the psychological link between the worms and me. They wanted to see if the worms also were able to connect with me in a relaxed state. What I discovered was that the vibration of my music transferred to the pool and worms. I could feel the change on my skin as they vibrated to the rhythm of the sound waves. How incredible that was. Entranced inside the tank I realized I could hear the council in my head. Or at least I imagined it was them. It was many voices, like an echo speaking or showing me foggy and distorted but very assertive images in my head, ordering me to come and see them. I focused on their words and suddenly the foggy images cleared leaving me with a clear head and an amazing buzz of thoughts. Some I recognized as members of my unit and others I assumed were the collective council. Am I really able to do this? There was a sudden hush of confusion as everyone realized I was fully among them. They were surprised that the council was ordering me to see them. Apparently 'seeing' the council was deemed redundant and unnecessary. In my case it was a privilege. The council was always only part of their mind not a body to be seen.

This unorthodox order was a short encounter. I saw them fleetingly then just as quickly the gateway was closed and I was blind to it once again. It was weird. Just for a second, I had a taste of what it must feel like to be part of a collective mind. Still lazy within the pool but sharp of mind, my unit arrived to escort me. They were relaxed and sure again, I could almost see them smiling as they collected me for the summoning. I knew where Rogers was so the council knew everything, but had decided to ignore the insubordination. Drak and my unit were happy in sharing the unorthodox news with me, not knowing that I already received the orders directly. The scientists extracted me from the pool, patched me up as best they could and covered me in gel for rapid healing. My gamble had paid off. I was hopeful and I was super curious about the council. If nobody ever saw them, what did they look like? Where did they hide? Were they walking among us unrecognized?

Why the big secret? The only thing I knew about them was that they were everything to the Dracos, shrouded in secret and left to the imagination but real enough to lead the Draco community. Whenever the Dracos needed guidance or support, the council was always present and ready to help. They were part of every Draco's consciousness and the basis for all decisions and actions. The Dracos never had a need to physically see them or be with them in the same room. So why me? I knew now they were always in my head, so why the need for physical exposure? With every step closer to their chamber, I grew more restless. At first I was excited, feeling like I was going towards some kind of recognition. It was unlikely. The only other conclusion I could imagine was that they were going to pass judgment. I had been involved in plenty of activities for them to judge.

Overpowered by a guilty conscience, my steps became smaller and slower. Drak and Rogers could clearly feel and hear my concerns. Determined to support and protect me they decided to follow me into the chamber. Rogers, disguised as a Draco guard was-three steps behind me while Drak walked directly in front of me to make sure no surprise came from there. I felt protected, but at the same time concerned that if I was right, both of them and my team were once again putting their lives at risk, for me. I was so tired. None of this was something my brain wanted to deal with. I hoped the council had not read any of our minds and did not know about Rogers's presence, directly behind me. If I did not offend them up until now, this would definitely be up there on the list of wrong doings.

I decided that it did not matter what the council had in store for me. I was going to get a chance to explain the peace treaty between the Dracos and the Hexadoids and the opportunities it held. In my head I was imagining all possible scenarios, pro and con trying to determine what they could possibly object to in this alliance. As proud as I was about developing the treaty I was finding it hard to create arguments against it. Who didn't want peace? I had the feeling that whatever debatable points I came up with, they would not be enough for the council. They could still surprise me and not honor the newly formed peace between the two species. Call me skeptical but I knew humans would do the same. My ace in the hole was Rogers. My plan was simple. Let them hear from Rogers directly, face to face. As the Hexadoid representative Rogers could demonstrate his desire to honor their terms. I was hoping that his presence would speak to his character, show his commitment to peace and outweigh preconceptions of violence and hostility previously associated with his species.

Drak and I were the only two allowed to advance into the next room. We walked into a dimly lit, cavernous room, which initially appeared to be empty. My guards followed close behind but stopped short of the entry, waiting and on guard. My plan was dependent on Rogers being present. To my surprise, the council requested that Rogers join us. Did they know it was Rogers? The three of us did not know how to react to the summons but at this point it did not look dangerous so we complied with the request with a grain of caution. We could barely see the three huge Dracos, draped standing in the far end of the room–in fluid, foggy gowns made of nanites, distorting their shape, making them mysterious and unrecognizable. The fact that they knew about Rogers and were not alarmed was very promising. The three of us walked as close to them as they would allow us, with me in the middle, Rogers on my left and Drak on my right just slightly behind me. It was me after all they primarily wanted to see.

Expecting anything but what followed, I witnessed my own judgment. Clouded with an echo of their verdict, I was still grasping for–a way to counter their logical argument. I was reckless, irresponsible, impulsive, selfish, self-centered and moody. Call me human, but it did not made any sense. Standing there under fire, my two companions were infected with my confusion and aggression. I could feel the anger creeping to the surface. Risking the council's wrath, I tried to win more time, but their decision had been made. Spreading the rage to Drak and Rogers and paralyzed with the repeating question "If I just could see the reason for their uncharacteristic decision…"

I neglected to foresee the next event. The council ordered two Dracos to take me for recycling. Before I knew it, Drak and Rogers attacked the guards. It was a blur and over quickly resulting in the two guards' deaths. I felt horrible seeing what my emotional influence had done to my friends. I immediately fell to my knees, accepting the council's decision and begging for Drak's and Rogers lives. This was not going to have a happy ending. I knew that. We were in the center of the Draco Station surrounded by thousands of Dracos all telepathically linked to the council. I knew it was a matter of seconds before we were surrounded and dead. I screamed for Drak's and Rogers lives to be saved, while stretching my arms out to the sides and holding both of them back from doing something even more reckless.

Following my lead Rogers shifted back into a Hexadoid, revealing his secret shape shifting ability to them. With Drak translating, he offered himself for their studies, and to take me off their hands. Arguing, if I caused them so much problems his people would take care of me and the Dracos would no longer need to deal with the unexpected fallout of my actions. Following Rogers lead, Drak offered to go into the Hexadoid camp with me, as my permanent guard and suggested that the entire unit would go with us. This would solve the double clone problem. Drak and Rogers were prepared for any offer, just to put a stop to the madness. I looked at Drak and Rogers, than at the council, knowing nothing about the Draco council and everything about human leadership. I was afraid that after Drak and Rogers killed those two guards there was no saving me, but maybe at least some chance for them. I hoped that if I put Drak and Rogers' life before my own, this sacrifice would show my loyalty to the council. I took my gun and I directed it at my head right after I flipped my emotional switch, planning to fire.

Unfortunately no matter how distracted Rogers and Drak were, they still had a direct link to my brain and knew what I was going to do before I did. I was out maneuvered. Everybody was in shock. Nobody saw this coming, other than the council apparently. The three huge Dracos backed off, taking their fog of nanites with them, revealing a large pool of worms behind them. A creature formed out of the worm pool, which addressed us with thoughts. We realized that the worms were the council, not the three dummy Dracos that had stood in front of them. We got it now. As I looked at Drak, he did not seem surprised. These worms were different than the ones on the planet, in size, shape and coloring. Never the less, they were worms. Now it almost made sense why the Dracos were so obsessed with the worms. I was still puzzled by Drak's reaction. I looked at him and caught a glimpse of what I had failed to notice earlier and more of the puzzle fit into place.

This pool of self-aware worms was either the descendants of, or the original biological beings on the planet Draco. The Draco clones were made thousands of years ago from a human template and modified by the worms, after they found a stranded spaceship with some dead human remains in it. These were not the worms of today, which needed to be studied and protected, but intelligent worms who back then inhabited the planet. This is why the Dracos were humanoid in appearance. The Draco's true origins were worms, and now their fascination of and by the worms made sense.

Forewarned of a natural catastrophe, the intelligent worms escaped from this planet, always planning to return. When they came back thousands of years later another, less intelligent worm population had evolved. What puzzled the council was the improbable ability the new worm species had to create portals almost unconsciously. Not only were the portals more numerous but also opened unlimited dimensions of time and space creating an infinite number of destinations. I would have loved to know this before, when I asked so many times who they were. Apparently it was not relevant information since appearance had no meaning to the worms.

If I were to follow the logic, each Draco was, at some point, a pool of worms. Drak could not understand why his origins were even a matter of interest. I was not a human anymore either. To this statement even I had to twist my head. All this time I had been thinking I would eventually go back home. But to what? Rogers was facing the same life altering realities and had reached the same conclusions. We looked at each other and realized we had been sidetracked. We were still standing in front of the council, and my situation was still unresolved.

The council knew my thoughts and always did. So why the charade? Was this a test for me? Drak? Rogers? My unit? I got my answer. They prepared this test for Rogers specifically for the peace treaty. Slowly it occurred to me that the Draco worm mind reading was limited and did not extend to the Hexadoid nanite hybrid. They needed to determine Rogers' loyalty, trust and nature as well as the remaining Hexadoids. The council gambled, casualties were expected, sacrifices were made, and chaos was avoided all for the good of the whole. The decision to terminate me was just another ruse to provoke Rogers and Drak and test their determination and loyalty, which they valued more than anything. Because I had recklessly infected Rogers, they needed to witness whether he had any lasting resentments or plans for retaliation or hidden agendas. Rogers as well as Drak's response to my circumstances and their determination to protect me from my imminent demise, which resulted in the death of the two guards, had proven their pureness of heart. On the other hand, my attempted suicide was not something they had anticipated or seen coming. I remained an open book to them. I was surprised to note that I was a source of amusement and entertainment. This is, was and forever would be the main reason I was not already dead.

I was not to be recycled. The danger to Rogers and Drak was gone, but I now had to deal with the fallout of my little stunt with the both of them Lucky for me, Drak was only mildly annoyed, but Rogers... Uhhh... Rogers was pissed. Still in Hexadoid form? I could see him struggling with all of his murderously enraged emotions as they crossed his face, all directed at me. Finding it hard to ignore his silent onslaught, I was mentally trying to stay calm and ignore what those looks meant for me but I still had to deal with the council. The council was not done with me. There was still the issue of my reckless behavior. In my defense, I was a teenager and would someday grow out of it. Obviously, that day was not today, and their concern was still valid. I needed to remind them about all my current accomplishments. The council after reviewing everything was convinced that all of my success was due to luck and persistence and not any skill on my part. They had to credit me with something. I had to have some redeeming qualities in order to get back into their good graces. The council conceded that my unit had evolved since their short exposure to me and my way of thinking. The council was hesitant to comment on the unfortunate outcome but indicated that they were watching. Of course I was not to be left to my own devices. Snake Eyes and Drak were to be my permanent watchdogs until further notice. The council wanted to have a conscious filter stop in place to counter, what they called, future reckless acts of abandon. Rogers laughed which sounded like crickets in his present form. He was betting on me to break them. I shot him a look but he just smiled smugly.

Knowing now that the Dracos were genetically related to the worms I felt the time was right to argue for a mission to stop the blobs. After all they were killing the worms, their close relatives. Now I also knew that if the council did not want to interfere in the natural worm-blob survival of the fittest battle, they most certainly cared about the portals, which were disappearing with the worms. Until now I-had the feeling that the council was all knowing and above it all, but my request was worth considering. It was strange to see these superior creatures taking my word into account. It was clear now that they wanted to stop the blobs but were at a loss as to how. It took me a minute to realize that I was the solution. This time I actually had an idea. They had read my mind saving me the trouble of explanation. I thought I had all the brilliant life saving ideas. They thought I was unpredictable and that no sane creature would be able to anticipate my moves.

We were going to need the cooperation of the Hexadoids to succeed. With all the forces combined we could see what we could do. In exchange for their assistance, the council agreed hesitantly, to find a suitable uninhabited planet for the Hexadoids that was suitable to their reproduction. Of course we would first have to go to multiple portals and find one. That would mean finding a way to travel in both directions. The council knew how unlikely this prospect was when they agreed to it.

The only condition the council made was that we could not kill the creatures. We knew we could dismantle the beast. Even if we discovered that the creatures could regenerate, the council insisted we find a way to either relocate them to a different part of the planet without the worms or find a different way to feed them. For whatever reason, eliminating the creature was not an option. All I heard was, we had permission to stop the creatures before they destroyed my last hope to go back home.

The council suggested that we return to the site of the monsters and gather more information. Additionally they generously recognized we were facing one unknown factor after another. Since none of the Draco commanders were equipped to deal with unknown variables, I should be in charge of the battle itself. Therefore, I and my unit would stay on point on this mission, and partner with the Hexadoids. The council was as nonchalant about the partnership as if it had always existed. All it took was a gruesome test to make them get on board one hundred percent. But what was I complaining about? I accepted the challenge and I was put in charge of a mission with serious magnitude. Damn the consequences, I was back in business.

Investigating the creatures

Back at the scene of the battle, we surveyed the area. It was a mess. There was so much death around us, between the dead worms and the creature's residue. I was glad that I could not remember all of the details of the incident; it was too awful to imagine. I didn't have to, I was there. I was terrified by the sight, the smell, and the morbid feel of this place.

Drak spread the nanites over the area to get some readings and better understand what happened. Rogers, mistrustful as he was, had his gun up and was scanning the area. This place represented pain and suffering and not just mine. It felt like a graveyard. So much had happened here and I could still feel the echo of the violence. I went down on one knee, touching the ground, hoping to recall specifics about that day. My fingertips grazed the soft surface below the giant's ashes. Weirdly, I could still feel the life force of the being. It was as if some residual energy was lingering, waiting for a new charge like a ghost. I looked at Drak and his nanite scan, hoping I was wrong. His expression confirmed my suspicion. Drak rearranged the nanite scan and tried again but the results were the same and confirmed it. The creature was still present. Not powerful enough to assemble itself but here. Reacting to my thoughts, Rogers pointed his gun at the ground beneath us, ready to shoot.

Drak drew his gun and pointed it at Rogers, I walked between them, deliberately faced Rogers and with my back to Drak, walked slowly towards Rogers and grabbed the muzzle of his gun. Maybe the rules weren't clear. We don't exterminate, if we don't have to. However, Rogers may have had a point. If the entity was not destroyed it remained a ticking time bomb. At the moment it was not a threat, but it could at any time gain access to energy and reestablish its form. We wanted to avoid a repeated encounter with the creature. Why couldn't it just stay dead? I did not disagree with Rogers, but if we could understand them better maybe we could find another solution before they reassembled. I looked at Drak and I swear I saw pride in his eyes. It felt good to get his approval.

Rogers wasn't happy but was willing to indulge me. Drak still pointed his gun at Rogers. It occurred to me that I had never thought about the will it took for them to work together. Sworn enemies for so long, past prejudices were ingrained and instinctive. Their scars were hard to overcome. It was clear to see that the alliance was still too new and we could anticipate some setbacks. After all of our work, could they go back to being enemies? They both had grown close to my heart. I wished that the point of no return was now. Or at least they would bury the hatchet for my sake. I hoped they knew by now how much each of them meant to me and what it would do to me if they ever hurt each other.

Crisis momentarily resolved, I went back to the problem at hand. Using the council parameters I had no doubt that they would not object to a mass scale disabling of those creatures. The question would be how? The worm's future depended on it. We had to determine their numbers and somehow work out a way to monitor them. Piece of cake as far as I could tell. Give me a week or so.

I was dreading what we had to do next. The only way we knew how to disable the creatures was for me to enter the worm pool again. The last time brought pain through torture and the worm pool was almost destroyed. We needed to discover what the scientists had been unable to discern during all those days in the lab. I had not thought of my father in a while but he came back to me again and told me to take a proverbial knee and think. What do we know? I was in the pool and I lost consciousness. The worms were fighting for survival. Was I somehow essential even though I was not in control?

Between the little fighting worms and my unconscious body, how did the worm creature unify to take its form? All species follow a signal from nature on special occasions, which overrides all thought and makes them react on pure instinct. Was that what we were dealing with? Maybe some kind of chemical pheromones? Middle school science had not held my attention but I did recall being entranced with the thought of communication between ants using chemical pheromones. Whether it was to procreate or survive did not seem to matter. Do the worms do the same? Either way, if my half developed telepathic mind was subconsciously sending signals which they related to on some primal level it might explain why they morphed.

How was I the catalyst? What if my unconscious, primitive, basic instinct mind was vibrating on the–exact frequency the worms needed to understand and they simply just followed? We needed to test this theory. But how? I really didn't want to be tortured or scared to death. We could render me unconscious with Rogers' stinger, but there was no guarantee that I would duplicate the same sense of distress since I trusted Rogers. I would just be an unconscious body among the worms.

Why didn't I think of it sooner? How else can you unconsciously enter an area without actually being present? The avatar chair. Sure the technology is sketchy at best but the connection between Drak and I was unique enough to succeed. This was an opportunity to test another theory. The only hesitation I had was that I would have to allow Drak full access in my mind again. I was reluctant since I was finally gaining some personal distance from him. I did not want him to have to choose between me and his values. But without Drak going into my mind we could not test it. What the heck. I could tell Rogers was not convinced that was the way to go. The whole avatar idea was preposterous to him. Giving up control like that to another being was foreign to him. It was the ultimate act of trust to relinquish yourself, not just your body but your SELF, to another. As a human, we understand there is a certain amount of trust, in any relationship, required for survival. We are meant to find and trust another one. Hexadoids are designed to be individuals, never giving up control even in the very end. This acknowledgement was concerning on many levels. I hoped he would change his mind, given our opponent.

It was settled; the avatar chair was our best option. I was scared. Rogers and I were at the scene of the dormant creature standing in the pool of worms Drak retrieved the remote avatar chair and was connected to it with a chip at his temple. I was ready to give control up to Drak. Rogers was very uneasy with this whole process and I could see his hesitation so I grabbed one of Rogers's arms and looked into his eyes. Not for support but for understanding. I wanted him to know I trusted Drak and I was sure I wanted this to happen. Rogers fulfilled his part by gently placing me into the pool of worms after he injected me with his stinger, relieving me of my consciousness. Rogers left the pool to take up a protective stance alongside Drak, who closed his eyes and went into my mind. All of my strong, intense and confusing emotions had left their imprint on his subconscious since he had been directly exposed to them before. The most trouble he had was with the emotions I had about him. Determined to get it over with, he flipped on his Draco switch. In other words, he went totally cold to all emotions including mine. Unconscious or not, I was getting all this. I felt like an observer seeing everything as it was happening without any ability to influence it. I felt the ice cold chill as he turned into a one hundred percent Draco.

I looked at the virtual version of him in my head and wanted to connect to him, but I was limited in my involvement. I now understood that I could only helplessly witness it all. I could imagine how hard it would be for any Hexadoids to take part in this play. Once inside the pool, we still had to get the worms to make a connection with me. Drak tried moving around but they just accepted my body and moved with me, virtually unaffected. I could feel his frustration and wanted to help him out, but I was at a loss with that myself. Then I thought maybe for him to awaken my adrenalin he had to be terrified. He would have to flood me with emotions since I was not able to.

This whole mind into mind and out of body experience was so confusing and scary. This would work; I was convinced. But how could I convey it to him? I could not interact with him at all. Hmm. I was restricted from interacting with my controller? Could I maybe flood my body with adrenaline? I searched my memory bank trying to recall how scared I had felt when in the pool last time. I focused on the pain and concentrated on it until there was nothing else. I was in a black void enveloped in pure pain. I could not breathe. I was suffocating. I could taste blood in my mouth. Panicked I realized, I virtually recreated my own nightmare. So that's what it is like to be in your own head. Peripherally, I could feel the worms reacting to me, it was working.

The worms started massing gradually around me. I felt their slippery bodies and I felt my anger and fear flowing to them. It was more than I ever wanted to feel and more than I thought I could handle. This time I was conscious. Pale like a ghost and covered in virtual blood, I felt I had nothing to lose. The worms followed. Now I had to watch Drak driving this new mounted entity like a puppet. I never imagined what price I would have to pay to make this happen. Defeated by my self-made mental agony I decided to never do that again. The plan was a bust.

After the poison in Rogers' stinger wore off I regained consciousness. Not knowing what I went through while being driven, everybody thought it was a raging success but me. Resigned and emotionally drained I did not have the energy to explain to them how wrong they were. I felt violated and drained. Willingly I flooded myself with all this pain and anger, it overwhelmed my senses. I wanted to fold myself into a ball in a dark corner. I wanted to disappear into a dark hole. Drak and Rogers felt my distress and got me into the shuttle. Reading my mind they slowly got the message. They looked at each other and sat right beside me. We needed a new plan. I knew it would take me few days to get over my experience and I needed to do it alone.

Back on the station, I kept my distance from everyone, hoping to avoid all telepathic intrusions. I barely ate, slept alone in my pod, and went to the OT by myself, practicing until I went numb. I was deliberately reckless, welcoming injuries in order to feel anything other than the black space in my head. Day by day it got better. Yet each day I had to restrain myself from going to Drak for help. I needed his warmth and shoulder to lean on in the worst possible way. But that would be selfish. That would just load my emotions right onto him. It was clear to me that if I was having trouble dealing with all this then, he wouldn't be able to deal either.

At the next Unit meeting, Snake Eyes noticed I was distracted, and given the importance of the mission, she analyzed the situation and determined that humans needed emotional stability as much as they needed water and food. Stability derived from a close relationship. I was impressed with Snake Eyes' ability to analyze human relations. Laid out like that in front of all the others, it sounded calculated, logical and frivolous at the same time. With everyone staring at me like a specimen under a microscope, I was trying to decide whether to be insulted, but she was spot on. I had no counter argument. But when she stood in front of the entire unit and put the entire unit to be at my disposal to take care of it, I realized there was a problem.

Hell no! She cannot plan my emotional stability and offer a relationship for me just to keep me focused! I am not crazy and it is none of her business or anyone else's. I was upset and could not fathom what just happened. Did they even understand what they were proposing? I looked at all of them staring at me and could not believe this was happening. Drak made a step towards me and it almost looked like he wanted to go into details about it. This was a nightmare. I demanded they stop treating me like some object they needed to analyze and fix so I wouldn't go postal on them. They should continue with the mission talks and find a way to deal with the monsters.

We needed a new plan. I did not see a possible way the avatar idea would work. It took me for a spin. How could I possibly ask anybody else to expose themselves to this if I was not sure I would be able to do it again? We planned to use the avatar to lure all the blobs in the biggest pool on the planet, which coincidently was the one I fell through. We would use the portal closing thumper, modified to send fragments of the pools energy around the planet like an appetizer, to get as many of the blobs as possible to one spot. With the help of the Hexadoids we could then mount more than one worm entity and fight them all at once. If I was willing to repeat my nightmare we could take them on one by one, but it would take forever. But I was scared. I was not willing to go through it again. I wanted us to look for another idea. Another plan. I knew none of my unit would understand that but Drak and Rogers did.

But Snake Eyes' comment made me feel worse and I could not focus at all with all the thoughts going through my head about what she had just proposed. Mostly I was bothered by the fact that my relationship with Drak would be ok now, as long as it was practical and useful to the mission. How could they change their minds like that? I adopted the whole 'no relationship' theory, but now they flipped the coin on me? Being snappy as Snake Eyes was, she proposed to shoot my hand to give me the needed clarity. In her mind I was not about to use my hand in the immediate future, so I did not need it. How thoughtful of her!!

I was embarrassed and walked away but Drak followed me, and obviously for him the subject was not over. We walked by a few rooms. I walked faster because I felt like he was stalking me. I just did not want to get into this embarrassing subject. It was hard enough for me to stay away from him and I did not need to have to fight something I did not want to fight anyway. All I wanted was to fall into his arms and let his strength melt me away. But instead I was tortured day after day with his presence, knowing he was unattainable for me because he would never develop real feelings for me. With this new idea from Snake Eyes, now he was offering himself to me like an object, which part of me wanted even though it did really come from him. The illusion would be enough to begin, and then maybe he would be able to learn to feel for me with real human feelings. Realistically, however, this would never happen. The Draco genetics were perfected over hundreds of cycles, and the Dracos eliminated the weak parts of their clone bodies in which they felt emotions. How could I, in just one cycle, think I reversed this process?

I rejected his offer because I wanted him to want me for me and not because it was logical and had a purpose. My resistance to this super logical step was simply not sitting well with him. Despite my obvious resistance, he pulled me into the next lab we

197

were walking by. As a melting notion, he exposed his upper body to me from his nanites and placed my hand onto his chest. I knew what that meant and I was not about to continue. Instinctively, he pulled me towards him with his other hand, placing his palm on my cheek and searching for an answer in my eyes. Here he was, with the body of a god, seven some feet tall, covered in beautiful scars, offering himself to me. It took all the strength I had to resist and pull myself away. In his confusion, he was desperate to understand why I was against it. It did not make any sense to him. So he did the one thing I know by now was an absolute no-no for the Dracos.

He connected to my mind, without permission, to the part I kept private. He knew this was where he would find the answer to why I couldn't let him in. Unfortunately this was the part where I hid my overwhelming desires for him. I learned this trick after I shot the Hexadoid. I learned how to keep a piece of me hidden from him. I saw in his eyes the change, when he felt what I had been hiding. It was like looking through a piece of glass into your inner soul. Nobody should ever see you like that. His eyes were flooded with a primitive, instinctual and very basic desire as he was now looking at me. His heart was pumping miles per minute and his body felt increasingly hotter. I knew I was really in trouble. It was hard enough to fight my desires inside me, but fighting them in both of our bodies… dear lord, I was screwed.

He pulled me closer to him, placing a kiss on my lips, melting the nanites from both our bodies in between. I was seconds away from giving in and slipping into the biggest mistake. No matter how much he appeared that he wanted me, I loved him too much to let this happen. He needed the space to learn how to want me all on his own, without my control. No matter how accidental that was. With the rest of my remaining strength, I escaped and left the room before I changed my mind. I avoided Drak under

198

all circumstances. I did not know how long the mind melt effect would last or how long he would feel my desire for him. It was safer for the both of us if I hid from him and avoided him until the next mission meet, where we would be in the group performing our duty. But that was not what he had in mind. His persistence in finding me was everlasting. In addition, he always knew where I was and what I was thinking. I had to come up with a new strategy because, short of fleeing the station, I did not know where to go.

A little trick I learned was how to plant small, really microscopic feelings into the Dracos of my unit. I noticed it the first time after I had the accident with the avatar chair and then again with Snake Eyes. I continued to do it incident after incident with all of the members of my unit. The closer I got to interact with them, the stronger my feelings affected them. So it was time to try to feed them deliberately with some handy desires. First, it was Snake Eyes needing to go over some inventions with Drak just before he found me once more. Another time when I was about to go to get my chow chow and Drak was conveniently waiting for me at the lab, Skinny had to suddenly go over some data with Drak in the central command. My little influences continued time after time. Drak did not notice them because they were not thoughts, only desires planted surgically into their minds. I just had to outlast the mind meld he exposed himself to. And just before I thought it would never end and I ran out of ideas of how to keep him busy and in company with other Dracos, I felt it. He was all himself again. This was just what I needed since I avoided sleeping out of fear he would find me there. I was so tired. My lesson learned was that I would never have an uncontrolled mind meld with any Draco. Just imagine if they tapped into the part of my brain where my sorrow, anger and rage are located. It would be like putting a nuke in a reactor.

But they were right; I needed a friend, an emotional partner, someone I could share my thoughts and emotions with without worrying about the consequences. I needed a pet! This thought occurred to me while I was still hiding in the lab and standing next to the tank with the worms. I suddenly wondered whether one of those creatures could become my little pet. Disgusting, but what other choices did I really have? Not social by human standards but social by nature, those creatures were usually pack animals. They needed to be with a minimum of a dozen other worms from the same pool or they would wither away. They needed each other to bounce their vibrations off of and stay calm; otherwise they would stress out. The Dracos had tried to integrate worms from different pools by putting them into one container but soon realized that they would repel each other like oil and water, keeping only to worms from their own pool. This made sense since each pool had a different, very unique, frequency.

Carefully, I reached into the container and withdrew one of the worms from the tank and cradled it in my arms. Filled with curiosity and abundance of need I looked at the worm, I felt for any sign of discomfort or a change in behavior. After a long moment of nothing, it was safe to say this worm was domesticated. It was time to take it for a walk around the station. Knowing I could not surprise anybody on the station anymore, I didn't even try to hide the creature from the Dracos. The further we traveled away from the tank, I was expecting the worm's demeanor to change, but he just continued to lay in my arms, like a blob, vibrating calmly. Just in case there were lingering judgments about my companionship, I avoided Dracos from my unit and especially Drak. Feeling confident with my new friend, I decided to take my little pet with me to the pod. After all this walking, the both of us were tired, and I wanted to see if I would be able to accept the worm as my slimy stuffed animal. I cuddled the slimy creature against my skin, and let out a surprised yelp. It had attached itself to me, like a leech, taking energy rather than blood from my skin. However, it seemed to be transferring the energy to my suit. Hmmm. Who would have thought, the only creature which did not need me to provide it with my energy, took what it needed and transferred the excess to my suit. This is, after all, why the Dracos were so careful with them.

I now did not need to charge the suit. After every feeding my pet would take care of it. The next day I woke up in the pod, rested with my suit fully loaded from my pet. I wanted to see if that worm was special or if any worm could be domesticated so I went to the tank, put my pet back in and grabbed another one from a different pool. This new worm acted similar to my first pet, in other words, a lot of nothing. I was feeling for its purr or for any change in this worm's disposition. While holding my newest pet I looked back into the tank and noticed that the first worm did not return to a group but rather slithered around the tank touching and mixing with all of the other groups. It looked like he was searching for me, or at least a way out. But then I noticed that slowly the individual worm groups were adjusting their vibrations and were almost in synch with each other. My worm had infected all the groups with his newfound frequency and now they all were acting as one group following him in his search. One pool! My thoughts were quickly picked up by the scientists in the room. I was unceremoniously pushed to the side still clutching my new pet while the scientists studied the tank. I tucked my new pet under my suit and thought about the new worm behavior in the tank and what it might mean to the mission. Now I had a pet and a new hobby. I wanted to discover what else these worms could do and hopefully keep it as a secret for myself.

Some time passed and my unit met again with all the test and simulation results for each of the plausible scenarios they created. There was a problem with each one. Based on the test results, the missions would fail. My preference would have been to just go in and do it, but I was hoping to be smarter this time and decided to try the Draco way and not rely solely on luck. Unfortunately our plans did not work in the test phase. We had to go back to square one.

We brainstormed some more, and returned again to the notion of using avatars. And not just one with me in the middle, we had to find a way to replicate the conditions with others in the worm pool. Unfortunately, the Dracos could not go into the pool. One stab from an angry worm and the Draco would be toast. That limited the pool candidates to me and the Hexadoids. We needed to test the Hexadoid ability to motivate the worms with their subconscious. Perhaps with some assistance, I could show them what I went through, get them to mimic the sensation and influence the worms. This was a big obstacle to overcome.

In addition to testing the Hexadoids' abilities to control worms, we had to convince them to participate in the avatar, which would mean the Hexadoids would have to trust the Dracos and let them into their minds. This was a deal breaker for Rogers. He did not believe any Hexadoid would allow another being to drive them like a puppet and decide their fate, particularly the Dracos, who generally do not care whether they lived or died. Why should they, when reincarnation was just one clone away? Based on past experience with the Dracos in battle, I knew where Rogers was coming from and I suspected we were going to have to work hard to convince the troops.

Rogers knew that my unit was different. Physically the same as any other Draco, because of me, they were now individuals with a finite life span. There was no clone waiting for transfer of memories and consciousness after death. Engraved with my human loyalty, my unit would not be leaving anyone behind, not even the Hexadoids. Rogers reluctantly agreed to the avatar with my unit. His involvement may sway the other Hexadoids but he was not promising anything.

I faced the fact that the Hexadoids were as emotional as humans. They would create the same emotional turmoil in the Dracos as I did. Additionally, the emotional prejudice the Hexadoids harbored toward the Dracos might cause problems. The thought of leading two culturally different war-like units was daunting. What was I expecting this would lead to? The thought alone scared the crap out of me; it was clearly dangerous but I felt we did not have a choice?

I suggested a 'Trust Camp.' I came up with the idea from sports movies. Two disparate groups are thrown together; chaos ensues until an understanding develops, as they begin to understand each other and the need to cooperate to achieve the goal. It is always easier said than done and there are a lot of fights, blood and tears before the units gel but the result is a strong unity. I needed help from Rogers and Drak to set up the physical and mental exercises. All participants needed to be mentally and physically protected from each other as well as the artificial enemy. I had Drak and Rogers working independently and cooperatively to build the camp while I worked on making the experience more real and challenging. Of course I did not share this with Drak or Rogers, effectively keeping this from their people. It was not that I did not trust them, but they were conditioned to sharing any information they could. I did not think they would appreciate the importance of surprise.

Visitor on the Station

I woke up in the pod with Drak beside me. It was nice having everything back to normal. He was so peaceful. With my hands on his chest, I cuddled myself to him enjoying the time with him. But I realized his skin was cold to the touch, he was stiff and I could not feel his heartbeat. Something was wrong! He did not respond to my attempts to wake him. Overwhelmed with panic I tried to open the lid of the pod to get help but the lid did not respond to my command. Using my feet, I tried to force it open; it did not budge. Desperate, I started shaking Drak. Nothing. I needed to take a moment to think and calm down.

What was going on? Was Drak empty of energy? Was the pod empty of energy? Well if that was the case, I was grateful we invented the spinal belt. If that was all it was, all I needed to do was to recharge Drak and the belt would do the rest. I placed a gentle rejuvenating kiss on Drak with all my heart and all my feelings out in the open. I just had to remember what we did when we hid in the worm pool from the Hexadoids. Driven by my memories, fueled by my love to Drak, my body expelled energy into him. I could feel his pulse coming back. I could feel the warmth of his body returning. His strong heartbeat pounded inside his chest. He started moving. First his fingers, then his hands, followed by his arms right until he gasped for air and his eyes flew open.

He turned his head towards me with an inquisitive facial expression and his hand went up my cheek wet with tears. He looked into my eyes with so much love, as my tears dripped unchecked onto his chest. Overcome with joy, I started laughing. He did not know what happened or why I was laughing. I was so happy I got him back; I could kiss that spinal belt. Touching his soft and toasty cheekbones, my nerves started to calm down and I started thinking. If the power outage took him by surprise, maybe this was not an isolated incident; maybe the whole station was shut down. OMG. What about the rest of our unit? My heart started racing again. I needed to get out of the pod and check on them as well. Drak had the same idea. Together we forced the pod lid open and climbed down the assembly of other pods, since our pod was not in the entry position. The entire station was dark. It looked as if it were frozen in time. Dark! No movement in any direction. Like the castle in Sleeping Beauty, nobody was awake, dead bodies everywhere. Heavy hearted, I was glad my unit had the spinal belts, designed to keep them alive if they were ever without power, until help could rescue them, but this was not true for the rest of the Dracos.

They did not need to keep their bodies alive. Their back up was the clone lab. Now we had two priorities. First, get to our unit members ASAP and revive them. Second, make sure the clone lab was intact and functioning, or none of the dead Dracos would be able to be revived. No matter what was going on, we were short on time and completely clueless as to what caused this power outage. Drak had never seen anything like that before. The power generator took bursts of energy on a regular basis from the planet. With a reasonable back up supply, it never needed to take more than the planet could spare. Most importantly it never ran low or was at risk of being empty.

So what possibly could cause such an outage? The spinal belts were designed with a distress signal so Drak could identify the location of all our unit members. Luckily for us, I was with Drak in the same pod when it happened. Since I was the only one in the unit that was not able to receive the distress signal, without Drak I would have had a hard time finding my people. I decided to correct this oversight for the future, but for now the two of us found and revived our group one by one. Our final destination was the clone lab. Thankfully, it was on a backup generator separate from the main source. I did not know how long that went on already, but chances were the clone lab was low as well. When we made it inside the lab, we saw that all the Draco scientists were dead on the floor.

I could try to fuel the lab with my energy, but I definitely couldn't keep it up for long. We needed to find out what the problem was and fix it. When we arrived at the generator, it was still pumping energy but the energy was being diverted somewhere. We followed the energy path to find the leak and it led us right into the shuttle hangar. The entire station was laid out with veins supplying the station and all its inhabitants with energy. These veins, or nervous system, lead right into its source, the generator. A massive nanite creature was plugged into one of the veins and was feeding from it. The massive nanite certainly looked like our nanites, but our nanites had never done this. Confused, we did not know how to react to it, until I remembered our suits.

The nanites seemed to develop a mind of their own. Could it be possible they were lashing back at the Dracos? Could I have caused this with my modifications to the suits? I was paralyzed with doubt until Drak yanked me out of my self-blame. He was certain it was not the nanites lashing back at the Dracos. He was convinced he would have heard them in his head. Not entirely convinced, I wanted to go with an alternative theory. But what else could it be? What if, and this was a big stretch, but what if the creature from the planet somehow got onto the base and used the nanites in the same way it was using the dirt particle on the planet? That would mean the nanites were enslaved to the creature. Following my thought process, Drak started plotting a defense plan with our unit which had joined us as they became activated. But how did the creature come to the station? I was more concerned with the how than with the why.

Drak and I disagreed on strategy. His plan involved lots of shooting and distraction; I wanted to take a page out of Rogers's book. I had to consider the possibility that the nanites assembled to create the creature were unwilling participants. While Drak did not see them as a life form, I kind of did. Besides, brute force was not my style. Uncomfortable with Drak's plan, I adopted a strategy from Rogers using deception and laying traps. I reasoned that it might be safer to get the creature away from the power reactor before we started shooting. Drak's approach had taken the loss of the generator as acceptable collateral damage; I thought that was not quite necessary. Still in tune with my thoughts and willing to postpone the attack, Drak waited out my theory development. We were angling closer to the creature for a better view when suddenly, a spark leapt from my skin onto Drak's. We froze.

I was under a lot of pressure and scared? Did my nanites react to that? Seeing the sparks, I was afraid that my inadvertent fireworks display had given away our position to the creature. The element of surprise was lost. But the implications were larger than that. In fact, this little spark could possibly be the solution. I remembered how willing the worms were to feed from my energy when we were in the pool. They loved it. What if the creature liked my energy more than the generator? It was different. It was exotic. I needed to try. I might be able to lure it away from the generator before we started firing. Maybe then the generator could be isolated to prevent the creature from latching back on. Maybe we could save the nanites, reclaim the stolen energy and reroute it back into the generator. But how? I started rambling again. Drak tried to follow but got confused. The only part he understood and agreed with was luring the creature away from the generator before the attack and shielding the generator. This would improve the station's chances of survival. It was worth the risk. Our focus shifted to the generator. We split into three teams.

Drak and I were the decoys, Snake Eyes was leading a team of three to create a shield around the generator, and Skinny and the remaining unit members were surrounding the creature, ready for a full on assault just in case. Everyone was on standby until we lured the creature away. It was a relatively simple plan with everything depending on my nanite energy. I was nervous, scared and operating under an assumption that I could produce enough energy to appear more interesting to the creature than the generator. Look at me! Taste my energy sparks! I was about to potentially commit suicide, if I was tasty. Was I completely nuts!?

I went to work, but as nervous and scared as I was, I was unable to expel enough energy to attract the creature. It was seriously pathetic what I was spewing. Not even worth the creature's attention. Drak noticed my dilemma and took charge. He jumped in and started kissing me. This would not have been my first option, after all we had just recovered from our last encounter, but the lab was in trouble and together we could do it. I welcomed his embrace and immediately got lost in his kiss. In fact, I almost forgot that we were involved in a life and death situation for the Draco lab when I felt a massive charge dispersed from me to Drak. Drak fully loaded, went into a deeper kiss as the gel he was covered in diverted the energy back into the generator and right past the creature.

I can only imagine the flavors that were infused into this sparking energy which Drak and I created. This new energy essence was unique enough to attract its attention. I was vaguely aware of the creature as it disengaged from the vein and followed the new energy looking for its source. Lost as I was in the sensations our kiss invoked, I was cognizant enough to read his plan without too much trouble. He had no intention of leaving me, as soon as the creature got close enough, Drak was going to sacrifice himself to ensure my safety and the station's. I could not let it happen. I had a Plan B that I kept hidden from Drak.

The creature inched closer. When the time was right and just before Drak made his move, I sent a massive charge towards Drak. With the strength of a lightning bolt, it tossed him across the room and into safety. Now alone, I was exposed to the creature, and I was okay with it. After all, we did not know what the creature could or would do to me. Theoretically, I was immune to it. The Dracos would not shoot at the creature as long as I was inside it, so I had time to formulate a plan while force feeding my happy memories and I was not in any pain.

Being embraced by the creature was similar to being engulfed in the worm pool. As long as I was feeding it energy, it was content and peaceful. Who knew how it would react when I stopped. I recognized the nanites the creature was utilizing. They were the shuttle nanites. This would explain how they were able to gain access to the station. What if I could get it off the station in the same way? Curious to see if I could move, I started walking slowly. The creature moved with me, and then I knew what I needed to do. The force field to space was right in front of me. I was a pilot and knew how to fly the nanites safely. Since I needed two brains to operate the shuttle, I wondered if the creature's brain would do. Well what did I have to lose? Shooting at the creature and trying to deplete its energy on a station filled with it was not a good plan. Even I knew that. The Dracos did not work "on the fly" the way I did.

Still connected, Drak was objecting to my actions but not providing any alternatives so I continued towards the force field, slow and steady, constantly observing the creature's reaction. I wondered if it would see right through me. The worms did. They could read my mind. They could connect to me. I was hoping the creature was nothing like them. It got a little bit dicey when we approached the force field. There was no keeping it a secret anymore. My anxiety grew. I had trouble keeping my plan to myself, while feeding it with pleasant memories. My energy flow declined and the creature noticed. I kept walking, but the creature stopped moving, allowing me to walk from its embrace. My plan was failing I needed to step up. The creature was now separated from me and the generator. I had to keep the creature interested in me.

Then I remembered how the intensity of my feelings were directly proportional to my energy output. This was the ace-in-the-hole I needed to make the creature come back to me. Boy did this work. Opening my mind to my feelings for Drak and letting it feed the energy flow was just what the creature needed. The force field was easy to get past now, but as soon as we were through, the shuttle needed to take form. I was protected from space by my suit, but only for a short while before I would run out of air. For the nanites to change into a shuttle, the creature and I would have to work together. I signaled Drak to close the force field behind us, protecting the station, but what about me? I didn't know if the creature would die; I most certainly would without the ability to breathe. Lots of assumptions—I put my life on the line again. I thought about how little I had changed and how short my life was. Then I felt myself slipping away.

Depleted of air and crossing into unconsciousness, I stopped producing energy. The creature lost interest in me and realized it was not able to get back into the station. The creature did not connect to me as I hoped but it did the next best thing. It used the nanites' memory to create a breathable bubble for me. We were both exiles outside the station. Or was I a hostage? I knew it was not going to kill me. So what now? It had to understand we could not let it back onto the station. What was its plan? The Dracos were low on energy and needed to reboot the station.

Inside the station, the Dracos could not find the council. We never needed to worry about them or know their location, until now. Stranded outside I could only watch while my mind searched for a solution to find a way to get myself back in or return some of the energy the creature had stolen from the station.

Nothing came to my mind. I wondered if there was any way I could connect to the creature. Maybe I could talk to it. After all, how bad could it be if it had not killed me? Eventually I would need to eat. The energy transfer was draining and I knew I could not stay out here forever. If there were residual nanite memories creating the bubble, what else could I get out of them? Maybe the nanites were my link to the creature and I needed to connect to the nanites, not to the creature directly. The last time I tried to connect to the nanites directly, beyond the programing, was when I redesigned the suit. Still connected to Drak, I could hear them planning aggressive strategies to destroy the creature. I was running out of time. If I just had another brain, I could fly us down to the planets' surface, separate from the creature and return alone.

No Draco could survive so close to this energy draining entity, which was why their solutions were destructive and militant. I was panicking. There had to be a way we could all walk away from this. I wished more than ever that I would wake up from this nightmare. I could feel Drak's fear for my life. He was conflicted about what needed to be done and what he wanted to do. Desperate to help me fly that ship, he stepped into the shuttle conduit we had in the shuttle hangar, the one we used to practice flying. He plugged himself in and activated the nanites shuttle mode. Now the nanites took on a shuttle form and were ready to receive the flight instruction. I did not understand why Drak tried to show the creature what it needed to do. The creature was confused and honestly so was I at the moment. Not knowing more about the plan I assumed that he must have known that the link between the shuttle and the conduit was limited. Unless he was physically on the shuttle, we weren't going anywhere. Not understanding his approach, I went with it. I closed my eyes and using the nanites connection to the conduit, I mind melded with Drak. Confused and angry, the creature changed the shape of the nanites into a random blob. Drak insisted on a shuttle shape using me to increase the dataflow to the nanites surrounding me in space.

It was a battle of wills between Drak connected to me and the creature connected to the nanites. I felt the creature's frustration and shared it. The idea of showing the creature what we wanted was good but felt more like a stick than a carrot. I needed to change that. The carrot was my energy. Each time Drak changed the blob into a shuttle, I released energy to the creature. When the creature changed it back, I stopped my energy flow. It took a few tries before the creature was learned. Hungry for my energy, it left the nanites in the shuttle shape but I could feel its resignation and contempt. Drak was pleased and hopeful that we could actually save me. There was no way Drak could remotely move the creature's nanite shuttle, but maybe I could. I closed my eyes and repeated the procedure Drak and I had practiced so many times before in the conduit. Theoretically, flying a real shuttle should be no different than flying a model.

However, after giving all I had the shuttle was not moving. My chances for success were dwindling. I knew that. I had tried so many times before with Drak and I barely got it to work; now I was alone. I knew I possessed all the info I needed in my head, but Drak was the other half who kept me organized and steady. No matter how much I wished I could use the creature's brain or whatever it had to think, if it even did think, it would not have been enough to compensate for the elements provided by Drak's brain. I was antsy and running out of patience. I found that the more I concentrated on flying, the less energy I supplied to the creature, which made it agitated. I gave up and I was forced to think pleasant thoughts about Drak, while waiting for my death and worrying about my unit, my people and the station. Talk about multitasking.

Suddenly Drak had an idea that I should have come up with. If our pilots took another nanite encased shuttle and flew around the creature, maybe it would learn by example and be compelled to follow. The attempt would use energy the station was already low on, but we had to try. I couldn't imagine the entity planned on being stranded in space, nor did I think it would like it, so it was worth a shot. Drak insisted on piloting the baited shuttle and Snake Eyes volunteered to be co-pilot

After launching from the hangar they positioned themselves in front of the creature. Content with my energy trickle, still in shuttle form, the creature did not react to the arrival of Drak and Snake Eyes. They were cautious, staying a safe distance from the creature, hoping to avoid an attack on their energy source. I sent Drak the image of a pesky fly at a picnic, in hopes he would replicate the movement with his shuttle and get the creature motivated enough to go after them. Drak's first attempts were ignored but as his maneuvers became more aggressive, the creature was all over it, obviously annoyed at the maneuverability of the other ship and frustrated at its own lack of movement. I was hopeful that it was motivated enough to fly and work with me. Between me and the nanites, we had all of the requirements to fly. I closed my eyes and opened communications with the nanites the same way I communicated with Snake Eyes' and Skinny's suits. I was sending the creature nanites images of us flying. I was sending the nanites images of my brain connecting and being in balance with the creatures. I was sending the nanites images of a partnership between the creature and me; all in hopes the creature would retrieve those images and help me find a way to make it work. With each image I made sure some of my sugary sweet energy was transferred to the entity, all in the spirit of the positive reinforcement or carrot approach.

Now all I had to do was to wait. Drak knew my approach so he and Snake Eyes gave us the distance and time we needed to figure it out without being distracted. Hovering adjacent to us, the situation seemed harmless for a moment, until the creature reshaped, extending a tendril of nanites like a lasso around Drak's and Snake Eyes' shuttle. Freaked out, I thought that was it. Flooded with panic, my heart almost stopped, and before I stopped my flow of energy n I noticed I was still receiving Drak's thoughts. The creature did not kill them. In fact it did not even damage the shuttle. It just connected itself to it. Wow. That was intense. Still concerned, I think I understood the new plan. After a short reassurance from Drak and Snake Eyes that all was fine, I sent a massive shot of positive energy to the entity. I could be wrong, but it seemed like the creature had chosen to be towed to the planet. It was the only smart solution to our situation. Of course I didn't know what the creature was planning to do once we were safely on the planet. Either way I was willing to participate, given I currently had no other option.

Following my instructions Drak and Snake Eyes towed the shuttle to the planet's surface. Slow and steady we approached the planet, passing multiple worm pools. We were unwilling to drop the creature off near a pool knowing it would kill the worms, so we flew to a secluded area a safe distance from any worms. All the while, I kept a steady stream of positive energy flowing to the entity hoping it would release us after we arrived at our destination. My nerves were a wreck. The closer we got to our destination, the more agitated I grew. It was too much to hope that it would just let go of Drak's shuttle once we were close, I was worried that once we were safely on the planet, we would become the creature's hostages.

Fortunately, once we touched the ground the creature released the shuttle, formed itself into a blob, and released me. Free of its hold, we were still within its reach and not clear of danger yet. Not having any prior experiences with it, we did not know the extent of its reach. I stood in front of it and waited, continuously sending my positive energy. I was drained and wanted to get away but did not know if the creature would allow us, especially my feeding energy, to leave. I wanted it to understand that I was not feeding it just to get it to cooperate. Even though I kind of did.

We were at a standstill— all parties just looking at each other waiting for someone to make the first move. At this point all indications were that the entity was relatively harmless. I chose to ignore the, not insignificant, detail that it had attacked us on the station and chalked it up to a misunderstanding. I was also skipping over the fact that we were in a full on war with them. But something made me want to reach out to it. As predicted, Drak disagreed as I walked towards the creature with an out stretched hand. My move was unexpected and the creature retracted a little bit before it let me touch it. With my hand connected to the nanites, I sent images to the creature to tell it to keep the nanites and use them to stay in touch with us. I also sent an image similar to a batman signal, encouraging the creature to send an energy spike towards the station if it needed my help. I kind of thought this is what I would have wanted if I were stranded on this planet with no friends.

Going with my gut and my heart, I waited for a response

from the creature. I was shocked when I saw the entity send a massive lightning spike towards the station. My heart sank as I thought the station was blown into pieces, but almost immediately, Drak received a communication that the station had just received a huge energy surge and it resumed basic functions once again. Assuming, this was a peace offering from the creature, I thanked it. Knowing it could have gone the other way, I was relieved. Glancing at Snake Eyes I saw she was looking at me like I was nuts. The last thing she would have done was offer the creature, which had almost destroyed us, a peace offering. So yes, in her eyes I was an idiot. Not expecting any thanks from it, I wanted to give positive reinforcement to the creature. I closed my eyes, touched the creature and smiled while feeding it one more time before I walked back to Drak. Still puzzled by my choices, but acknowledging the results, he waited for me at the shuttle.

I was stepping into the shuttle when he grabbed my arm, turned me around and placed a kiss on my lips. With his hand on the base of my spine, he pulled me tight against his body. He had never felt this way before. His kiss was deep and warm and I felt it in my toes. For the first time I felt a heat coming off of him. He felt something. It was a feeling of attraction, from him. My heart was pounding, jumping out of my throat and a smile escaped my lips. My hands were around his neck and I thought he would never let go of me, when Snake Eyes walked by and yanked him to the side. She made it clear that she wanted the creature dead. NOW. It had killed hundreds of Dracos, endangered others, almost took out the station, set us back by months maybe years, and on top of everything may have lost the council. The kiss she just witnessed was frivolous and had annoyed her enough to blame it for delaying our return. I was just happy that we had escaped with our lives. Snake Eyes was business as usual but Drak had changed.

Trust Challenges

Worried that the creatures could repeat their attack on the station, defeating them became a priority for the council. Of course I continued to wonder whether we could come to an agreement with the creature without having to battle. But the Dracos were determined; the danger was too great and the avatar plan was back on schedule. I was not asking for volunteers anymore. The council insisted on me making it work. Everyone was a candidate for the avatar project. We met with Rogers and laid out the facts as we saw them. He read my raw memories and paid attention to what it had taken to coax the worms to follow. I was worried that the circumstances surrounding worm participation would cause the Hexadoids to reject the partnership. However, to my surprise, confrontations which were brutal by nature were what attracted Hexadoids to the fight. They considered torture and pain a bonus and a badge of courage. I was impressed when I realized that, because of the torture and pain they would be exposed to, the most ruthless and strongest of the Hexadoids leaders would volunteer for the mission. Rogers selected 11 of them to partner up with my unit. Those were his terms for the plan. It was difficult for me to realize that the Hexadoids highly valued the risk of dying, and they were more than eager to face the challenge. Despite the need of partnering with a Draco, they welcomed the threat and inevitable confrontation. Apparently they were growing bored fighting each other and were looking forward to the fight.

I had to come up with a plan to create a partnership between each Hexadoid and their Draco partner. Not just any partnership, but one that they all would trust. Nothing less would get them through. The challenge was not just communication, but the lack of understanding of the Hexadoid culture. I had no idea what would get a Hexadoid to trust a Draco. I had no idea what would make a Draco trust a Hexadoid. I needed to create a brotherhood between the two partners that they could rely and build upon. I put my iPhone on play and sat down along the wall of the shuttle bay. Rogers and Drak observed me with huge skepticism. Amused, Rogers wanted to see what I would come up with next. Drak, on the other hand, lacked the necessary imagination to understand my dilemma. I remembered a movie where a football team made up of two groups from the opposite sides of town had to learn to work together. This was a methodology I could apply here, but each scenario I came up with ended up with either a Draco or a Hexadoid observing the demise of the other one and many times having a helping hand in this demise.

How can you build trust in a few days when there are years of hatred and distrust between the groups? I looked at Drak and Rogers standing beside each other with the guns in their hands. Those two were the perfect representation of the problem but also the solution. They hated each other more than anything and now they trusted each other with their lives. I needed to take a page from their book and find a common reason to fight, for both species. For Drak and Rogers that reason was me, but the others did not have it. I needed to help them find that one thing they all wanted to protect and were willing to overcome their instincts for. They all were clear about the dangers these creatures were posing. I needed to create a very personal gain for each and every one of them. This would only be necessary for the Hexadoids. I asked Rogers to figure out what each and every one of the Hexadoids wanted the most and publically commit to get them this when the monsters are defeated.

The Hexadoids wishes were split between relocation to another suitable planet, staying on the planet with the ability to reproduce, and pure revenge, with the satisfaction of killing their former enemies. Some had been thinking about this for a long time and would not be satisfied with just killing a clone only to face it another day in a new body. No. They wanted to actually kill a Draco and know it would never be resurrected. My unit was outwardly stoic but inwardly shocked when I agreed to terms allowing each Hexadoid to kill their Draco partner after the successful completion of the mission. My unit, conflicted and confused, did not object, understanding that the mission was priority and was to succeed at any cost. They were used to sacrifice. This was a necessary sacrifice for the good of the whole.

Snake Eyes and Skinny were spending more time with me. They were having trouble understanding why I was acting out of character, but took it as a sign that I was finally thinking logically first, like any other Draco. Rogers and Drak could not understand my sense of obligation to the Hexadoids at all. To me it was simple really. I was gambling that after they fought side by side, despite their reservations, win or lose, the camaraderie would be so strong they would forget their hatred and find a way to coexist. If my plan did not work, I would offer myself as the object of their repressed anger and hope they would be content with it. Yes, I sort of lied. I was willing to do whatever it took for them to work together and hoped Rogers and Drak could not see through my deception and if they could, that they would understand and keep my motivation a secret for obvious reasons. I was getting good at keeping secrets. Besides, it would keep everyone alive long enough to accomplish our mission. And it was a good exercise, the Hexadoids would keep the Dracos alive long enough to exact their revenge. The Dracos would do the same. Hopefully everyone would notice what can be accomplished as a team in the pool with a common enemy.

At this point in time, Rogers and his people did not know about the spinal belts. This worked in my favor. I needed to create a situation that appeared life threatening and dangerous but in actuality was fairly safe. In order for this to work they needed to believe they were in peril. Knowing that Rogers's first loyalty was to his people, I scouted and prepared the venue by myself. I took the shuttle with Snake Eyes since I needed a second pilot and without her in my head I was safe from any mind intrusions. We flew over the planet's surface looking for the most hostile area. I remembered where Rogers and I spent time together learning their language and knew the Hexadoids would know this territory by heart. On the flip side this place was unknown to the Dracos. It would be the perfect place for the Dracos to need the Hexadoids help to survive. Or so they thought.

I had already decided to bring additional creatures to this place, but I did not want Snake Eyes to know it. When we returned to the station, I requested an audience with the original commander and his current unit, Drak's replacement crew. It was bizarre standing next to Drak's clone. He had as many scars as Drak by now, his eyes were so familiar yet looked dead, like Drak's did when we first met. This was the first time I saw him under circumstances where I could not help but touch his face. I wanted to know if I could get the same awareness from him as I got from Drak. I wanted to see if my connection to Drak was a chance occurrence or something more. Drak's clone was puzzled by my cursory attention. Accommodating my need, as any good soldier would, he bent down so I had access to his face. My hands followed the new scars in his face. The spidery lines gave Drak's clone character, so different than my Drak. I felt sorrow, knowing that history would just repeat over and over again, with no hope for change unless I do something about it.

The connection was not there. Was I relieved? I needed the certainty that what was between Drak and I was unique and our own. I would have to think about that later because although that electric something Drak and I had was not present, I was aware of an emotional closeness to him and his unit. Looking into the faces of my cloned unit, seeing all my people reflected in them, I could not help but put them into my heart. I instantly wanted to protect them. A notion I learned to ignore. My instinctive impulse to save the Dracos had already proven fatal. I was determined to avoid repeating my mistakes. I squelched my emotions like a good Draco would and moved on with my mission plans. With the help of Drak's cloned unit, we picked up enough dangerous predator specimens to keep my unit busy and relocated them in the Hexadoids territorial maze of mountains, forests, caves and wetlands.

Using gaming techniques, I hid eleven objects throughout the vast territory for the teams to find and bring back home. The challenge was straight forward giving everyone a mission with targets and goals. It was dangerous, but I had to believe that the Dracos telepathic connection would alarm us if needed and that the Hexadoids knowledge of this planet's wild life, as well as this area, would give them what they needed to succeed. Now was the moment of truth. Drak and Rogers assembled the troops and formed into their pre-chosen teams. The targets were randomly assigned. I was continually on guard, Drak and Rogers kept trying to get into my head and retrieve any information pertinent to the exercise, but I knew I could not trust them to keep it to themselves. I kept it all hidden as the two leaders stood by my side, watching their people pair up and begin the mission. This was not the first time they had not led their people but it was the first time they had to lead from behind with an unknown ally. It did not help that neither team knew what to expect. It was nerve-racking and uncomfortable for them and exciting at the same time.

Confident with their knowledge of the area, the Hexadoids

took the lead of their teams and entered the playing field, leaving the Dracos to follow. Used to following orders, the Dracos automatically assumed a covering position and protected the Hexadoids back. Recklessly, the teams had underestimated my ability to manipulate the local wild life, and almost all the Hexadoids ran into the traps, dragging their Draco partners with them. Using Drak's telepathic connection to his unit, we viewed their misadventures on a modified 3 D holographic platform within the ship. It was scary to just stand by, even though I was ready to provide assistance if needed. It was more than just watching their movements, tactics and collaboration, or lack thereof. I was in a position of responsibility. I felt how much Drak and Rogers trusted me with their people lives. It was on me if anything happened to them. I was jumpy. While I was secretly happy to see that almost all of the teams acted as I had expected, I knew there were too many of them, to be saved if they all ran into trouble at once.

Without Drak and Rogers's knowledge, I had instructed the clone unit to wait in standby behind force fields throughout the course. Their presence would eventually reveal my trickery on the exercise, but I needed to keep the moment of surprise to myself as long as possible. Keeping track of the eleven teams as they ran in different directions, we noticed one team was able to avoid my little traps. The wild animal I had released in their sector, attacked as planned relatively early in the game. Skillfully as a unit and without any delays, they trapped the animal and advanced. I was mildly shocked to discover that the team was made up of the most fearsome Hexadoid Commander and Snake Eyes. Feeling the hatred emanating from him, I had thought he would try to kill her, right at the start, disqualifying himself from the trials. The last thing I expected was for him to accept her as an equal and be so in synch with her.

It made sense that they had the most run-ins in the past.

They each were the right hand of the most successful unit leaders on the planet. They probably took practice shots at targets embossed with the other one's face. They completed their mission and were on their way back in no time. I was impressed. However, my respect for Tiny, my nickname for Snake Eyes' Hexadoid partner because of his enormous size, was premature. Fresh from a huge win, I would have thought his respect for his past enemy would have erased some of the animosity he felt. I watched in horror as he hit her in the back of her head knocking her off a cliff. Momentarily frozen, I held my breath as her unconscious body tumbled down the steep decline. I started breathing again when her nanite suit curiously caught onto a small outcropping.

The nanites suites were not designed to act independently like that, but without this little unauthorized act, she would have fallen and been lost to us. From that height, not even her spinal belt could have saved her. We were all relieved to see her unconscious body hanging from the rock face, as her distress beacon activated. The beacons were designed to activate if the Draco body was in distress, not just simply unconscious. The incident happened so quickly that by the time the distress beacon activated, Snake Eyes would have been long dead. So what saved her and what activated the beacon prematurely grabbing our attention towards her distress? I groaned inwardly when after careful deduction, I suspected my modified nanites suit was more modified than I originally planned. I meant for that suit to be fashionable, not develop a mind of its own and especially not its own consciousness. I knew this had consequences that I would have to answer for; but for now I was immensely grateful for that little oomph.

As quickly as possible, we retrieved her from the cliff and got ourselves back to the rendezvous point to wait for the unsuspecting Tiny. Rogers was furious and embarrassed by his commander. He wanted nothing more than to separate Tiny's head from his shoulders. I, on the other hand, had to agree with Drak. We needed Tiny and although this appeared to be a setback, we knew it would not be easy. Clearly it was a stretch to expect lifelong enemies to put their differences aside and work together so quickly. After calculating the risks, Drak was hoping this was an isolated incident. As soon as Tiny arrived and presented us with the trophy, Rogers smacked him down. Tiny tried to convince us that Snake Eyes had an accident and that he had tried to save her, but unfortunately for him we knew otherwise. Instead of giving in to Rogers's desire, we placed him under a restraining force field and shifted our focus to the others. Snake Eyes joined us in the observation lounge after a small recovery. Understandably she did not want to work with Tiny again.

In the wake of the Snake Eyes disaster, watching the other teams deal with the traps I set for them was nerve racking. Drak and Rogers disapproved of the team's challenges and the traps I set. They made it clear to me that the planet was dangerous enough without the traps and that I went overboard with this challenge. We needed every able body alive and well to fight the monsters. Trying to kill them before the battle was not the idea. I, however, was convinced we did not stand a chance on the battlefield unless we could trust each other with our lives. Standing my ground, I kept staring at the display, hoping nothing else would go wrong. While all the time keeping in mind that the nanite suit acted on its own in Snake Eyes case. I was worried about Skinny. I could not expect the nanites, once they developed a mind of their own, to act on Skinny's behalf if needed. It could go the other way. They could act up and surprise him in the worst possible moment, causing him to fail or, worse, get hurt.

I kept looking back at Drak, searching for any sign of disappointment about that. Ironically, right now Drak's face matched Rogers in tension, disapproval and worry. Playing all the different what if scenarios, I did not have to wait long for the next incident. I had to witness Skinny and his Hexadoid partner, who I called Grumpy because of the permanent structure of his facial features, get trapped in a cave. Contrary to Rogers, we did not know enough about this planet to know just how much danger these two were in, until we looked at Rogers's reaction to it. Two of his hands grabbed the nearby standing console as soon as he saw their predicament and squished it so hard, the hard shell gave in underneath. This was not a scenario I had envisioned, nor was it one of my traps. Those two had easily fought and defeated the swarm of deadly bugs I sent their way, using Grumpy's knowledge of the insects. They should have been clear to retrieve the target and return to base, but now they were in a real uncontrolled exercise. I wondered if Grumpy knew the grave danger they were in, or even how to get out of there.

I would have loved to know what we were dealing with and knew without looking that Drak was thinking along the same line. We scanned Rogers' thoughts and were surprised to see that they had a seventy percent chance of not making it and we still could not discern the danger. Whatever the circumstance, the outcome really depended on Skinny and Grumpy communicating together for real this time. This was precisely why the negative outcome percentage was so high. It took me forever to learn the verbal Hexadoids language. How was Skinny supposed to communication non-verbally with a partner who did not read minds? I was suddenly distressed, as familiar features triggered memories of Rogers and me in a similar environment. This was not a cave at all. They were inside a creature. Dormant on the surface of the planet the giant creature was so large and still that it was not easily recognizable as a life form. The two had managed to find their way into its digestive system. One wrong move and they would either disappear completely in its maze of organs or trigger the digestive fluids to be released.

This instinctual release would dissolve them beyond repair long before any reinforcements could even think to rescue them. I turned to Rogers looking for options. I was ready to annihilate the creature using the ships cannons, or any means available to me, including the standby clones, in order to liberate them from danger. I placed myself in front of the control panels. Rogers placed one of his hands onto my shoulders, stopping me momentarily. Confused by his reluctance for action, it took me a moment to understand. Skinny and Grumpy had stumbled into the situation; the creature was innocent and ignorant of any activity. Blasting at it would only infuriate it, sealing their fate. I grabbed the large laser canon strapped onto the wall of the ship, ready to jump in and save them myself, but Rogers once more slowed me down, calmly gripping my hand. His unshakable hold told me all I needed to know. There was no way I could help. Nobody could. They had to recognize the danger and quietly get out of there before natural instincts took over and they were summarily dealt with. Any additional bodies in the creature would only irritate the situation making their presence known, causing the creature to react.

I was scared. I asked Drak to convey the situation to Skinny. Drak had already been in constant contact with Skinny, who knew what needed to be done, just not how. Although familiar with creatures of similar composition, Hexadoids had poor eyesight which made it difficult to navigate the digestive track. Fortunately for Grumpy, he was lost with a Draco who had excellent vision. The question was whether Grumpy could work with Skinny to get them out of there safely. Skinny led the search for the exit. Slowly and steadily, they moved one step at a time. Occasionally, Grumpy would grab Skinny's leg to stop it from stepping on a bad spot. Skinny observed the arteries of the creature, and with his fingers, he signaled to Grumpy as much as he could. Based on that, Grumpy provided the correct direction. Without speaking, they communicated! They relied and trusted each other! My heart pounding in my chest, barely breathing, I keenly observed each and every one of their moves. While happy with the communication success, I was mentally chastising myself. I now wanted to abort the entire challenge. I wanted to pursue alternatives, safer alternatives, to achieve the same outcome and get them to trust each other, but Drak and Rogers refused. Skinny and Grumpy displayed a partnership they never could have hoped for and fast.

Confident that the existing plan was worth the risks, they kept me from cancelling the exercise. Skinny and Grumpy were working their way through the creature. Meanwhile I had nine other teams to worry about who were also struggling with unforeseen challenges and pitfalls almost as bad if not worse than Skinny and Grumpy. It was a bad luck epidemic. Everyone was in danger of losing their lives. It was too much for me. I stared at the 3D display numb, unfocused, not really registering the action. Drak and Rogers, on the other hand, were in their element observing the teams, unaffected by the near misses, concentrating on the interaction and ingenuity of the pairs, invested in it more than ever. Snake Eyes was right beside them, eyes glued to the images, nodding when a new procedure was executed correctly and to their satisfaction. My face was tight, hot and filled with tears. My hands were shaking. I was living my worst fears. This was a nightmare. How could they just stand there, watching, waiting, as if awaiting the outcome of their favorite action movie? Once the horror of the situation eased up, I recognized that I had forgotten the sad fact, that they had been living this horrible reality for a very long time.

I was not meant for this. Who did I think I was? And why were they all listening to me anyway? I now understood that I was not a commander. Nor was I a soldier. What was I really? I could not see it through. I did not have the nerves for this. I revealed to them the location of the clone ship and took a back seat to the farce of a self-made show. While I was beating myself up it dawned on me that I was the only one agonizing over my mistakes. There was continuous danger, pain and struggle, yet almost all of the teams displayed an enormous amount of trust for their partner, teamwork and ingenuity. Given the choice, they all decided to cooperate with their former enemy and chose to complete the challenge and win. My plan was bold and reckless maybe even coldblooded, but it was working in the eyes of Drak, Rogers and Snake Eyes. They let the challenge run its course. Multiple times I was ready to send in the rescue teams and ships to retrieve everyone from their close calls, but Drak and Rogers wouldn't allow it. It was their call now.

Or so I thought. I may have resigned my control to them, but the responsibility stuck with me like a starving tick. It did not matter what I told myself, nor did it matter that Drak and Rogers were impressed with the success of the challenges, I felt responsible for every, nick, bruise, pain and suffering inflicted during the exercise. I was a monster in my eyes. Who does that to the people who trust you and love you? I was deeply confused and conflicted. I remembered I still had to deal with the fall out of changing the programing on Snake Eyes and Skinny's suits making the nanites act independently and possibly self-aware. Later that night, lost in my own thoughts and lying in the pod next to Drak, I found myself not able to sleep. The challenge haunted me. Unaffected by any of this, Drak was fast asleep. I kept looking at his scars and found myself comparing them to his clones. Freaky how they were the same and yet so different. I pulled myself up, closer to his face.

My fingers gently outlined his scars while my mind

remembered his clone's scars. Pain, sorrow and despair were written permanently on his face with each and every one of them. My emotions were all over the place, alternately hot and cold, high and low and drifting further from any peace I intended to garner. I loved him so much it scared me. If anything ever happened to him I would be lost. My mind was roiling with the events in the past few days. I was beginning to envy the emotionless Dracos and started wondering if introducing emotions was the smart thing to do. After all, look what it was doing to me. Everyone was better off without them. They were in peace. Knowing how important it was for me to sleep, Drak decided to end my dilemma and opened his eyes. Positioned as I was, inspecting his scars, our eyes were at the same level and locked on to each other. He lifted his head closing the space between us while bringing up his hand up to cradle my head in a possessive manner and kissed me. He knew well enough that this would yank me out of my self-pity.

Connected to my thoughts he decided to roll with my emotional roller coaster and join me as his kiss warmed my insides and I started to melt against him. I almost forgot why I could not sleep when his strong arms pulled me on top of him, still locked in our kiss. I stretched against his body feeling safe, content and warm as his hand traveled the length of my body in lazy circles. I had a second to realize where this was leading and once committed, we would be hard pressed to stop. I was enjoying every sigh, breath and caress but it wasn't about me. I was determined to grow up. From now on my Draco family would come first, before anything or anyone else, including myself. I placed a final, lasting kiss on his soft lips, snuggled my head onto his shoulder and closed my eyes. I pushed all my self-doubt into the part of my brain I kept hidden from Drak and went to sleep. This way, Drak thought he accomplished his attempt to distract me and I did not burden him with it any further.

The Avatar Chairs

Trust challenge out of the way, we still had to modify our avatar conduits for the Hexadoids brains. We needed to download their brain pattern into the hub, which was not easy. If we could convince the Hexadoids of the necessity and they agreed, we would have made great strides in trust because, this was like giving the Dracos their souls. While everyone had gained some level of trust for their respective counterparts, they did not buy into the peace treaty completely. The Hexadoids were a convenient ally but the alliance could go sour at any time. What assurances did the Hexadoids have once their services were no longer useful to the Dracos? This was all very new to everyone involved and the rules of engagement were not yet comfortable.

Eliminating their enemy when they least expected it was exactly the type of move the Hexadoids would make. How could I convey to the Hexadoids that the Dracos would not download any of the Hexadoids secrets, when we all knew that by downloading their brain patterns into the hub, the Hexadoids were handing over everything the Dracos needed to have the upper hand? Rogers knew this. It was, not easy for him to intentionally hand over the will of his people, to anyone. This was an individual choice which Rogers looked at dispassionately, knowing it was the right thing to do but also knowing that he had no right to expose and potentially weaken his race. His people's fate would be in our hands. I had to help Rogers come to terms with his decision. A compromise that leveled the playing field. Something we all could live with. I retreated back into my dark corner at the other end of the station. It was quiet there. I needed to remove myself from any distractions.

A giant force field was the only thing between me and space. It helped me to think. I needed to free my thoughts, silently hoping a solution would float to the surface. My mind began to wander and I found myself thinking of home. Back on Earth, wanting to keep my adventures and black book from my father, I saved everything on a flash drive. A flash drive would limit the Hexadoid vulnerability to its Draco partner. The plus side was that the Hexadoid could keep the Draco close to safeguard its essence. The downside, The Hexadoids would surely destroy all connections to their entity once victory was assured. It was so clear; downloading the Hexadoid brain patterns into their respective partner's spinal belts would serve as the flash drive. I had promised the Hexadoids that they could kill their partners at the conclusion of the alliance. Their counterpart deaths would destroy the only copy of their brain pattern. Their secrets would remain safe. Secretly I was hoping, the Hexadoids would learn to forgive the Draco they were partnered with, and they would trust their Draco partner to keep their secrets.

It was a stretch, but worth suggesting to Rogers. No longer able to shoulder the responsibility of lives that were not my own I was determined to involve Drak and Rogers in all future decisions. The Dracos did not like to mix their back up brain pattern stored on the same device with the Hexadoids. Those were designed as a backup in case they died. What if the information on the spinal belt became corrupted and mixed up with the Hexadoid? Reluctant to participate but understanding the reasoning, my unit complied, leaving me feeling guilty. This was not what any of my unit wanted, but they were good soldiers and willing to compromise for the sole purpose of succeeding. To avoid the over whelming guilt and sorrow I kept my distance, stayed focused on the mission preparations and surprised everyone around me. I played a Draco better than expected. Not surprisingly, it made Drak suspicious.

Drak knew I was keeping something from him and he gave me lots of time to share whatever it was, but this was more than he could handle. As we passed in the corridor he grabbed my hand and turned me in a pirouette leaving me pinned neatly against his chest looking up. He kept looking deep into my eyes as if he tried to see through them into my mind. He did not invade my privacy as he had previously. He was giving me the chance to tell him what my thoughts were but I knew that every time I articulated my feelings and Drak appeared to empathize, I was transferring that part of myself that the Dracos had managed to eliminate. Empathy and emotions had no place in him. Getting hurt, almost dying, pain, suffering, even my venture through space and time, all of it was nothing compared to the real problem I now faced. After spending some time all to myself not distracted by the daily plans and exercises, I came to a terrible conclusion. I was a virus, infecting them, the very people I loved and tried to protect.

It was simple. They did not have the antidote or the skills to deal with the corruption of their quiet order. My emotions and social etiquette were changing them into something they were not. Drak pulling me to him and, in his own way, demanding answers, was just one of many examples of this. I recognized it as impatience, curiosity, and frustration. He clearly did not know how to handle it. Without hesitation I stared back into his face, searching for signs that told me Drak was ready for full exposure to the turmoil within me and what I felt for him. Though his face would never be able to display complex emotions, I still hoped for something. I wanted to show him my anxiety and what I saw as the inevitable outcome. With full disclosure he should be able to utilize that logical brain of his and know that everyone would be much better off if they let me keep to myself. I wanted him. But I wanted him to stop pushing for me to open up all the time.

Leaning against Drak with his arm wrapped around me, I

suddenly realized I was very tired. Mentally tired. Maybe if he understood how dangerous the real me was for them, he would let me keep to myself. I had to be careful. Looking into his face, I started opening up little by little, watching his eyes to see how it affected him. I did not want to hurt him and I was not sure if, in all this time alone, I brewed some feelings he was not ready to receive. Looking into his wonderful eyes, I was uncertain what my future in this place would be. I was scared. Mostly I was scared that I was doomed to be alone. I had imprinted on Drak so if I damaged him with my mental anguish and hurt or lost him, I could never forgive myself. Drak took my hands into his. I could not see any change in his face. He remained calm as he absorbed the information pouring from me, including all my split convictions. Could it be that he had grown immune to my mood swings? I had the sudden realization that it was not up to me anymore. I was drained, Drak had read it all and for some unexplained reason he still wanted me. He wanted to be part of me, feel me inside his head. He did not like secrets. My secrets drove him crazy, and not in a good way. He could deal with my mood swings.

Now that I had opened up to Drak, I had a problem in the form of Rogers. Ever since I learned to shield my thoughts from everyone, Rogers felt resentful towards me. Almost as if I had betrayed him. He did not mind if I kept myself distant and hidden from Drak, but he saw our relationship differently. Deeper and clean, like a best friend. He never trusted anybody before he met me and that meant something to him. Shielding myself from him signaled that I felt differently. He took it personally and initially searched for ways to fix it, but had to give up when he realized no matter what he did, I was not going to open up. This drove a wedge between us I imagined that Rogers would be hurt when he learned that I had opened up to Drak before him, that he was not on the inside. Once I decided to open up to all of them, I would have to show that I had changed and the circumstances that changed me. The person who killed a Hexadoid and tortured her own unit without a second thought. This was an ugly side of me that I was ashamed of and did not want to share. Unfortunately, when you have a secret, it is like a cancer, spreading its ugliness deeper and deeper inside you until it destroys you from within. I had been struggling with this for far too long Knowing that it was growing beyond what I could bear, I decided to open up to both of them. Slowly, a little bit more each day. If I couldn't trust them, who could I trust? Leading by example, I was going to expose what I was hiding, cross my fingers and answer the question that had been running through my mind in a constant loop: how could I expect anybody to build trust around here, if I didn't show them how?

Convincing the Hexadoids commanders to surrender their minds to their Draco counterparts was not easy. Getting the Dracos to mix their Hexadoids partners' minds with their own back up was not easy. The real challenge would come after the two shared their brains in the avatar chair. Both parties would be vulnerable, exposed to things they might not understand. We were asking a lot. It was difficult for me to observe myself being driven by Drak and unable to do or influence anything. I could only imagine what the Hexadoid were going through. Emotions were needed to get the worms to connect and act as one. They were also the Achilles heel for the Dracos and motivation for the Hexadoids. This was a perfect recipe for disaster. I had been worried about this for some time but did not have the means to articulate my fears. The need to share this fear with Drak and Rogers was strong. Perfect timing. Hadn't I just resolved to involve them in all decisions?

Snake Eyes was partnered with Rogers for now but would get another Hexadoid partner later. Neither one wanted to be a bystander and welcomed the challenge. Drak was confident that he could help Snake Eyes if she became lost in Rogers avatar.

He knew her well enough to help her out as well as the fact that Rogers was different. We feared exposure from the other Hexadoids, who by the way did not know about his hybrid status yet. I shared many things with Rogers including my experience as a ghost of myself which he conveyed to the others. I shared in a way I was unable to do with the Dracos. I empathized with their worries and fears and understood their hesitation. I knew what was at stake if we failed. I knew what motivated them. I sold a challenge, with retribution as the prize, knowing that I hoped to convert their beliefs, hating myself while I did it. I was about to inflict my assumptions upon everyone again. My upbringing and gut tells me a true commander is someone who stands by his people, especially when all goes wrong, is ready willing and able to make the hard decision, even if success is minimal. In all reality, I was not able to do that fully the last time, because my feelings got in the way. I knew I was risking their lives. I knew what I was asking them to do. I would swallow my gut feelings and do what it took. I saw my father in my actions and determination and knew that I was first and foremost my father's daughter and I could not escape that upbringing. I was suddenly and unexpectedly appreciative of what he had dealt with, babies, death, soldiers, and how insignificant my life was, when compared to all of this.

The bonding experience between Rogers and Snake Eyes, outside of the pool, was bumpy at first but ended successfully. It was time for the others. Hopefully they fared as well. Snake Eyes removed the avatar chip from her head and looked at me. She had just successfully driven Rogers and spent some quality time in his head. Her gaze was intent making me wonder what she had seen in his head to make her look at me so creepily. Her attention was so intense that everyone was starting to stare, at me. My Draco unit walked up to her in a futile attempt to connect and find out what her plan was, but nothing. She just stood there, staring, twisting her head from side to side slightly. I was starting to worry that this was brain damage, but the medics would have noticed and attended to her at once. What was she so confused about? Unresponsive to the unit's attempts to connect to her, she finally approached Drak and forced him to mind meld by direct Draco touch. It was a special connection Dracos had between each other. After a few minutes I noticed that Drak placed a hand on her head.

Drak had done this to me few times. I understood now that it was not a gesture of comfort but an attempt to reboot me. Luckily for me, my brain did not respond. He connected to her mind and pulled her out of an endless loop, which allowed him to analyze what triggered her to loop in the first place. It was me! She saw me through Rogers' eyes. She experienced his blind trust for me. Emotions are tricky enough to deal with even when you understand the basics, but the Dracos didn't even have a benchmark in which to start. I was encouraged to see that Drak was not overcome with the emotional turmoil inflicted upon Snake Eyes but it was becoming clear that we had to develop a strategy to help the Dracos compensate for their lack of emotional understanding.

Until then, Drak was the only one with the necessary skills to quell the emotional loop created in the avatar chair. I feared that Drak would be exposed to multiple mental states. I had mixed feelings about this. Drak might find that my neuroses, mild, compared to the others, but exposure to so many other beings' mental disturbances might make him go absolutely mad. Even I might not be able to reach Drak this raw manifestation. It was going to be a long day. I took the time to examine the Hexadoids while Drak was working with Snake Eyes and thought I recognized a smug look of pleasure on their faces. Seeing the Dracos struggling with their cultural personalities was more fun than they had expected. The Hexadoids were now interested in the avatar for the discomfort it would cause the Dracos.

Pair after pair, test after test we decided to share the avatar experiences as they were completed, hoping to spare the remaining members of my unit the shock of cerebral consciousness from another species. Together Drak and I used the avatar chip to troubleshoot, soothe and reboot the Dracos troubled minds. I found myself challenged to create clever methods to help Drak conceptualize the concepts of the emotional conditions as he encountered them. We knew we could not shield them from the effects but we could introduce them to 'AHA' moments. Aha, so that is what happiness is. Aha, so that is what fear looks like. Aha, so this in annoying. That one made Snake Eyes smile. I guess I struck a nerve or two there. Walking my unit through emotions 101, I felt a kinship as I watched them struggle to accept what they were feeling, and it made me feel closer to my unit than ever before. I could see them understanding me better with each of those emotions. Short of taking notes, they were able to recognize and compare each emotional example to something I had done. I did not mind. Whatever helped them understand was fine with me. It also helped me accept my mistakes and I was finally able to laugh at myself as I watched everyone take turns mimicking my more memorable antics.

After a while, I noticed they were more empathetic and seemed to appreciate what I had to go through every day, dealing with confusing subjective input that lacked order. It was like flooding your mind with junk while trying to retain clarity. Having won their respect for managing white noise, I relaxed. To defeat these creatures they had to recognize the "junk" for what it was and leave it out of the decision-making matrix. That was the goal. And it appeared to be working. Each new experience meant a new connection between a Draco and a Hexadoid. The Hexadoids had to watch themselves while their Draco partner took control over their bodies. At the same time, the Draco driving them struggled with the good and bad memories of their Hexadoid partners. After the incident on the cliff, Snake Eyes struggled to understand me. I noticed because she made it a point to spend more time with me than usual. Historically she avoided me, especially after I created the modified nanite suit for her and Skinny. She went out of her way to let me know how annoyed she was with the spontaneous changes the suit was making for itself.

I often wondered if the goal was to get me to return her suit to its original default settings, but now, after the cliff, she stopped rolling her eyes at me when the suit looked different. If I didn't know better, I would say she liked the changes it was making. It was unclear if the change was due to empathy with Rogers during their link or a new understanding that the suit changes had saved her life. Either way, things had changed and she seemed happy about it. One could accuse her of being grateful, but only if one wanted to die. I began to suspect that it meant like Drak, she was starting to have deeper feelings. She was accepting her humanity and learning to live with it. I worried what effect the avatar training would have on the others and whether it would prompt them to further emotional exploration. I was imposing upon everyone foreign cultural stimulation without context or forewarning. I was influencing them and changing their customs. How ironic, that it all started because instead of recycling me, they tried to integrate me into their society. I was hoping it all would go back to normal or level out, once we defeated the creatures.

It was time to test the avatars in a pool. The Hexadoids were about to enter into one of the pools we chose for testing. If they could get the worms to mount together with stimulation, then the exercise would be considered a success. This was the most exciting test for me. The entire plan to defeat the creatures depended on its success. If this failed, I would be the only one with the ability to unite the worms into beating the creatures and that would be not enough.

Rogers injected Skinny's partner with the venom as he would during one-on-one hex combat and we watched his body pass out and submerge into the pool. Skinny was standing a safe distance away on the edge of the pool, linked to his partner. I was nervous about the success of the exercise and anxious about the wellbeing of my unit. Waves formed but not with the intensity required to unite the worms. I communicated all I knew, which was not much, regarding worm stimulation, but getting an explanation of an emotion is not the same as actually experiencing one. This was my moment of truth. As a resident expert in all emotions, was I good teacher? I almost gave up hope, when Drak's hand squeezed mine. He did not say anything, well he never did, but his squeeze conveyed the message, have patience, wait. Breathing deeply, conscious of the closeness and thankful for the moment, I relaxed a little. It seemed to take a very long time but eventually there was a slight variation in the vibration, almost too slight to notice. But slowly it got stronger. It was happening.

All Hexadoids United

I watched as the Hexadoid-Draco teams created one worm creature after another. It was impressive what they were able to accomplish. I applauded our success. I was jumping up and down inside but I could not help but wonder if it would be enough. Finally, something was going right for us. Sure we didn't know how many of those monsters were out there or what varieties they came in, but we had worm creatures on our side now. I wondered if it would be enough. We couldn't kill them, which made it way more challenging. We were being held hostage by our own limitations in this case. It would have been nice to overpower them with overwhelming firepower. Watching the Hexadoids working together, it could have been wishful thinking on my part but they seemed to be enjoying their undertaking with the Dracos. This partnership only involved a fraction of the Hexadoids planet population. Rogers' clan was only one of many. If we wanted to engage all monsters on the entire planet at once, we had to engage all beings on this planet. With full understanding, Rogers turned immediately towards me and shot objections at me in rapid Hexadoid. The Hexadoid clans were on their own for a good reason. They did not interact with each other in fights or in tough times. Cross clan integration was not only discouraged but it was the unspoken law every Hexadoid knew and followed. He was not about to disregard it. Not even for me.

I needed to think, I needed another perspective. After spending some time alone, wracking my brains, trying to think like a Hexadoid, looking for motivation, commonality, something to unite everyone, I had an idea. The only way disparate Hexadoid tribes would cooperate was if they believed in a greater cause. To negotiate with the other tribes I would have to respect their boundaries and venture into their territories alone. Just me as Rogers's presence would agitate the tribes and ruin any chance of an alliance. To keep my promise to myself, I would have to get the commanders to meet and agree first. All by myself. Draco involvement would be a sign of aggression as well. So I couldn't take the Dracos, not even Drak. I did not need him to get in the way of my bullets. I wondered what it would take to impress upon the Hexadoid tribes the benefits of the proposed alliance. Brainstorming with Drak and Rogers did not help. Their idea of impressive always involved massive firepower—nothing like overpowering your opponent into submission. I would need a different approach.

After hours in my thinking place, I finally found a possible answer. I needed help and I knew just where to get it, Snake Eyes and Skinny. Drak and Rogers would try to stop me if they read my mind and discovered my plans. With help from the dimensional observation station, Skinny helped me find the nanite creature that had invaded the station. Next we borrowed one of the transports and Snake Eyes and Skinny dropped me as close as they dared to the creature. We parted company and I left them with instructions to monitor us and only get me if the creature sent an energy beam towards the station.

I planned to get the creature to work with me. Not giving myself the option to fail, I cleared my mind and moved purposefully to the creature resting next to a pool of worms. With the ecosystem in the pool still intact, I assumed the creature did not need to feed yet. I thought of it more like a dog acting on pure instinct and I did not believe it had the capacity to restrain itself from killing the worms. I had this somewhat crazy notion that I could communicate with the creature on some basic level and entice it to work with us. Problem was, what if I was wrong? Truth be told, my entire plan hinged upon the creature cooperating

241

with me. I needed an ally when I engaged/negotiated with the splintered Hexadoid clans, and I did not want to face this pure energy creature in battle. Alone I knew I could communicate with the creature by sending images through the nanites, and that the creature had the ability to download them. I got close, proceeding with caution. After all, I could have been wrong. I could be in mortal danger right now. Yet, I had to risk it. The calculated risk was minimal based on prior exposure to the creature. I was semi-confident my plan would work. Standing at a safe distance, I started emitting images intertwined with my signature energy.

Starting with my happy childhood images on Earth, followed by my thoughts of lots of energy on this planet recycled and increased by the worms. Then I sent images of dead worms, depleted clouds, and a wasteland covered by blobs starving for energy. I wanted to show this creature their future if they didn't stop. Judging by our previous encounter, I was convinced this creature was very smart, and I knew I was giving it something to think about. The question was whether it cared for the future of this planet and if it saw this planet as its home. Was it going to work against its own kind or be as loyal to its own kind as any of us would? Honestly I did not have an alternative solution for its predicament. It needed the same energy as the worms. I was essentially asking it to starve. Still, I had to try. I wanted to show the creature that on its current path it would end up starving anyway unless it had a way off this planet.

I tried to communicate that without the worms; there would be no renewable energy for them to feed on. I was freaking out waiting for its response. I figured if I was to impress the other Hexadoid leaders, I had to show superior leadership abilities. I could not imagine anything more impressive than having one of the creatures at my side. This was my only chance to make it work. If I was lucky. While waiting for its response, I fed it with my energy. Bored out of my mind and antsy as I was, I kept thinking about my home and about my family and our happy times together. With my energy, the Earth images of Earth seemed to arouse the creature's interest. It wanted to see more images of Earth. Saturated with wishful thinking, soaking in hopes and dreams, I kept imagining how wonderful it would be to get back home. For a brief moment, the two of us traveled back in my memories. I loved it. I shared a piece of myself with this creature I never thought possible, creating a unique connection worth building on.

Without even realizing that it had happened, the creature agreed to join me in my quest to unite the planet. Unlike us, they did not feel loyalty to their own species. Things progressed nicely after that. Thrilled, I asked it to travel with me to the next Hexadoid camp. Anticipating my actions and accommodating my needs, the creature shape shifted its nanites into a platform or raft of sorts, similar to the one I had played with on the other mission. It engulfed me into itself in the form of a shuttle to keep me safe from the environment, but it was not a shuttle, which would have required two minds working together. It was more like a hovering vehicle that could be used to glide over the planet's surface and sometimes go up if I fed it lots of energy. My night vision provided us with enough visual acuity to maneuver safely in the darkness and shadows, and the nanites sent me images back when I was inside. The planet was vast and we had a lot of ground to cover in a short amount of time. I continued to feed it with memories of my childhood to keep us occupied and energy to keep the creature complacent. We had fun. Or at least I did.

The planet had many large, barren patches, seemingly without any life forms, as well as areas rich with plant and animal life. I referred to the deserted patches as the dead lands because nothing lived there. The creature carried me across the dead lands, but in populated areas, I ran alongside the creature, while it was shape shifted to match the surrounding to avoid detection by prying eyes. It was amazing what my new enhanced body could do. With every passing day, we became more and more in tune with each other. The creature adapted quickly. We were a team alternating between raft and itself at will. To navigate the raft safely, all the skills I needed were in my head. The creature only had to take the images I provided and follow them blindly. We became one, which was something I could not do with Drak. I was enjoying the bond and the shared experience so much and wanted so badly to include Drak that I almost forgot why we were traveling together, until we spotted two scouts just outside our first Hex camp. I communicated to my companion that I was to be dumped mid-air and that it should keep out of sight. The fall was hard but necessary. I could not risk the creature being discovered. It was a partnership made in heaven. I was operating on the assumption that the Hexadoids would be afraid if they saw the creature. I asked it to blend into the foliage giving the appearance that I was alone when we approached their camp. I was hoping it would follow without too much explanation. I approached the Hexadoid camp seemingly, on foot, unarmed, and unprotected, I must have looked funny and ridiculous when I made my entrance into their camp, because they did not even bother to draw their weapons.

The Hexadoids parted like the red sea as I made my way into camp. Without knowing who their commander was, I became engulfed by the mass of Hexadoid bodies. My plan was to keep walking until one of the Hexadoids stopped me. Based on my knowledge of Rogers's clan, the alpha Hexadoid would be the one to make the first move toward any new comer. Almost at the center of the camp I came upon an enormous older Hexadoid with long deep scars across his entire face. He was a scary looking dude. Even with the knowledge of my own formidable backup, I was intimidated. He exuded strength and intelligence. If I didn't have the creature hopefully watching my six, I would have felt compelled to run for the hills. I tried my best to appear calm and unafraid, although adrenaline was filling my veins and my heart was pumping overtime as I approached the leader. He was downright surprised when I started conversing with him in his language. I was grateful for Rogers's teachings in this minute. Surprised about my boldness and that I spoke his native tongue, he granted me the courtesy of listening. I realized I was more of a novelty than a serious ally to the skeptical Hexadoids but I believed I was ready for all possible scenarios. I had to convey to him why it was not just beneficial but imperative for his clan to join Rogers and the Dracos against the creatures. As I anticipated, aside from the amusement I provided, there was no incentive for him. Skeptical about a joint venture between Dracos and Hexadoids, he had little faith in either the promise of a possible relocation to a suitable planet, or our abilities to succeed in such an undertaking.

This was the moment I waited for. As soon as he was done explaining why he wouldn't help, I signaled the nanite creature. In a beautiful display of slow and steady change, the nanite creature appeared behind me. First, the commander thought we were being attacked and asked the entire camp to draw their weapons, just as I planned. Rather than attacking, the creature shape shifted into a platform for me to step on. I knew this would display my elevation above the commander standing with the remaining Hexadoids and show my superiority over him. After all, as close as he allowed the creature and I to come, into the heart of his camp, he compromised the security of his people already, and therefore showed his lack of competency. Displaying the creature's obedience to me got me his attention. If I could order around Dracos, Hexadoids, and the pesky creatures, he saw me as a worthy adversary and was willing to listen.

He had no choice but to admit that I won our little display of power and, therefore, I was maybe capable of winning a war. After a moment of deadly silence, he looked around into the faces of his people, who were shocked and humbled at the same time, and then looked up into my face. Without consenting to defeat, he demanded an audience with my unit and the other Hexadoid clans before making any commitments on behalf of his tribe. I won! It took everything I had to keep myself from jumping up and down. I contained my enthusiasm long enough to soberly thank the Hexadoid leader for his gracious offer and suggestion, assuring him that the meeting would take place in a neutral location.

I was hoping that by not forcing him to commit right then, especially after I had embarrassed him in front of his people, he would not feel too resentful. Hopefully, then he would be open for a partnership. Once clear of the clan my partner and I raced to the next encampment. I was running, trying to rid myself of the pent up energy and excitement I felt from my victory and just anxious enough about the next encounter. The creature glided behind feeding off my excess energy as I relived the confrontation and thought of ways to improve the next meeting. We had to repeat this performance as many times as there were tribes on this planet. Running on foot from camp to camp was much easier with my new Draco body. I could run the entire day with minimal rest. I ate what Rogers fed me while I was learning the Hexadoid language. We moved quickly during the night. I had to conceal the creature from patrolling eyes during the day, but felt safe utilizing the creature's services during the night. The suit and the creature were taking care of me, keeping me warm, cool and protected when required and in return I supplied them with energy and dream entertainment. It was so quiet with them. No other thoughts were cruising through my head. I was alone.

Other tribes were not so "open-minded" at my arrival. A lot

of them sounded an alarm and assumed defensive positions as soon as they became aware of my existence. Short of firing at me, they did all they could to defend themselves against me. In some cases I had to succumb to beatings, not too different from those I received from Rogers, before I was allowed to face their leader. Others escorted me at gunpoint into the center of their camp. As varied as the reactions to my entrance were, they all had one thing in common: it got me in front of their leader. And as long as I took the beatings and did not react to the guns, I was safe until their leader decided otherwise. Each and every time, once in contact with the leader, I had to demonstrate my superiority. On cue my creature friend would make an appearance resulting in a commitment to meet in one cycle at the Earth portal.

As I arrived back at the station, my successful little adventure was shared with the others. They saw it as bold, strategically far beyond my young years, and they oddly admired my ingenuity. They were maybe unable to cheer my homecoming, but turning eyes in a place where I previously seemed invisible to everybody but my unit was an amazing feeling. As successful as I was, I realized that this was a small victory. Now I had their attention to meet, but I still needed to get them to join us. I needed their respect. We needed to combine Rogers' unit with Drak's unit under my leadership to show them that we could work together and succeed. When I got back to the station, I told Drak about my exploits and what I learned. He agreed that Rogers should meet with us and discuss our options. It would not just be the first time anybody attempted to get the two species into one unit, but it also would come with other challenges. The first one being the communication hurdle and the second challenge the fact that each one of the commanders had their own unit they needed to command. Why would they be subordinate to a human? What possibly did I have to offer to get them to surrender to me? Each unit already had a substitute commander leading them during the battle. I needed to crack the communication hurdle. What if the Hexadoids got a modified version of my neuro-converter? That way they could communicate with the Dracos the same way I did. The issue would be the use of nanites. I had them inside my system. They did not and would never have.

Driven by my new project, I pulled all the Dracos and Hexadoids into the station lab. I presented my issue and made it a competition project. The same pairs in the trust challenge were to come up with an idea. This way they would work together once more and try new things. The Hexadoids needed the competition factor to be motivated, but I knew that the Dracos exchanged information between each other anyway to support progress. This way we would not be reinventing the wheel. It was super fun to watch them working like that. Coming up with all sorts of crazy ideas and seeing their process and progress was awesome. After a few days into the challenge, we had a solution. Not being allowed to nanite the Hexadoids, we had to use an external viewing source combined with a neuro-modified reader. Or something like that. I would have suggested to introduce some colors and patterns to those cool shades as I called them, but Rogers caught me mid-suggestion with a firm hand squeeze and a disapproving look. That thought was not missed by Snake Eyes, who didn't see why the Hex should be spared from my style modifications and thought that we should give it a solid try. Anyway, it looked like skin over the Hexadoids' eyes, giving them protection in battle and viewing the Dracos communication at the same time. To send information the Hexadoids had to think about their message and the Dracos had the same kind of eye viewer to receive it. I liked the additional protection feature and loved the fact that the Dracos could now communicate with their partners. But would this be enough to get them to work together?

Now I could inform all of them of what I was up to. I

explained my worry about not having enough firepower, which everybody agreed with, naturally. I mean they're soldiers, they never have enough firepower. When I told them my intent to unify all the Hexadoid tribes, the reaction was complete silence from the Dracos and Hexadoids. Everyone must have thought the communication device was broken and were waiting patiently for me to clarify. Although Rogers knew of the plan, he looked disappointed in me. He had expressed his objections earlier but the arguments were self-centered and towards me not the plan, almost as if I had determined he was not enough for me. He was taking this very personal again. Additionally, none of the Hexadoids thought I could get them to even listen. I was met with immediate ridicule and judgment, until I surprised them as I did to the other commanders. I loved to observe the shock on all of their faces, including my mute friends the Dracos, as the nanite creature underneath me transformed into a circular pedestal and elevated me above all of their heads. I did not need to express myself beyond that point. Their silence was my success. While they were listening I informed all of them about the existing commitment from all other Hexadoid leaders across the planet to meet in only a couple of weeks. All we needed was to find a way to impress them and convince them to trust our ability in this undertaking. I looked at Drak and he was genuinely surprised and perplexed. His subtle facial expressions were not so subtle anymore. Rogers on the other hand changed his anger into recognition. I think for the first time in a very long time I impressed him. Maybe the first time ever. This was a great feeling.

This was only the beginning. It was time to meet the clan commanders at the Earth portal, I hoped we were ready. We were not the first to arrive. The Hexadoid commander from the wetlands was already waiting for us. Distrustful and not wanting to be surprised by my creature again, he had his people all strategically located and armed, at the ready, waiting for a signal to attack. Taking a page from my father, I had anticipated a similar move like that from at least one of the Hex commanders. I was prepared to act dumb which would give them the impression that they were in control but allow me the opportunity to gain their trust. With the help of the clone Dracos as security, I made my first move. I had the Draco-Hexadoid partners lined up to display respect, with pomp and circumstance with as much formality as we could manage, to all arriving Hexadoid commanders and their people. The amassed numbers of Hexadoid clans covered the same area as a giant worm ocean. Due to the disconnection between the clans, nobody ever realized how many Hexadoids were on this planet. In daunting numbers, they divided the field into sectors. Each respective commander stood in front of that claimed sector.

It was up to the commanders of the Hexadoids to vet my ability to lead. They were not willing to risk their and their people's lives to an unworthy leader. They walked up to me and continued to Drak, Roger and their people. The display of a Draco and Hexadoid leader guarded by a nanite creature was extremely impressive, but the Hexadoid commanders wanted to taste blood. Walking around us like a swarm of bees, they accused the Dracos of coming up with this scheme to kill all Hexadoids and they used the nanite creature as their example of me twisting all the facts. Their argument was that since I could tame one why couldn't we tame all of the creatures the same way. They called Rogers and his people traitors, and started pushing them around, provoking any response, which would start a fight right there and gave them a reason to leave.

The biggest and most vicious leader of the wetlands tribe drew his gun and pointed at Rogers head. Anticipating protective response, his group drew their guns and pointed at Rogers' people. I looked at his body posture and facial expression. I knew enough about the Hexadoids by now to know he was not bluffing. He was trying to undo my efforts to unite the tribes. In his rage about being put in this situation, he decided to kill Rogers and everyone who stood by him. Knowing that nobody would challenge him in order to avoid a blood bath, he held all the cards. It was a matter of seconds before it would be too late and without undoing my efforts I was at a loss what to do. Luckily for me, the work I had done with my two units was more successful than I thought. I placed myself in front of the gun to shield Rogers, and immediately all my Dracos did the same thing with their respective partners. With this quick response, we displayed our willingness to risk our lives for the Hexadoids and with one strike won the respect of the Hexadoids. Even the biggest skeptic had to hold their breath at our little unplanned demonstration. It was scary but beautiful. Going forward we had no resistance, even from the wetlands commander.

After laying down the rules of engagement and momentary peace, we headed back to the station. I was exhausted and headed right for the pod. I was imagining the battle. Thinking about the amount of troops that had to be coordinated and strategically placed, I realize I was way over my head. I needed help. Thinking about how my father would do it did not help. They had all this technology at their disposal and a well-tuned and coordinated war machine. I had the same equipment, but I was a novice leader.

Drak advised me that I didn't have to lead everyone. If I melded with Drak and Rogers during the battle, the three of us could coordinate everything. The idea of a mind-meld scared me since the last time I'd done it, it got Drak all confused and in my business. Melding with both of them was a disaster about to happen. It was a possibility but not my top choices. Instead I could link myself more intensely with Drak and Rogers. This would establish not just a telepathic link but sort of two-way highway. Our thoughts would be thought by all three of us at the same time. With the growth of my abilities, I discovered for brief moments I could do that. While not as efficient, I thought it prudent to leave the emotional aspect, which a mind meld would bring along, outside the battlefield. We just needed a way to strategically coordinate the battle as one and communicate to all troops.

Suddenly the council came to mind. They'd already done it. Hell they perfected it. I needed their help. It would be bold, but not impossible, for me to ask them to play the role of coordinators for the Draco troops during the mission, while receiving our orders. But what about Rogers' people? How should we get the messages to the Hexadoids if they were disbursed over a huge territory? We needed to invent a way for the Hexadoids to get along and communicate between groups. Again the challenge was clear. With the teams in place in the research lab, the competition could start. By now my little games gained reputation and merit. Each time a different team won, soaking in well-deserved recognition, it boosted the connection between the teams and the teammates.

I stood in front of the observation window with Drak and Rogers by my side. I watched them work together, find solutions together, and succeed together. I wanted to believe this all was for something. I could feel Rogers and Drak's mutual agreement. I actually could feel Drak's sympathy and friendship for Rogers and Rogers' for Drak. I was so busy working on the connection between the teams, I forgot about the missing connection between the two most important people in my life. Here it was. It caught me by surprise and took my breath away, as tears made their way down my cheek. I guess I did not have to worry anymore whether they would stand at the end of each other's gun barrels anymore. In the midst of desperation and an unknown future, I found myself enjoying a moment of happiness. I guess this is what life was about. This was all I could hope for in the end of a good day. This is a moment I would cherish.

Before the battle

There was a lot of preparation to be done before the battle. I kept thinking of all the scenarios of what could go wrong. I asked the teams to come up with their own doomsday scenarios. With all the negative energy, I was getting cold feet. There was just too much to account for. Too many variations of what could happen. While I could prevent some negative outcomes, I couldn't prevent them all. After listening to the Hex-commanders and Dracos suggestions of different strategies, I realized how much experience they all had. How their lives were entangled in battles and war, as they were a part of everyday life. The death they all lived with. Once again, I felt under qualified for my position. Feeling my panic, Drak and Rogers reminded me that with all the knowledge in the room I was the only one the monster will not see coming. I was the only one qualified to surprise them and wise enough to know to listen to others, which made me the perfect leader for this mission. I wanted to hug both of them for their confidence in me but was stopped mid thought by both of them. While they were talking and thinking strategy, I was occupied with protection. In simple terms, when they were talking strategies and worse case scenarios, it was in relation to the battle strategies. Me, I was thinking what if they get hurt or die!

After the incident on the station I asked them to equip me with a receiver so if any member of my unit needed help I would also know. Of course my first thought was to put all of our units in a big protective safety bubble. If only! I did not want even one man to fall, under my command. Not realistic in a war. Unfortunately this was my main concern. So how do I protect my people from getting hurt? I realized with my people I was thinking about thousands of soldiers! The Irony did not escape me at that moment. The station's energy shield was my first choice of such a protection. Once more the council disagreed and was against using a shield or sharing the shield technology. And before I could start arguing about the merit, they simply showed me the incident with the nanite creature. The shield was the only thing standing between the station and total annihilation in the end. Despite their perpetual war with the Hexadoids, the Dracos were a peaceful race and the shield was their only passive technology protecting them from a full-scale attack from anybody. Sharing it was not on the table. I could not argue with this logic and had to move to other protective ideas. We needed a way for our wounded to be protected. The Dracos did not care about it and it was not in the Hex nature to need or want protection. Their priority was always offense rather than defense. It was up to me to ask for this type of invention and see the implementation all the way through.

Using our teams challenge spirit, this was added to our list of gadgets to come up with. Shortly after Skinny's team came up with an invention of a nanite suit adapter, to be able to morph their suits into a Hex form, if a nearby Draco got injured, died and did not need it anymore. It was a way of recycling a perfectly good suit in the heat of the battle I guess. The programming was complex. The Hex had a totally different physiology. Their skin, just like mine, would not by nature be able to load the suit with energy. I found a way around it but how would the Hex do it? I was reminded that the suits were only temporary protection until the battle was over. Dah, what am I worrying about? It would just fall off.

I expected a little difficulty convincing the council to proceed with this invention. I argued that we already provided the Hex with modified weapons to fight the creatures. This was only for defense. Technically we would not suit them up with nanite armor; we would only recycle a suit from a dead soldier. I argued that the

Hexadoids had salvaged Draco technology for years. I could feel the council's lack of enthusiasm for it, but at the same time their lack of strength to fight me on all of my "out of the box" ideas. In their infinite wisdom they chose their arguments with me.

In the hours spent arguing with the Hexadoids and Dracos about what's important to pay attention and worth protecting, one idea came up multiple times. We needed a backup plan in case I got killed—a scenario that honestly never crossed my mind. Unthinkable as this might have been for me, it was a possibility. Ideas like a clone, a shield, putting me into a ship far away, or even leaving me on the station and making me lead the battle remotely, came up. None of which I was entertaining. If I was to inspire others to give their lives for this cause, I would have to lead by example not hide like a coward in a remote station. Nobody is irreplaceable or above approach, although I understood the protection of their council this way, I did not see myself as important as them. Not even I was that delusional. No matter how much they compared me to the council in this case, I still remembered how I watched from a safe ship, while my unit partnered up with Hexadoids and fought for their lives. I remembered the sick feeling I had, and the promise I made to myself to never feel like that again. The best I could offer was a backup plan.

My back up would be Drak and Rogers. They were connected to me, and knew what I would do. With that in mind, I thought about the Dracos and their unique way of avoiding true death. If any Draco fell during the battle, they would be activated back at the station inside a new clone. Ineffective, if mid battle, firepower wakes up back at the station clicks away. Ideally ships should stand by, full of clones ready to drop them to inflict more damage. That would eliminate any delay in replenishing the battalions. To minimalize the effectiveness of the attack from our enemy, the Dracos devised a procedure to release the physical energy from the clouds negating their renewable power source. We diverted all cloud energy into the worms, saturating them, just in case Dracos ended up in the pool. Additionally, we needed better ways to divert the energy from the monsters to reduce them in size rather than just to disburse them.

On a personal note, I was worried about the Hexadoid leaders. Their acceptance of me as a commander and person of knowledge without challenge was unnerving. Not only was I not of their species, I was small in stature and built with less muscle than a male representation of my species, appearing weak. Would they see me as a pushover for power in the near future and try to kill me? I had just argued against having a clone made in my image. Considering it, was I being short sighted? I knew at least one of the Hex leaders was ready to sabotage or challenge my leadership. The confrontation would be quick and arrive without warning. Not likely a premeditated attack but one of opportunity and instinct. I couldn't ask Rogers' for advice, for that would question the devotion and honor of his own people. I did not want to risk upsetting him. Nor could I ask Drak, knowing how overprotective he was. I was in fear of being assassinated at any moment. Tunnel vision and dizzy spells were becoming my norm as I struggled with sharing my fears and watching my back. I had a premonition that something would go wrong and it was causing havoc with my nerves and stomach. I realized that I would have to be mobile to see all the battle at once. Maybe I could use the hovering vehicle to move around the battle scene and send ground or aerial support when it was needed. Or maybe I should just eat something.

Everything was in place. I was anxious and unable to sleep. Drak must have felt the same. We were lying next to each other in the pod, restless, when Drak opened the lid. He needed to recharge for tomorrow, but instead he got out, grabbed my hand and pulled me out with him. We walked into the lab. The lights were dim and I was curious. Why were we there? He did not do anything without a reason. Standing in front of me, our eyes locked on each other, he placed something in my hand. I unwrapped it from its nanite cover and found a spinal belt. Tears threatened my eyes. Without consulting me, Drak had commissioned my very own spinal belt. It was visibly different than the Draco units, which made sense since I did not have Draco skin. The data storage was visible, which told me he was worried about losing me in the battle. The belt enabled him to come to my rescue or, worst case, download my consciousness into a clone. I laughed as I noticed that this model also had the protection feature. Its construction clearly contained more metal, bio-tissue and nanites than the Draco version, and I was apprehensive about how it would be attached to me.

I did not have to wait long to find out as Drak walked behind me, moved my hair to the side and rested the upper part of the spinal belt onto the base of my skull. With additional pressure, the neuro-connectors attached themselves against my skin. The pain was short lived as it quickly became a dull tingly vibration. Pressing the rest of the belt along my spine, each side of the belt extended its nanites tentacles into my skin and attached to my spine. Not having Draco skin this was the only way the spinal belt could do its job. It felt good feeling his fingers along my vertebrae. His other hand was on my hips holding my body in place for the process. My suit armor moved out of the way as it came into contact with Drak's fingers, exposing my entire back to him. After few minutes, I realized I was enjoying his attentions way too much. Expecting nothing but the obvious pressure of the belt on his side, I slowly turned around and noticed quite the opposite.

His eyes were the shade of red again and almost sparking

fire. The same eyes I noticed right after I infected him with my desires. This time those eyes were self-initiated. Could it be he was enjoying applying the spinal belt on me? I turned back letting him continue. His attentions resumed as if uninterrupted by my brief inspection. He continued touching my skin, sliding his fingers over it. I could not help myself but emit my energy right into his hands. My skin was covered with electrostatic energy, leaving my body in a form of mini lightning, into his fingers. Searching for an argument to stop this, I rendered myself helpless to his touch. There was literally nothing I could come up with to flee the scene. I was not imposing anything on him. I was not transferring any of my thoughts to him. He was under no orders to satisfy my needs and there was no practical reason for him to continue. His eyes clearly revealed that the emotional part of his brain was fully engaged. Hopeful and desperate for this moment, I had almost given up hope, but there it was. The basic human need for connection. He was experiencing it for the first time with me. We both knew tomorrow could be our last day and maybe that was all it took for him. I didn't care. After this, I would be ready for anything. I stood there, letting him peal my nanites away and I feared to turn around and look into his eyes. If the fiery eyes were gone I would be disappointed.

Was this the moment I was waiting for all along? I was scared. Feeling his fingers over my shoulders and down my side, the tingle leaving my skin and the nanites fleeing the scene, exposing my entire body to Drak. The tension overwhelmed my system to the point that I could do nothing but turn around and join our lips together. He hesitated; cautioning me of his insecurity about what would come next. He had no idea where this was going, only that his mind was forcing him to continue. His feelings reflected in his reddish eyes were speaking volumes and I was so ready for this. Charging him in the pod was not needed anymore, nor did the station expect the sudden inflow of massive energy as our exploration continued. We continued for hours discovering the human-Draco limits before the dawn diverted our attention to the day ahead. You don't know love until you are entirely satisfied in the moment, unwilling to continue to the next. Yet it was time. The day we all eagerly waited for was here. It was time for us to get to our predetermined place.

Battle

Still warm from the afterglow of intimacy, I was positioned on a hill, mentally reviewing the preparations that brought us to this point and visually scanning our formations trying to envision contingencies when one of the Hex commanders approached me from behind. My guard was down and I was not my usual paranoid self, still wallowing in the mellow zone I found myself in, since separating from Drak only hours before. My mind was sharp but I felt protected and safe, almost invincible.

The Hex commander stabbed me from behind with his long, venom filled scorpion stinger tail. The stinger was so sharp that it sliced all the way through my body. I could not understand what was protruding from my suit. Odd what comes to mind when you are mortally wounded. My first full thought was that apparently not all Hex are built exactly the same way. Rogers did not have that scorpion tail. Fortunately, Rogers was next to me and so was my unit, they had my six covered. Expecting this behavior from the Hex, they were staying close by, but not close enough to spot the assassination attempt before it happened. They killed the assassin before he could hit me a second time. After the poisonous stab, Rogers took the left over venom from the dead Hex stinger and injected a small pouch under his armpit with it. Then he took his own stinger and extracted the fluid in that pouch and used it to inject me. That was how they created an antiserum. Any other species would have died from that lethal dose of venom, but I was enhanced with Draco nanites. I was hurt, a fact that did not escape my attention, looking at the fist-sized hole in my guts. My agony infused muscle spasms indicated how much the venom stressed my system. Either way, thanks to my nanites, I would be ok soon. But not soon enough.

As the anti-venom and nanites started doing their work, I began to worry about the fragile relationship between the Dracos and Hexadoids. One of their own was killed. Any trust that may have started to form between us may have been irreparably damaged. This could be over before it even started. Fortunately, those that witnessed the attempt and aftermath waited silently only long enough to see if there was to be any fallout then the Hex went about their business as usual. I was patched up as well as I could be, and with the antiserum in my system, I was out of immediate danger. I had a battle to coordinate. I was fortunate to have Drak, Rogers and my unit at my side. Seeing me hurt, they took over the prep, not giving me a chance to intervene. My moment of self-reflection was interrupted by the pounding sound of the emitters. They were working overtime announcing the beginning of the battle as the creatures were on their way towards us, from all directions.

After all that excitement, the Hex commanders designated to drive the worm entities, found their positions in the pool. My unit was set and ready to drive the Hex commanders from the outer rim. The remaining Hex troops, led by Rogers, spread out around the perimeter of the pool. Drak was in charge of the Draco battle troops, including the replacement clone ships, and shuttles flying overhead. He was positioned near his battalion, on the ground, ready to attack. We quickly realized I could not coordinate multiple forces in my present condition. The field was so vast and multifaceted it was a stretch even when I was uninjured. My wound left me too weak for Plan A. I needed to go with Plan B and merge minds with Drak and Rogers. The last time I opened my mind to Drak was a disaster and I was afraid how it would look with the three of us. I was anxious and just hoped it would not be a total mess.

I could tell that Rogers and Drak were entering my

consciousness with care, taking time to watch my reaction and gently nudge my walls of resistance. The connection between the three of us took a toll on my brain. I went down to one knee, fighting my instincts to shut them out and for a brief moment seriously doubted this was going to work. But, there was no going back. Without the mind share there was no way to coordinate the looming confrontation. I mastered my fears and let them join me, as I mentally navigated my way through their minds getting comfortable with their reality without leaving mine. It was a mental dance. As long as no one stepped on the others toes, we just might come out of this unscathed.

My Unit and their Hex partners had become experts with the avatars. At the edge of the worm pool, the Dracos drove their Hexadoid partners who were located within the worm pool, who then generated multiple worm-creatures for our army. Everything was working as planned. The worm creatures were energized and attentive in the pools with the Hex avatars, the avatar controllers ringed the pool, the Hex tribes and Dracos backed the avatar pairs and the ships and shuttles circled near enough to replenish clones and back us up where required. We systematically took on the monsters, fighting side by side, gaining ground. Ships and shuttles fought from above, ready to deliver the final blow. We were winning. We were growing confident. Too confident. I surveyed the battlefield with a bad feeling it was all way too easy.

Then a new giant creature joined the battle. It was different from the other creatures in that it seemed to organize, plan and take charge of the other creatures. It looked like it was on fire, surrounded by an orange halo, bigger, and more vicious. Upon closer look, it appeared to be assembled from lava chunks instead of the ground particles, the others were made of. It quickly noticed and correctly determined that the Dracos/Hex partnership was enabling and controlling the worm creatures in the pool. With purpose the fire creature made its way around the shore. Snake Eyes was hit first. Helplessly we watched as she fought back with all she had, but the creature skillfully drained her energy leaving her body badly burned. Skinny was next. He saw it coming and tried another tactic, but even he too was powerless against the creature. One by one the distress beacons activated from the members of my unit as the creature slaughtered them. It targeted my avatar teams fast, determined and precise. Drak was tied up in his own struggle to keep his troops alive. Rogers tried to help but was too late. Without the Dracos controllers, their Hexadoid partners were nothing but stranded bodies, unable to hold the worm entities together. The remaining troops did not stand a chance against the creature without the worms. The creature was now free to attack and the tide turned. My unit was protected by their belts, but the other Dracos and Hexadoids were not so lucky.

I was sick with grief as they were killed and injured in vast numbers, and I was desperate for a way to rescue anybody alive in the pool and help them out. Out of nowhere, I was hit by an energy blast and everything went dark. My body lost control of the flying vehicle I was using. When I came to, I found myself stranded and helpless, on top of the worms, listening to Drak's distress beacon. Rogers was battling the lava monster and losing. I could feel his struggle and his determination, as he was pinned to the ground, fighting the boiling hot creature with everything he had. Others were falling faster than the ships could replenish the troops. And I was stuck in the ocean.

Finding themselves threatened and without a leader, the worms hardened until solid. I pushed myself up as far as I could and took in my surroundings. I was tangled among Hexadoids and Draco soldiers, some alive and injured, others dead. We were safe for the moment but it was only a matter of time before the agitated worms would turn into stabbing lethal weapons, killing anything in their ocean. It was too much. Worried about Drak, and unable to find him, I was paralyzed. I knew I was running out of time. We were losing. It was a massacre, and I was responsible.

Before I became overwhelmed with the finality and guilt ridden with the responsibility of it all, I concentrated on the knot in my stomach. I was becoming blinded by the tears in my eyes but fought them back knowing that I needed clarity and sight. Tears were a luxury that I could not afford just then. Looking around desperately for inspiration or a miracle, I felt the worms stiffening. I had seconds before the stabbing started. Mentally, I searched for Rogers. I wanted him to shake off the Lava Monster and find Drak and find a way to save him and anybody else if he could. I felt defeated. The battle was over. The stabbing had started but – I didn't feel it. I was boxed in. The nanite creature I had domesticated came to protect me. It created a cradle around me, which made me happy. I sent pleasant images to the creature as a thank you. I also, unintentionally, transferred pictures of my Hexadoid partners suffering in the worm pool along with my desire to help them. Soon, I could feel bodies being added to the bubble, one at a time, joining my protected space. Following, what it assumed was my request, it began collecting Hexadoids. Hopeful and grateful, I sent my positive energy in a steady stream. Fed with my energy, my creature grew stronger and moved even faster.

My moment of peace was interrupted when I felt Rogers distress. He was still battling the lava creature. He was exhausted and was losing any advantage he may have had. Fighting with all he had, it became obvious he was not going to make it. My already stressed body, once more, expelled a rush of adrenalin. I knew I had to make a hard decision. Save Rogers or my Hexadoid partners. It was not an easy decision but I had to make it, I could not save them all.

Just the way I had worked with the creature to travel the planet surface, I sent images to it, leaving the pool, dropping the unconscious Hexadoids on the adjacent shore near my dead unit's bodies, and with haste, retrieving Rogers from the lava monster. Soon Rogers was in the bubble with me and the other Hexadoids were lying by the pool. I knew even conscious as they were and protected with my unit's suits, they did not stand a chance unless we won. Mourning over their dead Draco partners, the fried Hexadoids re-grouped and one by one sounded an impressive battle cry while touching their Draco partner's corpses. Our troops were still fighting and dying out there without any indication of change. It was a merciless slaughter. With Rogers on board we barely escaped the creature, but what now?

As if the nanite creature knew what I needed before I did, it shape-shifted into a shuttle. Just like old times, I took my position inside the creature, navigating with my body, and off we went. This was all new to Rogers. He keenly observed my maneuvers, trying to make sense of the images he saw in my head. I needed to rise above the battle and take the proverbial ten thousand foot view. Misjudging my actions, thinking I was fleeing the scene, the troops on the ground looked after my ship, as it grew smaller. What they did not know was that I was staving off a panic attack that left me breathless. Terrified I froze during the avatar trials, and I could not afford to do that again. Observing our troops still falling in large numbers, I was short on time to come up with a game changing, lifesaving idea. I needed a miracle. From this distance, I could clearly see the monsters end game. They were forcing our unprotected troops into the deadly, irritated worm pool. Movement in my suit, reminded me of my little pet worm, which I forgot I still had in my suit and I knew what I needed to do, and what I had been dreading.

I needed to sacrifice myself and take my place in the ocean, without Drak. Under enough pain, I could maybe mount the entire ocean into one creature, pushing the battle back onto the deeper shore. Instead of diverting the energy, I needed to get the worms to do what they were designed to do and drain the energy from the monsters. Feeling what I had to go through last time, Rogers protested heavily, arguing that there were other ways than to be butchered, to win this one. In his optimistic view, the battle wasn't over until the last soldier died.

Meanwhile the lava Alpha creature began draining the clouds of energy and redirecting it to the monsters around it. We needed to stop the Alpha. Without him the remaining minions were disorganized and easier to eliminate. As we descended multiple energy beams crossed our path from below. They were directed at the Draco station. With no means to stop the massive charge, it hit the station. The station's reactor blew, creating a chain reaction of massive proportions. Caught in the after blast, I could feel and smell the burning nanites of our shuttle creature. Rogers and I knew we had seconds before we were toast. I felt something unexpected coming from Rogers. He was scared for me. Not for himself. Then we were overwhelmed with pressure as we flew into a bright light of some sort. The pressure in my ears was excruciating and my body was tossed in all directions. My last thought was, "Is this how it ends?" Then the pain stopped. The shuttle was still shaking. Still hearing a ringing in my ears, I opened my eyes and I could see the stars and the planet flash in front of my eyes over and over, as we spun away.

I could feel my pet worm, warm and squirming, next to my skin. I could hear Rogers' thoughts as confused and disjointed as my own. We were protected, inside the nanite shuttle, but the superheated air smelled burnt and seared our lungs. We appeared to be out of immediate danger but we needed to get back and assess the damage at the station. Also our troops still needed to be accounted for and I was desperate to find Drak. While spinning around, we could not see the station, so I assumed we were on the other side of the planet. The dark side of it. The largest moon was tidally locked to the planet; its rotation period around the planet was equal to the planet revolution period, and therefore, this side was never graced with its shine. The life here was ice cold, more hostile and more dangerous than in your worst nightmares. There were no worms, pools or oceans on this side. Therefore, the Dracos never explored this side of the planet, nor did any other species inhabit it; not even the Hex dared to occupy it. Honestly, the fact that we were on this side and would probably land here scared the crap out of us. We were in trouble, but even more concerning was the nanite creature. It was not responding to my movements. I was sending energy, what I had left to give, hoping to revive it from the shock I assumed it was in, but nothing. Rogers was comforting me with the voice of reason and hope as usual. It was maddening!

Based on the information I had downloaded into my brain during my futile attempts to become a pilot, I knew that we required less energy if we piggybacked on one of the smaller and closer moon's gravitational forces and slingshot back around the biggest moon, versus fighting current momentum to reverse direction and head back into the planet's atmosphere. Even for that we needed energy which I feared I could not generate. I smelled something burning. I knew that smell. The last time I smelled this was when my unit was scorched alive in the hangar. Was Rogers hurt? We both inspected each other, and when Rogers saw my back, his pulse accelerated. I did not feel the injury. The creature's nanites took the full blast of the explosion and through our psychosomatic connection, transferred the effects of the blast onto my body. Without the energy shield that protected a regular shuttle from any radiation or melting point heat exposure, the result was devastating. Rogers watched in horror as my eyes and hair turned white from pain I did not feel. What I did feel was my strength draining away.

I was burned, the nanite creature was MIA, missing in action and Rogers...well he was concerned. Just when I thought, the day could not get any worse, it did. We were helpless without energy, and we needed lots of it. Not only would the energy assist in healing my burning body, it would get us back to the battle, the station, Drak and home. Overwhelmed with the desperation of our situation I started daydreaming about my night with Drak. With the mind melt in place, privacy was out of question. Rogers was immediately interested. He was like an infant, always yearning for more experiences and information but this was something I wanted to keep for myself.

I was not about to give away the little bit of self-esteem I had, even if it would save all of our lives. There had to be another way. I looked at Rogers, into his big blue eyes and asked nicely, to leave this one to me. Disappointed but not surprised, he agreed almost too easily I managed to produce enough memory energy to keep the shuttle nanites afloat and heal. It was not much but it was sufficient to hold any deterioration of our predicament at bay since the nanites shuttle stayed intact. I could only assume the creature was still alive. Rogers was trying to be patient but this was too slow, his strength and abilities were useless in this situation, making him antsy. Our resources were diminishing slowly. Eventually we would run out of air if we did not do something in the near future.

Thinking we were about to die, I felt at peace. No more pressure to save anybody. I looked at Rogers and saw sadness in his eyes. I was tired and felt old, at least a hundred years older than the girl who fell through the portal, at the ripe age of 16. I noticed that Rogers tried to mimic my young age in his human form. I looked deeply into his blue eyes, red cheeks and knew without asking that he was not ready to give up and die. He was feeling helpless, not understanding my lethargy and acceptance of defeat. Things were getting continuously worse. After rebounding around the moon we were now caught in the gravitational pull of the planet, racing to the surface. If we did not burn up entering the atmosphere we were sure to explode when we crashed onto the planet's surface at great speeds. Neither the nanite shuttle creature nor I had energy. Rogers grabbed and shook me, demanding that I start fighting. For both of us. My heart was torn. I was hurt, resigned and bleeding, comfortable in my pity bubble, and willing to let someone else take up the fight. Then Rogers reminded me that there were still people I cared about that needed my help. Sleep and oblivion seemed so welcoming just a moment ago. Rogers wasn't done. He wanted me to use hate to recharge. But I could not feel any hate or rage towards the monsters. How could I? One of them just saved us and it was wounded and stranded alongside us hurtling through space. We didn't need to kill them; we just needed to stop them, before they destroyed the planet with all of us on it.

I didn't have it in me, but Rogers insisted that I think about that night with Drak, Rogers reminded me that he was still somewhere out there, counting on me to save him. Dragged out of my self-pity, I stared at Rogers. I didn't have the energy for a slingshot maneuver, or to fight Rogers. Why not? Easy! I closed my eyes, ignoring everything except the sensual memories of that night. I reveled in the sensations not caring that I had an audience or I was vulnerable. It was pleasant at first, soothing, giving peace to my heart and soul, and then it started making me feel stronger. More energetic. More motivated. I opened my eyes to see Rogers staring intently, inches from my face, mirroring the joy and satisfaction I felt. Optimist as usual, he saw us going home! Energy was now flowing freely from my body, disbursing so strongly that sparks were flying on currents that seemed to move around my body. Time seemed to flow differently, as if on a different frequency. I felt my worm had something to do with this. Rogers was moving but so slowly he seemed to have stood still with the smile permanently engraved on his face. I was unable to move myself as time or reality, or possibly both, slowed down. I felt the worm hugging me. Its purr and vibration was fast and steady, giving me all the time I needed to charge, plot the course, and get us on our way before the perfect window for the slingshot closed. I was sure the worm was doing all of it. When the station exploded it must have used the energy from the explosion to get us to safety. We always assumed that the worms needed to be in a pool to create portals or do any of this, but apparently we were wrong. All it took was one worm generating the right vibration, frequency, and an enormous amount of energy to do it.

As with everything, I had only solved part of the worm riddle. What I did not know then was that my pet worm took my wish about seeing Drak too literal. I turned the shuttle towards the moon and initiated the slingshot. Caught in the gravitational pull of the moon we then hitched a ride around its dark side until it was time to give it another burst of energy. After we left the moons orbit, we were heading back so fast, that I knew it would be dangerous without a shield. I turned the shuttle around once more so the majority of the burn from the planet's atmosphere would be absorbed through my back again. My nanites would heal me, but who knew how that would hurt Rogers. On atmospheric impact, some of the nanites scattered and broke away from the main body. The rest were exposed to immense heat and transferred it, once again, to me. Rogers held on to me as tight as he could, as if holding my body would keep it from falling apart. Or was it the shuttle he tried to hold together? None of it mattered, because we ended up unconscious. I remember mumbling something to Rogers about closing his eyes, 'the better to see me', before I opened mine.

Second time around

As if it was a dream, I was standing on the hill addressing the forces in front of me. I stood confused about what just happened. Déjà vu! I felt a large presence sneaking up behind me. Knowing what was about to happen but slowed down by my confusion, I barely dodged the attack. This time around the stinger didn't punch a fist size hole in my guts, but rather scratched the surface of my shoulder. I was still infected with the anti-venom. Fortunately, my unit prevailed. They killed the assassin right after his first attempt. With less venom, I did not get knocked out by agony infused muscle spasms. I looked at Rogers. I saw the same confusion on his face. We both knew! It wasn't a dream. The worm didn't just teleport us onto the other side of the planet, it brought us back in time!

The rest of the Hexadoids wondered why I had almost no reaction to this attack. I convinced them of my superior strength and leadership. They sounded a battle cry unlike anything I ever heard before. Filled with motivation and conviction they now independently positioned themselves rapidly around the ocean parameter. The pool entity drivers rolled right inside it. Confused about the already existing mind meld between Rogers, Drak, and I, Drak quickly picked up on the past series of events and transferred it to the other Dracos minds. Surprised and completely unclear about the details of my pet worm's abilities and my recent adventure, the telepaths knew what the possible future held for us. It was crystal clear to them; it was all or nothing going forward.

The creatures kept arriving around the pool, and both species were rigorously fighting side by side without prejudice toward each other using our new energy draining weapons. Just as before, we were winning the upper hand with the difference being that this time we knew better than to grow reckless and too confident.

We were waiting for the lava monster to show its ugly face, and we knew it would target the avatar drivers first, taking out our worm entities in the process. This time around we used the force field technology from the station to protect the Draco avatar drivers without the council opposing. We also protected them with the shuttles above just in case. What seemed like overkill proved to be a much-needed diversion for the lava monster. While it was busy plotting an attack on the avatar drivers and spending all its attention on getting to them, it was unable to organize its friends this time. As before, the other monsters surrounded our main forces, slaughtering them from every angle.

Determined to change the outcome, Drak ordered all cornered Dracos to kill themselves. Transferred into their new clones, they were now dropping from the ships in hundreds. The suits on the dead Dracos automatically formed a protective barrier for the remaining Hex. The only way the monsters could hurt the Hex before was by shooting at them with focused energy lasers. Now, thanks to the nanites mounting a massive nanites-shield around them, this was not possible. Unsuccessful with the inside attack, the monsters turned around to defend themselves from the outer attack. Free from entrapment by the monsters, the Dracos drew the focus of those energy beings and gave the Hex a window to break free. However, even with all this in play we still were not winning. We were not even making a dent. We needed to turn the tide somehow.

Meanwhile, not needed by his Hexadoid troops, Rogers had his own mission. Knowing that at some point Drak would go missing in action; Rogers, using his newly learned skill, flew the nanite creature to keep an eye on him. From there it was easy to rescue him when his unit was pushed into the worm pool. Now it was clear why his spinal belt did not save him last time. He was buried under a ton of agitated worms, draining him from all energy. He never had a chance to be discovered in time to be saved. With Drak on board, Rogers pushed his way past the monsters main defenses. Flying from above Drak kept shooting and diverting the attention from the monsters when it was needed giving his troops the advantage they needed. Fully engaged we all struggled to win the upper hand. Whenever we got one of them pinned and reduced to a manageable size, they got reinforcement from another one of their kind in the form of additional energy, and we were at square one again. The energy had to come from somewhere and I suspected it came from the lava creature. I was right. The alpha creature started draining the clouds of all remaining energy and sending it to the monsters. We needed to stop it before we could take care of the rest of them.

We needed to divert the energy from the monsters by getting the worms to do what they were designed to do which is drain the energy from the monsters. It was time for me to jump into the ocean. I didn't need to be tortured by the stabbing worms this time because Drak was safe and sound and ready to drive me. With the other Hex in the pool, I knew I didn't have to take on all the worms by myself. It was all or nothing; we had to try. The avatar driving Dracos, including Drak, joined forces and moved all of the worm creature drivers into one place. Against all odds, we managed to assemble three times as many worms as I had thought possible. Now matching the monsters in size and strength, we moved the worms out of the pool and onto the shore, going after the monsters. Walking out of the ocean was only possible due to my little pet worm. As he learned in the lab, he was free of the virtual pool limitation and conveyed this experience like wild fire to his new pool friends. Our giant self-made worm creature, moving like a massive blob on the ground, gave the rest of the troops the shield they needed to regroup. Rogers used the joined worms as a shield and shot from behind it at the enemy.

Understanding our plan, the other Hex clans started rolling in from around the ocean at incredible speed. The monsters followed, not knowing they were entering a trap. The battle scene moved away from the worm pool, inland. The ships still firing from above were separating portions off of the monster, now also amassed into one over my worm creature. We created an impenetrable wall and moved fearlessly forward.

Wanting to avoid overloading the space station reactor, we needed a new location to deposit and disperse the energy now draining from the monsters. Remembering how much energy it absorbed during its attack on the station, I knew the nanite creature could handle the massive amounts. I asked it to become our new energy dumping site. It was surprised when we started feeding it from all directions but hungrily accepted it. Rogers was flying and coordinating the Hex clans from above. Drak was connected to the ship and driving my avatar self, when the nanite creature positioned itself like an umbrella in the center of the battle, welcoming the energy influx.

The Hex and Draco soldiers were fighting back to back, surrounded by incoming monsters, when I ordered those Dracos who had died and were newly cloned to be dropped into the battle, without the latest download of data, to speed up their transition into the fight. A little confused and with gaps in their memories, they followed my orders, conveyed by the council, blindly. The new clones dropped in and automatically took protective positions next to their Hex partners. The Hex were not disposable and we knew we could only mend the injured Hexadoids, not the dead ones.

The occasional sacrifice of a Draco in order to protect a fellow Hex did not go unnoticed. This display of loyalty inspired the Hex to outdo themselves. The troops became more aggressive and their fighting spirit became deadlier. This push was all we needed to move the tide from losing to winning. Slowly but surely, we reduced the size and number of our enemy. Our injured Hexadoids were pushed into the middle of our troops and protected from further injury. The vast worm pool was empty as they mounted into deadly worm creatures absorbing and swallowing what remained of the monsters.

Surprisingly, as we depleted the energy from the lava monster minions the main monster grew stronger. We could not deplete its energy; we could not shoot it with weapons. Its impenetrable lava shielded skin seemed immune to everything. It went after us and the worms, leaving nothing but dead bodies behind and pushing the energy it took into its associates. We needed to beat it if we wanted to win. What use was it to kill a monster if it was just going to be resurrected by this alpha creature? The Hex clans were capable of taking on the remaining monsters themselves. I could leave the ocean to them. Being connected to Drak allowed me to convey all my thoughts. Separated from the pool, Rogers used his stinger to wake me up. It was time to come up with a new plan.

Pulled into the creature:

Since its exterior was impenetrable, the only option we had was to try to defeat the lava monster from within. If at all possible I wanted to understand what I would need to get in or encounter after. Would I be incapable of functioning after my torturous journey inside? I decided to contact the council myself. Nobody as far as I knew, had ever done this before. If we stood a chance I needed info fast and they were the all-knowing after all, although skimpy with sharing.

They explained that my body would be torn apart into atoms, exposed to radiation, and reassembled in the proper order, and put back together. If I did it right, and even then no human body would ever withstand this, but I had my nanites and a Draco enhanced physiology. Would that be enough? Not even the council had enough information to tell me that or what I would need to do once inside that creature. With the small ounce of hope they gave me, it was recommended that I go for it. I guess that's why I was put in charge. The Dracos dealt in logic not what if, maybes, hopes and wishful thinking, and it helped this time that for them our bodies were expendable. Time was running out. If I did nothing, the ability to travel back to Earth and protect not only my family but the family I had created here would be gone. It was all or nothing, I decided to go for it.

Forgetting for a moment the annoying connection to Drak and Rogers I found myself having company on my new suicide mission. They both left their posts and rushed towards me. In their opinion I was committing another suicide and they were about to stop it or be part of it. This time they were too late to stop it. All I had to do to create the right conditions to be pulled inside the creature was to detonate the antigravity charge combined with the pulse emitter, while holding on to the energy reversal field generator, just as instructed by the council. This trio was a perfect storm scenario. It should be enough to create a temporary pull, shifting me out of phase with enough energy to push me past the impenetrable skin and right into the creature. The only stupid thing was that Drak and Rogers were now with me in full range of the blast and in for the ride.

We held onto each other, but it was not enough. The body of this giant swallowed us entirely. A burning sensation came over our bodies while the pain felt like razor blades skinning us alive. Pulling and numbing sensations followed. We held onto each other, pressing so tightly that we formed a continuous ball of flesh with me in the middle. Drak and Rogers tried to protect me with their bodies. They covered my head between their torsos and curved away from each other forming a basket around me. The scorching heat, pain, pulling and numbing took only a few minutes, though it felt like forever. We ended up in a fuzzy and grey version of reality. We smashed into the ground. The burning and pulling stopped. It was silent.

We were lying on the ground, thrown apart on impact. The air was thick and laced with smooth streaks of what looked like molasses. I swiped my hand through one of the streaks causing it to swirl in slow motion, leaving the drops abandoned behind. We were back on the planet without troops, but we weren't. It was as if time slowed for everyone and everything, except us inside the creature. We could still see the action happening around us, but we were not participating. Then, one of the shuttles flew slowly right through me, like a ghost. It didn't make any sense. Did we cause the creature to phase out of reality with us? But why were the energy blasts emitted from it still visibly hurting our troops? This was a weird reality. Were we dead? I could feel Drak and

Rogers both mentally and physically. I could smell their burned flesh. I could feel their pain as if it were my own, and probably some of it was. While aching, I was grateful for the pain, since that meant we were all still alive. Drak and Rogers looked at me. Apparently the irony of being happy that we were suffering in pain was lost on the both of them.

If we were not dead, what was happening? I moved closer to them and grabbed their hands. Who knew, maybe it was not over and another funnel would take us in. I didn't want to be separated. Our nanites worked tirelessly and managed in just a little bit of time to repair enough of our injuries to make us functional. We had not moved but the landscape and our perspective had changed. We were definitely inside the still-moving creature. In a way, it was good news. This meant we had made our way successfully inside it, adjusted to its hostile environment, had a chance of destroying it and save the planet in the process, and then somehow find a way out of here to live to tell the tale. I was a little sketchy on the details but I was feeling optimistic. Something would come up.

It took a massive effort just to move; but there appeared to be no obvious way out. I crawled back to Drak and Rogers. They were still recovering. They had endured most of the beating since they had wrapped their bodies around mine. I loved them for this. They were my heroes. I kissed Drak and Rogers before helping them to their feet. Their energy was almost depleted but they managed to get on their feet and follow me. I was pleased to see how well they worked together, almost as if they were meant to be together. Drak pulled out his research module and started collecting readings. Rogers had more luck getting close to the creature's skin, which he inspected thoroughly, poking around, looking for weak spots. I sat down, exhausted and basically just looked around.

I had a feeling the answer we needed had to be here. How was this creature growing stronger? Where did it get the lava and the ability to stay on fire? Why was it different from the other creatures? All of the attempts to dismantle it were failing. Our people were dying trying to weaken it. I knew we were on the right track, fighting from within, but I did not see how...yet. The key had to be in the differences between this creature and the others. Was lava and fire the only difference?

Rogers was already looking at the physical being. Drak was scanning its make-up. The obvious was all covered. But I had a feeling. There was something . . . I closed my eyes and opened my mind and heart. I was getting pretty good at that. There was an edge to this creature. A feeling so intense that it was almost tangible. I knew this feeling, had felt it many times in my life, but nothing this extreme. This creature exuded it like cold molasses on a warm day. It felt like ANGER!! This entire creature was pure anger. It was furious. I closed my eyes one more time and placed my hands on the core we landed on. It was pulsing. I could feel its loneliness. In its funny make up, I wondered if this place represented the heart. Why was this creature so angry? The data from Drak's probe provided us with massive intelligence, which he immediately forwarded to the council. Rogers still poking at its shell was aggravating it from the inside. I could feel it getting distracted and maddened with every stab. A vortex was forming, multiplying in intensity the more he aggravated it. Could it be that easy? I asked Rogers to forget poking the poor creature and shoot the shell, just shoot it. And he did. The intensity of the vortex grew in size.

It was working. We just had to make it angrier, so it would destroy itself. Drak was still taking measurements with his equipment but his eyes were on me. I was still on the ground, with my hands on the core. The more aggressive Rogers became, the more irritated the creature was and faster its pulse. There was a noticeable shift in the monsters attention and I could feel the focus of the creature move inwardly to us and away from the outside attack. We were doing something right. We had to keep at it. Rogers kept firing. Drak kept sending the response of the creature to the council recording the attack which was now focused on the same place just from the other side. But there was more. I could feel it. The creature was pissed and the vortex was so immense that we had trouble holding on. We were drawn into the maelstrom and the pulse continued to rise. With the creature distracted, internally, by us, the external attack was gaining the upper hand on the outside and the creature was becoming less substantial. I started wondering what would happen if we actually won. Would we disappear with the creature or would we be free? Whichever way it went, we were staying for the long haul, win or lose, within the creature to the bitter end. The entire planet depended on this. We had noticed that the other creatures were energized and stronger once the lava monster arrived. Were they inspired by their leader? Assuming this was their leader, it seemed reasonable to suggest that if it were defeated, then the others would fall. That was the theory.

The attack continued from both sides. A coordinated assault on the creature. I kept my hands on its pulse following odd feelings, which helped identify places to strike. Some locations were unaffected by our beating on it and others drove it nuts. Obviously we kept hammering at the more sensitive areas. After a while, the creature was substantially smaller, gravity could not pull at us anymore. Its energy to fight back had finally subsided. We defeated it!

Suddenly, a pull and push, overwhelmed us. I could sense that we were about to be expelled from what remained of the creature. We couldn't stop it. Thrown around, we just managed to hold on to each other. The pain returned, more intense and once again nauseating. The scorching subsided as my nanite suit merged with Drak's and created a cocoon around the three of us. Just before we were expelled from the creature, it lowered his defenses, and I could finally identify what had been bothering me.

This monster was hostile for a reason. It was exacting its revenge for the monster we defeated the first time we encountered them, the first time I was tortured inside the worm pool and created my first worm-creature. It was its mate. I know we did not kill it. It was still alive, although present in its existence as an echo of itself. Could it be that this creature did not know that it was still alive? That would explain its intense anger. The monster must communicate telepathically similar to Dracos and therefore thought it knew everything that had transpired that day. Adapting, it had plotted its revenge by developing an entity so much stronger than the rest. If this creature was able to communicate, plan and have complex feelings, we had no right to just destroy it. The council was right! I was confused and sick to my stomach. We inadvertently, by our ignorance, had created this lava monster. How much of this disaster could be traced back to our misunderstanding, interference and influence? I had mixed feelings about our involvement in this battle. This was not feeling like a win.

Out of the creature, the battle continued for a while, until the very last one was defeated. As suspected, minimizing the lava monster was the pivotal point in the battle. Once depleted of energy, the others were easy. We lost so much that day. The monsters were no longer threatening the worm pools. I stood once more over a graveyard of bodies and felt sick to my stomach. This was not a victory. It was a catastrophe.

Help from the Nanite creature

I looked over at the nanite creature, which came to help. Or at least that was what we had assumed. How gullible we all were. During the battle it had drained its comrades of their energy, leaving them dormant and defenseless, unbeknownst to us, it had all it needed for its ultimate goal. Soon after the battle, my nanite creature positioned itself on the edge of the worm pool and started emitting a very deep sound. It was almost too low for my ears to hear, but my body clearly felt its vibration. That vibration was picked up and amplified by the worm pool, intensifying the affects a million fold. The entire field was vibrating in unison, creating an eerie thumping wall of sound, which made everyone sway as the air was pushed past them. It stopped as it started, for no apparent reason. The stopping was accompanied by a giant blast of air originating directly above the nanite creature. The blast emanated straight down with such force that we were all pinned to the ground. This new development could not mean anything good.

Filled with all this energy, the nanite creature had created and opened a new portal. How did it know to do that? Was it for me? I could only guess that it was going right to Earth since it was over the pool I was dropped into upon my arrival. It did not fit. It did not feel right. Call me skeptical but I believe in selfish reasons. So why would it open a portal for itself? Or for that matter, why was it helping us? Thinking a mile a minute I could only come up with one conclusion. Now I understood. This must have been its plan from the beginning. After it had fed from my energy, it wanted more. After sharing stories of home complete with crowded cities and towns, it must have thirsted for my home more than I did. How delicious it must have seemed, an entire planet with seemingly unlimited energy sources like me. An all you can eat buffet. Unable to open a portal on its own without a substantial amount of energy, more than I could create, it was happy with me until we diverted the energy to it during battle. What a windfall! It received more energy than it needed. It continued to help us because it now knew how to manipulate the worm pool and could generate all of the energy it desired. We delivered the energy right to it. We could not let it get to Earth. Earth was not ready for it. As the creature disappeared from view, I leapt into the portal. Unquestioning, Drak and Rogers followed. I was no longer concerned about letting them into my mind, I was grateful that they cared enough to join me. This was not their battle, yet they came.

In the portal I was subject once again to more pain, pulling me in all directions, trying to rip me apart. Thanks to my robust physiology, my body was able to hold it together and it did not hurt quite as much. We were together moving through the portal. I knew we had to stay together no matter what. I stretched my hands out to Drak and Rogers to pull them closer in to me. I did not want to lose them. Once again, despite their feelings for each other, they came together to create a shield around me for protection, and I held on to them with everything I had. We could only assume we were heading to Earth, but who knew where we were really going or what to expect on the other side.

www.ingramcontent.com/pod-product-compliance
Lightning Source LLC
Chambersburg PA
CBHW061948170626
46813CB00006B/2569